Bo

Piercing a Dom's Heart
Touched By a Dom
Domination in Pink

Holly S. Roberts

Published by Bad Luck Publishing
clubeldiablo@gmail.com
http://wickedstorytelling.com

Printing History
One Dom at a Time – eBook: August 2012
Piercing a Dom's Heart – eBook: September 2012
Touched By a Dom – eBook: September 2012
Domination in Pink – eBook: October 2012
Bundle eBook: October 2014
Bundle Paperback: October 2014

All rights reserved including the right to reproduce this book or portions thereof in any form.
This is a work of fiction. ALL characters are derived from the author's imagination.

No person, brand, or corporation mentioned in this Book should be taken to have endorsed this Book nor should the events surrounding them be considered in any way factual.

Club El Diablo Box Set Vol. 1-4

Book I

One Dom at a Time

Chapter One

The whip snapped with just enough force to bring a low cry from Angela. When I used the twelve-foot Australian leather in a scene, it always drew a large crowd. The sound of their breathing surrounded me and I could feel the sexual excitement in the air. I stayed in the zone and so did my sweet sub—Angela was one of my favorites to work with.

Moisture beaded along my hairline as my arm came up and flicked the whip again. Red welts systematically appeared down her body; just enough to leave a fine line but never break the skin. This is what the members of the Mediterranean Club paid for. Though calling it a club was going slightly overboard.

MC was a BDSM dive. I had worked here for three years and done everything from tend bar to discipline subs. My current role of enacting scenes for the questionable crowd was my favorite. I blanked out the whispered voices, the smell of sex, and too many bodies. Angela needed me.

I was fortunate the owner appreciated the crowd I brought in and let me decorate, clean, and maintain my own alcove. I also had a small office off the back where I could soothe and comfort my patrons after I finished breaking down their submissive barriers.

I gave Angela a brief respite so I could adjust the speed of the vibrator clenched within her tight pussy. Her moans became louder and I rotated my wrist ready for the next round with the whip. *Snap*, I loved the sound as it popped against flesh.

Finally she could no longer hold back her screams and she found release; her orgasm rippling through her body carrying the crowd with her. Many of the watchers pulled their subs aside to private areas for a small moment of relief before the next show started. I had one more exhibition for the evening and then I could go home. I hadn't used my vibrator in more than a week and I needed a little fantasy time.

I removed the juicy pleasure toy from between Angela's legs and assisted Raul in releasing the sobbing woman from her bindings. He carried her nude body into my small private domain and gently placed her on a tall padded bench.

"I'll take it from here Raul, thank you."

"Yes Mistress Lydia." His eyes never looked into mine.

Angela lay down on her side shuddering and trying to control her emotions.

I walked over, ran my hand gently through her hair, and helped her sit up to take the sip of the orange juice I offered.

"Thank you Mistress."

"You did wonderful tonight Angela, I don't think I've ever seen you more beautiful and responsive." I kissed her on the cheek then took out a bottle of my personal blend of special oils to coat the red welts I left on her skin. I also wanted to make sure I hadn't caused any lasting damage. There was no sign of blood or torn skin but I liked to assure myself my subs were okay before they left my private room.

"Lay back sweetheart and I'll get you fixed up so you feel better."

"Yes Mistress."

I helped her to her stomach and began soothing the oil into the soft skin of her legs, back, and ass. "Tell me about your week." I kept my voice gentle. This was her time and she needed a reward for giving me her trust. I listened attentively and made the right sounds of encouragement when called for.

"He didn't call. I waited all week and now I know he won't be back. I loved him but he couldn't accept what I needed."

"When's the last time you saw your therapist Angela?"

"I saw her two weeks ago and she told me Aaron probably wasn't the guy for me but I was still hoping he would give us a chance."

"Is that why you requested I use the whip tonight?"

"Yes Mistress, I needed to forget the rest of the world. Thank you."

My hands continued to glide gently over her firm buttocks and upper thighs. Angela's body was beautiful. If I were gay, I would be in love with this messed up beautiful woman. The men in her life were stupid. "Turn over and let me get the front."

I began rubbing the oil into her breasts, upper thighs, and stomach. Towards the end of the scene, I struck her perfectly groomed pussy a few times because I knew it would take her over the top. Now, I made sure I massaged the faint red lines to take away the sting.

Angela's breathing quickened but she knew my rules—no sex outside of a scene, or you were no longer one of my treasured subs. I was strict and never deviated from my rules. I also never took a permanent sub. It was all in the not so fine print of the contract they signed before I began working with them.

"You're beautiful Angela." I plucked her nipples with a little twist and she groaned in response. I kissed her cheek and helped her sit up. Grabbing a soft towel from a shelf below the bench, I wrapped it around her and took a quick peek at the time. I had forty-five minutes until my next scene. Angela needed me more than I needed my low-cal snack break so she got her wish. We sat on the couch and my sweet little sub asked permission to lay her head in my lap. My fingers ran through her blonde strands and I listened while she spoke more about her life.

This was the time it all became worthwhile and our poor fucked up lives took solace from human touch and caring. I sipped on bottled water and gave Angela a full bottle to make sure she stayed hydrated. I hated post scene sub drop and having this bonding time helped us both avoid the feeling of aching loneliness.

"Are you going home now or will you hang around for a while?" I knew the Mediterranean Club was not the best place after a scene but there was little I could do but ask Raul to keep his eyes open.

"I'm going home but I'll make an appointment with you for next week if I may Mistress."

"Yes, but I'll miss you until then." The towel slipped off her breasts and they begged for attention but it wouldn't be from me. I took her lips in a soft kiss. My gaze traveled up as the door to my private world opened. My hand clenched suddenly in Angela's hair though I softened my grip immediately.

"This room is off limits. Please leave and close the door behind you." I expected the door to shut immediately but an unfamiliar man entered and I could only stare. He was well over six foot tall, breathtakingly gorgeous, and ever so lickable. His aggressive stride brought him completely into my private sanctuary. It was more than obvious that this hot body didn't belong at the MC.

I held Angela still as her muscles tensed and she tried to move her head from my lap.

"If you take another step, I'll have security throw you out of the club and have your membership revoked." It was the best I could come up with when what I really wanted was to replace the date with my vibrator and use the stud standing inside my door.

"I'm afraid it's your boss who gave me permission to come in here." Dark dangerous eyes looked into mine. He gave a quick glance at the nearly naked woman in my lap but then zeroed in on me again.

His voice was sensual, deep, and commanding. Angela's body trembled in my arms. I began running my hand through her hair again though it was a nervous gesture on my part and damn I was never nervous. I now had a slight inkling of who was standing in my domain and I wasn't happy.

"Angela my sweet, our time is up. Thank you for sharing your beautiful body and giving me your pleasure. Come in early next week and I'll buy you a drink. I would like to try a new scene and I think it will push you just a bit more." Looking up into the intense eyes watching me I leaned forward and took Angela's mouth. This time I put a bit more carnal movement into my lips. As if on cue, she responded with instant passion. I knew better and I didn't mean to tease her but Mr. Dominance shook me up.

I pulled away from the kiss and gathered the towel around her shoulders. "Get dressed and have Raul escort you out. I'll see you next week.

I walked her past Mr. Umm He Smells Delicious and looking out the door, my eyes found Raul who was cleaning my area for the next scene. I gave him my "you will be punished" look for not warning me about my visitor but then I nodded my head toward Angela so he would follow. Raul and I were a team and he knew Angela required watching after a scene. I shut the door when the two walked away.

My eyes traveled slowly up the large yummy male body standing in front of me. He was wearing black loafers, black pants, and a long sleeved white dress shirt unbuttoned halfway down his remarkable chest. Clearly defined muscles bulged beneath his shirt which made the entire package sexier. They weren't the over the top muscles of a competing body builder but with a little oil, he would make a statement. His skin was darker than a suntan would provide and I guessed he had Native American, Hispanic, or another darker skinned race somewhere in his bloodline. He was gorgeous. I'd heard the rumors through the BDSM grapevine but seeing him in person was different. For the first time in years, my pussy creamed at just the sight of a man.

I was male exclusive when I fucked but it took a lot of work to take me over the edge. I had a feeling this man could do it without touching me. He was trouble and it didn't help that he knew how insanely sexy he was. I'm sure he just blinked those luscious dark eyes and most women drooled as an orgasm rocked their world. I hoped the saliva in my mouth stayed where it was and I could get through this without making a complete fool of myself.

When my eyes finally stopped on his heated gaze, he quirked his mouth slightly and I noticed the dimples that only made him more arresting. I bet he hated those dimples. I managed to control my breathing. I wasn't the best dominatrix in the state for nothing. My cool gaze met his—one master to another.

"Mr. Collins, you've taken me by surprise. I thought I was clear in my refusal of your offer."

His smooth chocolate eyes pierced mine. "I was told you only fucked men." He was obviously holding back a grin but purposely let his dimples flash in a well-practiced expression that had to drive women mad with lust.

My shoulders stiffened. "I don't discuss my sexual preferences with strangers."

This time he smiled full out and my knees weakened. Years of hiding my own inadequacies kept me standing in the face of Michelangelo's David. I was really in trouble.

His voice tightened, "I don't particularly care about your sexual preferences but I paid a lot of money to find out what makes you tick and I wasn't expecting surprises. I can't say I'm thrilled to fly halfway across the country to handle what should have been a cut and dry deal you couldn't refuse. I'm not fond of the word 'no,' so here I am at this less than stellar establishment. Seeing it in person is far worse than the pictures my team provided. I'm at a complete loss about your reasons for refusing to work for me."

This was his Dom voice and it was enough to snap me out of my love sick fantasies of taking his hard cock in my mouth and making him moan. Years of practice helped me gain control of my erratic heartbeat but there was nothing I could do about the fire blazing in my eyes. My complexion turning from pale to red was the bane of light skin, freckles, and red hair that hung in a single roped braid down my back. I had a Dom voice too. "You've wasted your time for nothing and there was no need for you to slum in my neck of the woods. My answer was final, is final. No!"

His expression remained intense. "Your boss feels differently."

"My boss can't afford to lose me." Johnny Ford knew I was his bread and butter and I drew beginners and BDSM legends to his slimy assed club. At five foot six and 140 pounds, I wasn't small and it took years to turn my extra pounds into muscle. Those muscles could wield a whip to perfection. I had come to terms with my large framed body. Damn, Damian Collins made me wish I were 5'2" and built like Angela. Argh, the man was a god or the devil as his name suggested. He needed to leave.

His eyes relaxed and his lips quirked at the sides. "Your boss has been well compensated for your time and he's placed you at my disposal for the next 30 days."

No fucking way. Hot fury rushed up inside me, steam should have poured from my ears and eyes. This Neanderthal was not buying me. "I am not for sale Mr. Collins, to you or by my ex-boss. Emphasis on ex." I stormed across the room and using the key I hid on top of the cabinet, I opened my locker and retrieved my large personal bag. It held my street clothes along with sub toys but there was no way I was changing. If a cop stopped me on my way home, he would get an eye-full and maybe I would get out of a ticket. I didn't see myself driving slowly and obeying the speed limit and I would pay the damn ticket if it came to that.

Refusing to look at Mr. Dick On A Stick, I made sure I had everything. I wouldn't be back and the sick feeling in my stomach only pissed me off more. I refused to let it sway me and only had one goal before I left. I would walk out of this room and kick Johnny Ford in the balls, as I should have done many years before. I was never coming back.

I turned to the door but the cream-dream fantasy man in my office blocked the path, his back resting against the scared wood.

"I'm taking you to dinner to discuss my proposal."

The arrogant ass. My eyes traveled to the corner camera. It might be my private room but for safety reasons the cameras were essential. The problem was Johnny knew how I would react, and I could only guess the amount of money it took for him to give me up for a month. Damn him, he wouldn't be sending a bouncer to get me out of my current predicament.

I had no choice and even with years of self-defense, I had little chance of removing my problem physically. His broad shoulders brushed both sides of the doorframe. God I loved a large chest and a man who made me feel small. Controlling my inner slut, I snapped out of lust and into disgust. My only chance of escape would happen after I was out of this office.

I met Mr. Dreamsicle's eyes. "Well, the answer is no but I wouldn't want to refuse a free dinner." I couldn't hide all my irritation but my voice dropped down a sexy notch. I was a good actress.

His grin flashed again and stepping back, he opened the door letting me precede him.

Chapter Two

I kept my office brighter than the low-to-no lights in the main part of the club. It took a moment for my eyesight to adjust. Unfortunately, this wasn't a good thing. I often thought blindness would be better than looking at the crappy surroundings. The darkness did nothing to hide the sleazy atmosphere.

I figured Johnny shopped at the BDSM equivalent of a garage sale or he gathered donations off curbsides where people hoped someone could benefit from their castoffs. Slimy surroundings went hand in hand with a slimy boss. No more, I was finished.

Damian didn't touch me but he used his large frame to crowd my body on purpose. The man had nerve and entirely too much alpha sex appeal. I cast an angry glare at a group of subs sitting on a garish couch with their mouths hanging open. Too bad I wouldn't be around to give a little discipline. I noticed Molly sitting with them. Like a good sub, she kept her eyes down. She was pretty but overweight by fifty pounds. I was sure she wouldn't make it past the door of Mr. Edible's private club. If I still weighed over two hundred pounds, I wouldn't be in my current predicament. Maybe I'd eat a cherry Pop Tart tonight.

I took a deep breath and as much as I hated to admit it, I was pissed at being forced to leave this smelly, seedy place that had become my second home.

Out of the corner of my eye, I caught sight of Johnny. My body turned but a strong hand grabbed my forearm and led me away from the hairy balls that needed my knee. "I'd like a word with my boss." My voice was sharp.

"No, and if you insist on causing a scene I'll pick you up and carry you over my shoulder. Your choice."

I came to a dead stop and looked up into the dark eyes that held a promise and looked like they would enjoy my humiliation. No one topped me outside of my bedroom but this Neanderthal Romeo didn't know that. He only knew I was dominant. Why did I get the feeling he thought he could control me. I'd had enough and if Johnny was getting rid of me and wouldn't be sending backup, I needed to handle this myself.

Using my body, I stepped into Mr. Deluxe Dimples. In perfect textbook self-defense 101, I grabbed his arm, tipped my shoulder, and bent at the waist. Taking another step in, I twisted and leaned to the side as Mr. Tall, Dark, and Airborne went flying. The entire move took less than three seconds. Before he made a solid thump against the cheap carpet, I was heading out the front door just daring the bouncers to stop me.

I cleared the entrance; debating if now was a good time to run. I wasn't concerned about what was ahead of me—I was terrified by what I left behind. I cast a quick look over my shoulder.

"Are you Ms. Simmons?"

Shit, I couldn't help my startled squeal. Two hundred and fifty pounds of double trouble stood in front of me leaning against a black limousine. I was so fucking screwed. At that moment, Mr. Maniac came through the door. His dimples were no longer showing.

"If she gets away, you're fired." His voice was deadly.

There wasn't even a split second to run as ham hocks wrapped tightly around my arms.

"Place her in the back."

"You son-of-a-bitch, this is kidnapping." I was scared but I wouldn't show it. My foot kicked out and Mr. Muscleman Number Two let out a grunt.

The car door opened and a not so gentle hand pushed me in the back. I was wearing knee high black boots and a short black leather mini skirt with a red thong beneath it. My knees hit the side of the limo and I fell forward with my ass in the air. A solid hand came down across my displayed cheeks and I scrambled inside. I crawled to the far corner and sat on the same afore mentioned now sore appendage.

I was beyond furious and like most women, even a dominatrix, I was about to cry. Things were not pretty when I cried. Biting my tongue finally caused enough pain to hold back my tears. I thought about screaming at the top of my lungs but I knew there was no one around to hear it but Mr. Moron and his muscle bound sidekick.

The car immediately moved forward picking up speed. I had a quick glimpse of Raul rushing out the door as he watched the tail end of my kidnapping. My head turned toward my nemesis. If this was his idea of a job interview, he was insane.

I had repeatedly turned down the offers to work at El Diablo even though it was the most exclusive private BDSM club in the country. Raul thought I was a fool but at the MC I ran things my way. I chose my subs based on my needs and theirs. I also understood that poor self-esteem brought many men and women into this lifestyle. I met the desires of the needy and I put up with fast-fingered Johnny because it filled an empty hole inside of me.

I wanted nothing to do with slapping my whip against the asses of the rich and lazy who thought their shit didn't stink. I sat in my corner of the limo and fumed for about sixty seconds.

"Where are you taking me?"

He didn't talk for a moment. A typical Dom response—build the tension and let the little sub know who was in charge.

"My plan was to take you to dinner but quite truthfully I'm now thinking my private suite would be the best place to put you across my knee and redden the rest of your sweet ass."

I inhaled sharply unable to keep the sound from escaping and received the slight quirk of his mouth again.

"You seem to have me mistaken for one of your subs. If you think you can beat me into accepting your job offer, you'll be disappointed."

"Oh? I have no intention of beating you in order to get you to accept my offer. I plan to spank your delectable ass to make myself feel better.

Chapter Three

Damian Collins was completely out of his mind. "If you hit me again, I'll file charges." As far as threats went, it sucked but this was all I had.

He laughed and I also heard a chuckle from the driver. "I assure you my team of attorneys will handle any legal problems you throw my way."

I knew he was right but there was no way I was giving in. "Why me?"

"That's the smartest thing you've said all evening. Your fame precedes you and I'm tired of hearing about the red headed Domme who attracts my rich patrons. They fly over here at least once a month just to watch you work. They pay your boss big bucks for a chance to have you top them but it seems you are rather discerning in your choice of subs. I only know of one person who managed to get past your selection process. It's been the talk of my club for months."

His eyes were dark and inside the shadowed interior of the backseat, I couldn't see them but I felt their burning heat. His Dom voice had turned low and sexy, with the knowledge that he was completely in charge. What I would give to tie him up and make him groan.

Inhaling slowly to gain control of myself, I decided to give my abductor a small amount of truth. "I know The Mediterranean is a rat hole but I'm not into perfect people. I like flaws. Your mega million-dollar followers spend enough money keeping their bodies beautiful to feed a small country. My answer is no."

"Hmm, you may have a point. They're beautiful but I believe most of them are mentally fucked up. Mommy and

Daddy didn't give them enough attention, rich Uncle Bruce got too touchy feely when they were small or better yet the dog was the only one willing to put out when they were juvenile adolescents."

"You're disgusting."

His voice went from sexy to stern, "And you're a self-righteous prude. I've seen your earlier pictures before your generous curves became muscled stealth. You put as much stock into your body as my millionaire club members do. I didn't find any evidence of plastic surgery in your file but borderline anorexia and maybe even bulimia are a given."

It was killing me that I couldn't see his face but at the same time, he couldn't see mine. My fingers trembled as I brought them to my mouth. It hurt—his words, his guess, and his obvious satisfaction in my humiliation. My hand went to the door handle. I was getting out even if I had to jump. The door wouldn't budge.

"Does the truth hurt? All of us are fucked up in this crazy world. You don't need to be into the BDSM scene to be crazy and we both know it. I think you will be pleasantly surprised with the diverse nature of my… followers, as you call them. I want you working at El Diablo. I'm willing to negotiate terms. I'll give you a one-month trial period, a deluxe suite at my hotel, and allow Raul to accompany you though he will officially work for me. You will work three nights a week but no tending bar, helping with accounting, or cleaning your own area. I'll triple your pay plus pay the rent on the one here so you have a place to come back to… if you come back."

He let that sink in but then blew my next 'no' all to hell.

"If you remain stubborn and continue to say no, I offer you a wager."

He had done his homework. He knew I lived for a bet. Once a month I took one hundred dollars to the racetrack and wagered on the ponies. Before he died, my father was a jockey. He never made the big time but he raised me at the track. He was five two and weighed a hundred pounds soaking wet. My mother was large like me but that's what turned him on. She died when I was a baby and he loved nothing more than telling me stories of the first time he saw her.

I shook myself mentally and snapped out of my walk down memory lane. I couldn't help myself, "Terms?"

His laugh sounded inside the dark interior and vibrated across my skin. It was almost sexier than he was. "If you accept the challenge I'll hold off on the spanking you deserve and drive you back to your car after dinner."

"Terms?" I said in my ultimate bitch voice.

"You have twenty-four hours to hide and then I have twenty-four to find you though I doubt I'll need it. If I win, and I will, you will work for me for the desired thirty days. If you win, I'll pay you fifty thousand dollars and walk away."

Fuck, he knew I wanted my own club and he knew I needed the money. Double fuck. "You have a deal but I have a condition about dinner."

"That's okay, Carl take us to Beasty Burgers. My lady wants her usual."

I was in trouble.

Chapter Four

They dropped me off at my vehicle with a full stomach and then watched until I drove away from the MC. I went straight home. Samson needed his walk and I needed to call Raul. I knew where I was going and I knew no dossier would have the details.

I opened the door and one hundred and fifty pounds of lovable Rottweiler bounced around like a toy poodle. Samson and Raul were my best friends. Both gave me so much more than I could ever give them in return. Sam followed me to my bedroom so I could change into my sweats and running shoes.

I also needed to get out of my red dental floss that passed for underwear. I unzipped my boots, removed my leather corset and skirt, and then peeled down my red thong. Walking over to the mirror was a mistake because when I looked over my shoulder at my bottom, a defined handprint was clearly visible, damn him.

I pulled on my favorite sweats hiding the evidence of Mr. Control Freak. "Come on monster, I have a Beasty Burger to work off and you need to do your business."

We ran five miles, taking breaks for Sam's personal needs. It felt wonderful. When I stopped running and began my mile cool down, I used my cell to call Raul. His mother had a dilapidated cabin she'd left him when she died. It was over two hundred miles away and we had only gone there once to clean and make sure everything was locked up tight. There was no electricity, no running water, and no way Mr. Delectable Dessert would discover my location.

Raul was waiting for me in front of my apartment with the cabin key when I jogged up to his car. "That man is edible. The rumors do him no justice." Raul was in lust again.

He was also gay and I wasn't surprised Mr. Hot Pants had that effect on him.

"I have no idea which way he swings so you might have a chance."

"Nope, I would have known if he shot my way. You better watch yourself because your voice actually goes dreamy when you *don't* say his name."

"Bullshit."

"Oh sweetie, I can see your blush."

"Stop, or I'll sick Sam on you and you'll drown in slobber. I'm taking a quick shower, packing a bag, and then I'm gone for forty-eight hours. Fifty thousand dollars will get us started Raul. The club will be small but with our savings and this money we can do it."

"I know baby-girl. Good luck."

I leaned my head into the car and kissed his cheek.

One hour later, I was on my way. Normally I would be asleep so I cranked the Rolling Stones up high and sang along. I wouldn't win any singing competitions but I knew every word to every Stone's song ever recorded. When it came to music, I was a seventies wannabe. George Thorogood's Bad To The Bone played next and I managed to stay awake. As the night continued, Samson whined in the back whenever I hit a high note. I continually looked in the rearview mirror making sure no one followed.

Finally, my headlights led the way through the trees, avoiding the thick brush trying to take over the narrow dirt road. It hadn't rained in several weeks and my old Subaru Outback had no difficulty getting through the deep but dry ruts. After the next bump, my lights shined on the small cabin in the distance. Samson would enjoy this. I had two gallons of water, dog food, some canned food for me, and a six-pack of Sterno fuel. My biggest problem would be using the outhouse for the call of nature. Yuk, but I could survive anything for two days.

Samson jumped out of the car as soon as the door opened. He immediately started stiffing out his territory and I grabbed my small overnight bag and made my way to the cabin door. I left the headlights on so I could see to get it unlocked. The lights shone into the bare living room. Thank god, I brought a book and candles to get me through the isolation. I carried my bag to the single bedroom that at least had a bed. The light barely made it around the curve of the door but I could see enough to place my bag on the foot of the bed.

I turned and then let out a blood-curdling scream as large arms shut the bedroom door and grabbed me in a steel grip, placing a hand over my mouth.

Samson hit the solid door with growls and barking.

A seductive voice whispered warmly in my ear, "I've won Mistress Lydia. Your flight takes off tomorrow evening. Get some sleep and then get that delectable ass of yours home. Pack a few personal items. I'll provide everything else. The plane tickets are waiting on your kitchen counter. Samson and Raul are both provided for and will be going with you." His hand lifted.

"You cheated." I said between gasps for air.

"You lost so take it like a Dom. Carl will pick you up at the airport in Houston. Now, I'll let you walk me out so your dog doesn't bite my legs off."

I could hear what sounded like helicopter blades in the distance. I was so completely fucked.

Chapter Five

"You gave me up." My snarled words spit out at my ex-best friend.

"If you stop yelling long enough to listen, I'll explain."

"There is no explanation. You knew I had no desire to leave the MC. You knew I'd refused Mr. Cheating Skunk's offer several times and you knew we needed the fifty thousand dollars."

Raul's hand came out of his pocket and he handed me a white slip of paper. My eyes briefly passed over the deposit slip and froze. There was one hundred and thirty six thousand dollars in the balance total. I looked up.

"He offered me a hundred thousand to give up your location. He might have found you anyway so I took it. He told me he would take the money back if I alerted you. We now have enough to fully start the club."

I had no words and looked back down at the total.

Strong arms came around my shoulders and brought me into his hard male chest. Raul was like a brother. How could I fault him for taking the money? Hell, I would have taken the money. Our dream was now sitting in the bank.

My eyes teared up. "You know I didn't mean what I said?"

"Oh but I liked the gay fag stag comment. I might use it sometime."

"You bastard." My arms tightened and Sam began to whine. He hated when he wasn't getting his share of attention.

"We need to leave. I hope they have a kennel large enough for Sam. I hear its cold in the cargo hold. Should I put him in his sweater?"

"I'm sorry but if you put that pussy sweater on him, I'm taking a different flight. Samson can tough it out like a real man."

"Says the gay man?"

"Oh honey, if dick size makes the man there isn't a *more* man than me."

"Argh, you're horrible. Use your muscle for something other than comedy and grab my bag. I'll get the leash."

The airport was crowded. We stood in line though everyone gave us a wide berth with Sam sitting at attention by my side. Finally, we made it to the check-in counter and Mr. Mogul's influence took over. A small electric cart appeared out of nowhere and the attendant ushered us on. Apparently, Sam was flying first class and had his own seat. I just hoped he didn't get airsick and barf all over me.

We bypassed the security checkpoint line and went straight to the front. Sam passed through the metal detector with me and we were off again. This time our destination was the Admiral's Lounge. I settled in with an imported high dollar beer that I didn't pay for. I could really get used to this.

Our flight was uneventful, if you didn't count the fact Samson wanted to sleep but couldn't get comfortable in his oversized seat. Finally, he was able to lie in the aisle and then he embarrassed me by snoring. Raul pretended he didn't know us.

Another cart picked us up at the gate and we sped along to the waiting limo.

Carl took my bag.

"How was your flight Ms. Simmons?"

"Fine, thank you. What should I call you?"

"Carl will do. It's a thirty-minute drive to El Diablo and Mr. Collins wants you there as soon as possible."

"I was hoping I could go straight to my room."

"Your suite is at The El Diablo. It's a luxury hotel and has everything you'll need. Mr. Collins wants to meet with you but I don't think you'll be working tonight."

We got in and Sam tried to sit on my lap but I shoved him over. He never figured out that he wasn't a lap dog and he always managed to finagle at least half his body onto mine when I sat on the couch at home. The limo was no different.

Luxury hotel was an understatement. The fountains looked like they came directly from the Bellagio in Vegas.

Carl drove away and we followed another man inside; same build, same good looks, and same demeanor. Why did the wealthy surround themselves with such extraordinary beauty? Normal people needed jobs too.

The inside was just as riveting as the outside. For thirty days, this would be my life. I inhaled the smell of money.

"Damian is eligible. He's hot and he's rich. You could do much worse." Raul's words whispered from under his breath while we walked to the elevator.

"Shh, behave smart ass."

We watched through the glass enclosure as we traveled to the top floor.

"We're at the top?" I asked our escort.

"Almost. There is one more floor but the only way to get there is to use one of Mr. Collin's private elevators.

Noticing the plural use of the word "elevator," I again realized how far out of my depth I was.

My escort placed a folded piece of expensive parchment paper in my hand. Five numbers boldly stared back at me.

"The access code for your rooms."

I punched in the number and entered a large foyer. Wow, it was incredible. Samson began to sniff out his new surroundings and I realized he needed a walk to take care of his business and I said so.

Follow me please. We followed him through the cavernous rooms to a set of French doors. Stepping outside, sparkling lights showed off an amazing outdoor oasis. The balcony wrapped around the building and was about twelve feet wide. A four-foot wall separated the garden from the Houston skyline. Real grass was under my feet, I could smell it.

"Mr. Collins assigned me and my co-worker to take Samson to the park when you're not available. Hotel staff will see to the dog waste left out here. I notified Mr. Collins of your arrival and he'll be here in a few minutes. Mr. Garcia, I need to show you to your suite."

My eyes met Raul's. I knew he wouldn't leave if I wanted him here. I was hoping he would be sharing rooms with me but apparently, that wasn't an option.

I gave him my brave smile. "I'll be fine. Get settled and call me in an hour."

He kissed my cheek and walked away. I knew my eyes were impossibly large. We were so *not* in Kansas anymore.

Once I was alone, I traveled down a large hallway and peered into several rooms before I located the master suite. There was another set of French doors and Sam whined to be let out again. He needed to mark his territory. I followed him and walked to the wall looking out over the city of Houston.

"I knew you would love the view."

I jumped and turned simultaneously. His dimples flashed and I inhaled sharply. The man, whose memory made my panties moist, stood before me. He was wearing black sweatpants, running shoes, and nothing else. His hand was holding a bottle of water and a fine sheen of sweat coated his incredible chest. He did this to me on purpose. I hadn't packed my vibrator damn it.

"Is the club here at the hotel?"

"So eager to begin working?"

"Yes, the sooner I start, the sooner I can leave."

"How you wound me Mistress Lydia."

"Do you want me for your Mistress? I would love to use a bullwhip on your damp skin?" I knew my eyes sparked with anticipation.

His laugh was low, sexy, and had my panties drenched before he finished. This man played havoc with my libido. "No, my fantasy is you tied to my bed, legs spread, and your screams filling the room while my cock slides in and out of your delectable pussy."

"And that will remain your fantasy." Dammit, I hoped my voice sounded stern enough. "For a hundred thousand dollars you might have talked me into whoring myself."

"Tsk, tsk, Lydia. It wasn't the money—it was the bet. I don't plan on paying for the use of your body when I know you'll willingly give it."

Damian obviously saw the lust I tried to hide and it only made me stiffen my resolve. "Most Doms respect a Domme and don't feel the need to control anyone but their submissive."

"Is that what you think?" His dark eyes caressed my body. "I guarantee every man who watches you wield a whip wants you chained and screaming." His gaze stopped on mine and heat sizzled between us. His voice lowered even further. "The difference is I'm not afraid of you and I go after what I want."

I gulped like a fool. "My body is not part of the deal." Even I didn't believe my own words.

He took a step closer and I took a step back.

"You know if you use your little flip trick again I'll go over the wall."

Oh, a chink in his armor. "That really got to you didn't it?"

"So much more than you know and I still owe you a punishment, but not yet. I'll let you worry about it for a while longer. The anticipation should make you wetter."

I wasn't going to lie. He knew every woman creamed when he flashed his dimples so I changed the subject. "When do I start work?"

"Tomorrow night."

"Then I need my sleep." I wanted him out of here.

"A late night snack will be here in a minute."

Samson heard the word snack and came running. He walked up to Mr. Wet Panty Advertisement and sniffed the hand Damian extended. He licked it and then licked again.

I had to smile. "He likes the salt on your skin."

"I'd like you to lick the salt from my skin but it's not my hand that's the saltiest."

Shivers ran across my skin. "Does that line work for your other Dommes?"

"I don't want to fuck the other Dommes and I'm afraid I never mix work with pleasure. With you I'm making an exception."

"Poor me."

His eyes glinted. "I don't usually care for ball gags but I might make an exception."

"Is that a threat?" God I hated him but I couldn't get the picture of licking his salty cock from my mind.

He laughed again. There was a soft chime from inside and Damian turned and walked back the way he came. Samson and I followed him around the outside of the apartment to the doors I'd originally entered when we first arrived.

Our waiter placed the meal on a side table. After a short bow, he disappeared. Damian poured wine and then we ate a cheese quesadilla sent down from heaven.

"Room service and anything else you need is available using the house phone. Just press zero. Your phone is programmed to call my suite too." His dimples flashed. "Just press 666."

I couldn't help my return grin. "You take this entire devil thing very seriously."

"It's my trademark and it's earned me a lot of money."

"I understand why you want me working at your club but why do you want me in your bed?" My voice went husky against my will.

"Hmm, I went to The Mediterranean already knowing what you looked like and how good you supposedly were. I watched the tail end of your scene and my cock got hard. In this business, you become jaded. Watching a simple scene doesn't usually do it for me but you do. Even dressed as you are now in your loose flowing hippie clothes, I'm hard. I kept these pants on because I knew I would be uncomfortable if I slipped on jeans. Really, I'm not sure what it is. You aren't the most beautiful woman I've ever seen, you don't have the best body, but you are sexy as hell. I want your braid wrapped around my hand and your mouth on my cock. I want red stripes across your ass and thighs. Then I want to kiss each one with my fingers buried deep in your pussy. When you come, my mouth will be licking every bit of juice from between your legs." The brown in his eyes had darkened even more by the time he finished his recitation.

I had trouble controlling my breathing but my ringing cell phone saved me. Fumbling, I finally managed to answer. "Umm, hello."

The phone disappeared from my hand. "She'll call you back in a few minutes." My phone disconnected with a snap.

He was close but he took a step closer. He didn't touch me but bent his head and soft warm air blew past my ear when he spoke, "Your shift starts at nine tomorrow night. You have a closet full of appropriate clothes. Carl will show you the way. Be on time."

He stepped back and then walked out the door.

Chapter Six

I admired Raul's closet full of BDSM attire. His leathers came with a small pitchfork emblem. Mine did not. He chose a set that showed off his nearly perfect physique and exposed his ass cheeks. I knew about the scars on his hip and upper leg from a motorcycle accident when he was a teenager. He usually hid the marred skin but with his choice of outfits, the scars were a statement and made him sexier.

"Do you think they'll fire me the first night for frightening the customers?"

"We're both walking away if they do but I've always told you your scars are exciting and they made me want to soothe you that first night I chose you for a sub."

"Still one of my best memories. Tell me why we became friends and you no longer top me?"

"Because you are much better as my assistant than you ever were as my slave. You cry too easy."

"Keep it up and I'll find some big bad Dom tonight and leave you alone with Master D."

"So it's Master D. now?"

"Well, you never use the same endearment twice and that man can master me anytime he wants. I hear he doesn't bang the staff. What a shame." He chuckled. "You're blushing. This should be a fun night."

"Let me dress and then we'll get it over with." I refused to acknowledge his teasing.

I went back to my apartment. The wardrobe selection I had was far more extensive than Raul's was and the closet was the size of my bedroom back home. There was a mirrored wall and a white plush bench in the middle of the room. This was mine for thirty days and I would enjoy every minute. I chose a black leather front lace up corset. There was purple ruffle at the top but it did little to hide the swell of my breasts and I knew there was probably a good chance my nipples would spill out at some point during the night. I chose black leather shorts that also laced up the sides. I didn't trust my crotch with Mr. Drip Fest around and I wanted it covered. I left an inch of skin showing down the center of the top and down the sides of the shorts.

My black boots back home were cheap and uncomfortable. I slipped on a pair of four-inch supple leather ankle boots from the closet and fell in love. They fit like a dream.

I didn't go for garish makeup but I did put on black eye liner with a slight curl at the sides. My eyes were a deep dark blue and one of my best features. My hair was in its customary braid but this one was high on my head. With a touch of deep red lipstick, I was ready, *not*.

My hands shook when I opened the door. Raul and Carl stood waiting.

Raul's whistle had me blushing, which was the biggest downfall of my pale skin.

Wow Chiquita, I so want to play."

"It's Mistress to you." It was time for the show and I wouldn't take any shit from Raul for the rest of the night. He knew I wouldn't discipline him but I had no problem finding someone who would.

"Yes Mistress." He tried to hold it back but I could hear the smile in his voice.

I turned to Carl. "Are my personal items set up?"

"Yes." Was his reply and I arched an eyebrow.

Raul answered next, "I made sure it was the way you like but my work was overseen Mistress." Raul was a tad disgruntled.

"Let's do it." I wasn't going to be more ready than I was now.

We followed Carl. He led us away from the bank of elevators we took the evening before and stopped at what looked like another guest room door. Carl entered a pin number and the door opened. An elevator door slid quietly to the side.

"Use your private suite code for this elevator and it will take you to the club. You may go there when you're not working but proper Domme or sub dress is required. If you want a non-kinky atmosphere, use the lobby or second floor bars. There's also an indoor pool and health club. Your room will have a list of everything the hotel offers. Use your room number on the bar or dining tab, everything is paid under the terms of your contract."

The door slid open and the world changed.

The lighting was low but spotlights to the sides softly lit up scene alcoves. The sounds of spanking and cries were normal but that's where normal stopped.

There was a real, honest to god carousel in the center of the large rotunda. It moved slowly and subs were riding brightly colored horses and moving up and down. Some had their hands chained to the pole in front of them while others just held on. The colorful lights glowed and turned a child's ride into an erotic wonderland. There was a spanking bench, no two, where the customary park benches should be. It was totally awesome and erotic. This was a BDSM playground for every wet dream imaginable.

I had trouble taking my eyes from the carousel. Displayed in all his glory, a young male sub was having a flogger used on his already pink striped ass by a Domme. My nerves settled. I was back in my world.

Finally, I was able to take my eyes off the erotic spinning wonderland and look around. There were three bartenders behind a thirty-foot bar. They wore black silk long sleeved shirts completely opened down the front with black bowties identifying them as El Diablo employees. Two of the bartenders were women and they wore skimpy black bras. All three had on skintight pants.

I noticed the cocktail waitresses had similar tops and bow ties but sported skimpy black leather skirts, black thongs, and high heels. A woman was lying face down on top of the bar and whenever a Dom sitting nearby placed an order, they delivered a hard slap to her naked behind. Her shoulders were shaking up and down and a small sob escaped with each blow. Bad sub.

A warm hand on my arm startled me but I didn't need to look to know who it was. Turning, I barely managed to get a breath in.

His chest was bare and smooth. His leather pants looked painted on and disappeared into black leather boots that stopped just below his knees. Each muscle begged to be touched. I barely had enough control to keep my hands off his sculptured chest. Slowly my eyes traveled back to his face.

Dimples.

His fingers released my arm and surprisingly, I was able to stand on my own. Even in full Domme mode, it was pure torture to be around him.

"Mistress Lydia." He took my hand and kissed the inside of my wrist. His tongue licked the area before releasing me. My pussy clenched.

"I have a surprise for you and I'd like to show you around."

"That would be wonderful." My Dominatrix voice sounded breathy in my ears. I had to get control of myself.

We walked closer to the carousel and I could see faces of men and women riding the brightly colored horses.

"If you choose a sub for the night they can wait for you on the carousel if you need to leave them alone. House rules keep Dom's from approaching another's sub on the Carousel. You can also see that discipline is one of its better features."

I looked at the sub flogged only moments ago. His mouth worked between the Domme's thighs and she was holding tight to a pole made for just that purpose.

The slow spinning movement stopped and a young woman stepped down. She held the carousel controller in her hand and approached us. My shock was apparent. It was Angela dressed in an El Diablo employee uniform. She went to her knees at my feet. My hand touched her hair but my eyes went to Damian.

"Permission to speak Mistress?"

"Yes Angela you have permission." Tears burned my eyes but I held them back.

"I arrived this morning. Master D. gave me a job and when I'm not working I'm a full member of the club."

I couldn't help my frown. "You traveled this morning and you're working tonight?"

"Yes Mistress but Master D. told me if I didn't take a nap I could not come in this evening. I only work for another hour but he wanted me here so you would feel more comfortable. I would like to write myself on your schedule for next week if it pleases you Mistress?"

"Yes it pleases me. Thank you Angela, you have made my evening brighter."

"Thank you Mistress, I must get back to work."

Yes you should, I'm not sure kneeling while you're on duty is a good idea."

Damian's voice interrupted, "An exception was made this one time. She asked and I granted her this small favor."

I stopped Angela with a slight touch to her arm. She turned and I gently kissed her on the cheek. "Thank you for being here."

"Yes, mistress." Angela gave me an incredibly sweet smile before she walked away.

"Do you like my surprise?"

I had to fight the need to wrap my arms around him. "Your control of my life makes me nervous."

"Too bad, you lost the bet." He smiled wickedly. "We need to finish your tour."

"You cheated." I said with a disgruntled voice though Mr. Nasty Nipples ignored me.

Curious eyes followed us. Damian took in everything with a sweeping gaze but for the most part ignored the patrons. The entire club was lavish and even smelled delicious; leather, wood oil and sex, nothing like the Mediterranean. Everything looked new, expensive, and clean. The lighting was perfect and the music in the background was subtle with a heavy bass. A group of people sat on low couches playing cards. Subs kneeled at their feet; some naked and others barely clothed. This was the world of pleasure and money—my world for a short time.

What surprised me the most was everyone was not beautiful. There was one woman who was pleasantly plump and wore the collar of her Dom who handed her a drink and sweetly touched her hair. She smiled and said thank you.

There was an older couple; both looked to be in their sixties. He was collared and appeared blissfully happy, wrinkles and all.

"Excuse me Master D." A bouncer spoke. "We have a matter that needs your attention."

Damian looked my way. "Come with me, please."

I so wanted to come with his cock buried deep inside my pussy but I nodded my head and followed.

We stopped at a corner station and I could hear loud sobs as we approached.

The bouncer wasn't happy. "Master Ellis was escorted out. His sub has a few bruises and he didn't stop when she gave her safe word. I'll have his file on your desk in the morning but I thought you might want to see to Melody sir."

Damian walked into an alcove separated from the station by lush plants. I could smell the rich soil and greenery. A thin woman was lying on the couch and Damian sat beside her.

"Are you okay Melody?"

"He hurt me." She sniffed while trying to regain control of her emotions. "I used my safe word but he wouldn't stop."

"Do you need medical attention?" His hand tilted her face up so she looked at him.

"No Master D. I'll be okay."

"Good, here sit in my lap." He pulled her gently over and cradled her like a baby. His hand pressed her head against his shoulder then went to her breast and kneaded the plump flesh tenderly. His other hand went to her shaved pussy and massaged her labia.

Fuck me, my gut clenched and my fingers tightened into fists. I was jealous. I'd watched this happen with subs hundreds of times and I had gentled subs this same way but I wanted those hands on me.

Damian kissed her. It was tender and sweet and I wanted Melody to die.

"Stephen please have Melody's preferred drink delivered here and find Kyle for me."

"Yes, Master D."

I continued to watch and Mr. Lusty Master continued to comfort the no longer crying female.

"You called Master D?"

He was tall, almost the size of Damian, and he was incredibly gorgeous, it was hard to tell who was the better looking of the two men. This hunk wasn't dressed as an employee he was a Dom.

"Do you have a sub for the night Kyle?"

"No, I don't."

"Melody has need of some TLC and I was hoping you would take her to one of the private rooms and make her feel better."

"My pleasure. I take it Master Ellis will not be returning?"

"No he won't and I want you to watch over Melody until a new Dom can be found for her."

"Again, my pleasure."

"I'm sure you've figured out at that this is Mistress Lydia. She's off limits except to the subs."

What? Did I just hear him right?

Kyle smiled and went to kiss my hand but a glare from Mr. Dramatic stopped him. Kyle grinned and tipped his chin down in acknowledgment. "It's nice to me you Mistress Lydia."

"Nice to meet you, Master Kyle." He dropped my hand and I couldn't help myself. My fingers grabbed his and I raised them to my lips. My tongue came out.

Kyle fought a full out grin and quirked his eyebrows at me. He then took Melody from Mr. Control Freak's arms and walked away.

"You will be punished for that too my dear."

"Promises promises."

I couldn't help but look at his crotch where his erection strained against his pants. "I see Melody has you hot and bothered?"

Before I could draw another breath into my lungs, Damian's arms wrapped around me and his lips took mine. They nibbled, they sucked, and then they devoured. My pussy went into overdrive and my pelvic bone rocked against his hard cock. His hand went to my braid and used it to tug my head back giving his mouth better access.

After I was thoroughly kissed—hot, bothered, and wet, his lips ended their assault. His chin rested on the top of my head and he said with a throaty growl, "We can't do this here. It will be bad for business and bad for you in general." His hand tightened its hold in my hair. Come to bed with me when your shift is over. We need to get each other out of our systems. I need to fuck you." He turned slightly and whispered in my ear, "Say yes."

I inhaled his musky scent slowly into my lungs. The soap he used and his spicy natural body odor were incredibly erotic. I exhaled. "Sorry but I must decline and I would prefer you not kiss me again." I was glad he wasn't watching me lie. "I'm not sleeping with you and I don't care if I'm in your system or not. I have sex with subs and my private life is my own. I might want to fuck you but I won't. Candy is not good for my teeth or my hips."

His chuckle was low and rich. "Oh! You stubborn bitch. I want your teeth on my candy." His hips ground into mine and then he released me. "I promise my cum is sweeter than chocolate and you can lick it off my lollipop stick."

"Argh, you did not just say that?"

"Oh baby, I want to talk dirty to you. I want…"

"Stop." My hand covered his mouth and the son of a bitch bit me. It wasn't gentle either. "Ouch. Okay Mr. Fuck Fangs, I'd like to explore your club and get to work but I need a sub. I'd also appreciate a recommendation. Tonight I want a male. He needs to be tall, with dark hair and eyes. Some heavy muscle would also me nice. If you have a twin brother, I'll take him."

Damian laughed full out. I loved the sound.

"Your wish is my command and I have the perfect sub for you. I want to see you work the St. Andrews Cross if your game?"

"My pleasure, Master D."

Chapter Seven

Adam was a hot cowboy. He was no Damian but I couldn't complain. I left his hat on along with his chaps. I worried that Mr. Fuck Me Tonight would give me a complete loser. It was nice to be wrong. However, it wouldn't have mattered because I was horny as hell and could get my rocks off just by closing my eyes and dreaming about Mr. Palatial Penis.

The crowd began gathering around the large area while I strapped Adam to the cross. It was top of the line and would lie flat, which was perfect for what I wanted later. "Your safe word?"

"Red Mistress."

"We've discussed your limits and I know you like pain but tonight I'm only getting familiar with you."

"Yes Mistress."

I kissed him. It wasn't anything like Damian's kiss but I liked to get to know all my subs this way.

Standing, I removed a cock ring from a tray on the side table and clamped it tightly on his erection. He groaned.

"Shh, don't make a sound or you won't like the punishment."

I used the whip. It was new. Just by warming up my wrist and snapping it a few times, my mind drifted to the deep dark place I craved. This was my own special universe where I could block out everything around me and concentrate on my sub.

Adam trembled when I ran my hands across his chest and then over his firm ass. I kissed his lips again and felt his heartbeat pick up beneath my hand. My fingers moved down to his cock and I ran them along the metal of the ring. His breathing accelerated even more. Mine was slow and steady.

"Shh, remember my command."

He knew better than to speak. I stepped away and released the coil. It dropped to the floor and I rotated my wrist one last time.

The crowd went quiet and waited.

I gave them everything they desired.

My sub was good and took the pain. I checked a few times and he assured me through gritted teeth that he wanted more. I would use Adam again. I liked choosing my scene partners depending on what I planned. Adam would make a good whipping post on nights when I needed a heavy workout. I also wanted to see what Adam could do with his mouth. I craved relief.

He broke. It took twenty minutes, but finally his yell resounded through the club.

My body was slick and sweaty. With two more strokes of the braided leather, I was finished. I walked to Adam and began loosening the turn wheels that allowed me to lower the cross. Raul helped. He didn't need to ask what I wanted—he read my mind. When Adam's body tilted back, we unbuckled him, turned him over, and refastened his bindings. I walked around and shimmied out of my shorts. Facing the crowd, I grabbed the bar above Adam and straddled his face.

"Lick me Adam, slowly, clean my pussy."

The crowd watched. My head went back and I groaned as my orgasm built. I closed my eyes imagining one mouth on my cunt, one tongue licking and sucking my juices. I pictured his face, his grin, and those sexy dimples. The orgasm pulsed through my pussy and I cried out. Yes, I would be using Adam again. I hoped he remained unattached.

Slowly, my eyes opened and burning dark orbs pierced mine though my sexual release gave me enough control to ignore his scalding gaze. This is who I was. I made no excuses.

I adjusted the cross and moved Adam to a standing position again. Pulling my shorts back on, I tied the leather strings and then walked around and removed Adam's cock ring. He groaned but managed to hold most of the sound in.

"It's okay, this is for you, and if it feels good I want to hear it." I ran my fingers over the side of his face and gently kissed his cheek.

I removed a cherry flavored condom from the tray beside me and rolled it over Adam's cock. I liked candy and this kind had no calories. I worked my tongue over him and then took him fully into my mouth. I sucked and moved my lips while slowly massaging his balls with one hand. His cries grew louder and finally he shouted and spurted into the condom.

I looked to where Damian stood but he was gone.

I began unbuckling the leather cuffs from Adam's legs first. Raul unstrapped his wrists and asked Adam if he could stand on his own.

Raul assisted him to the couch hidden by a grouping of plants that covered the alcove behind the scene area. Each station had a small alcove for after care.

Adam lay with his head on my lap.

"Raul, can you get us bottled water?"

"Yes Mistress."

"Tell me about yourself Adam."

And it began. I knew I wouldn't want to leave El Diablo when my time was up but I would.

Raul returned with our water and another thirty minutes passed. I could really use a glass of wine.

"Adam, would you be willing to finish showing me around? I'll buy you a drink. I would like you to continue as my sub this evening, are you interested?"

"I'd be honored Mistress."

Raul strolled over after we left the area.

"Do you have enough to keep you busy Raul?"

"Yes, Mistress. I have a Dom interested in me and I'll go up to my room and change if you don't mind."

"Have fun."

"I plan to Mistress."

I looked at Adam. "I would like to meet some of the other Doms and Dommes. Are there any you think I would like?"

"Mistress Anna is a favorite and Master Jordan. He likes fire play and he should be at his station soon."

"I'm not into fire play myself but I wouldn't mind watching. Lead the way please."

We walked out of the alcove and I noticed a large crowd a few stations down.

"Is that the fire play?"

"No Mistress, fire play is only performed at station five. You're looking at station three."

"Let's see what's going on."

We walked over and I could see between a few of the people watching. It was Damian and god he was sexy. The butt plug in his hand made me squirm. He had a woman displayed over a spanking bench. She was writhing and moaning loudly. His hand came down on her lower back and then moved to her rounded plump cheeks. Her body was lush and beautiful.

A scream rang out when Damian ran the butt plug along the crack of her ass. She was behaving badly and the damn thing wasn't even inserted.

Damian's hand slapped down hard across her ass.

"I don't mind hearing you scream when I give you a reason but I've barely touched you."

"I'm afraid, Master."

"I think I can help with that but I want silence for the next five minutes, understood?"

"Yes Master."

His finger entered her pussy. He added another and pushed in, then withdrew. It was slow torture and her rounded ass bucked slightly but she remained quiet.

With my very fucked up head working overtime, the scene didn't make me jealous, it made my cunt throb. I wanted to play too. Turning to Adam, I nodded to the floor and he went to his knees. My hand went out and pressed his head to my hip in a loving gesture. "Watch." I wanted his eyes on the scene and not me. I had a feeling I was giving too much away when it came to Master D.

When her orgasm started, Damian inserted the plug and Miss Screams A Lot let loose. It was high pitched and irritating but I guessed some men liked it. Oh Lydia, thy name is jealousy. I smiled and at that moment, he looked into my eyes. His ignited and I knew the flames in mine answered. I couldn't get away quick enough and poor Adam had trouble coming off his knees and keeping up.

It was two a.m. before the club slowed down. I spoke with several Doms and Dommes. They paid membership dues and looked at me as something of an oddity but they were nice. I really liked Anna, and we had plans for some shopping later in the week. Adam scheduled with me the following week and gave me the lowdown on several subs he thought I might enjoy. He also spoke more about his poor little rich boy life and Damian was right; money did fuck you up. At least Adam seemed happy now and he was working on his master's degree in psychology. Too bad I would be long gone when he started practicing.

I made it back to my rooms and let Samson outside. I fell into a fitful sleep and dreamed of Damian and his mouth.

Chapter Eight

I didn't see Mr. Lush Lips the next day but he escorted me to the club that night. He said a few clipped sentences but after that, he didn't invite conversation. What a grouch. We parted at the bar and I ordered a strawberry marguerite. Yep, a girlie drink but I didn't care. I never got drunk when I worked but I needed to get Damian's sour mood out of mind.

I worked with two different subs but didn't take any pleasure for myself. They never complained and both enjoyed pink skin along with several orgasms.

I had the next two nights off but had to be back on Saturday. I requested Angela for a new idea I was playing with and gave Raul a list of what I needed. I gave instructions to Angela not to shave or wax intimately before our session.

Shopping with Anna and Raul was a blast. Always take a gay man shopping was my motto. He and Anna hit it off and they made plans for her to use him in one of her scenes.

"I don't quite understand why you won't use Raul as your sub?" Anna asked when Raul took a side trip to the men's room.

"I don't know. It just doesn't feel right but at the same time, he's wonderful. What he really needs is a male Dom who turns him on and won't let him get away with any shit. Watch it or he'll be topping you."

She laughed. "I have a trick or two for naughty subs."

We both laughed and her eyes sparkled. "So give me the low down on you and Master D."

I could tell curiosity was eating her up. "There is no low down. I want him, he wants me, but we're not playing. Two Doms don't make a right."

She chuckled at my play on words. "Last night he was intense, almost volatile when he enacted his scene. He wants you bad and I've never seen him go after a Domme. There isn't a sub at El Diablo that doesn't want his collar. Every once in a while, he'll spend a private weekend with a sub but after that it's business as usual. Right now he's behaving odd and we all feel the tension."

"I'm only here for three more weeks and I can't see Damian with stripes across his ass. If he wants me, that's what it'll take."

"Oh girlfriend, that will never happen. What brought you into the scene?"

"When I was eighteen I fell for an older man. He was a Dom and I spent a very eye-opening weekend learning it was hard for me to be submissive. I was quite chubby back then and embarrassed about my body. I began working out, jogging, and then I ordered a bullwhip online. I disposed of all my apartment furniture, watched videos, and practiced for hours every day. I worked as a secretary during the day but little by little I began exploring the lifestyle at night." I momentarily looked away. I had left out so much. So much hurt and pain but I only shared those memories with Raul and Sam.

Saturday arrived and I was looking forward to working with Angela. Damian didn't escort me, he sent Carl. I refused to ask about Mr. Succulent Semen.

My scene was set up as I asked. This was role-play and I wanted to have some fun.

I tied a silk scarf around Angel's eyes and whispered in her ear. "Do you trust me?"

"Yes Mistress."

"Okay, remember your safe word. I won't take you farther than I think you can go but tonight I'm pushing." I kissed her forehead.

"I want you on your knees in position."

When I was ready, I placed her on the St. Andrews Cross and using gel, I shaved her pussy while I massaged her rounded bottom. I never touched her cunt with my fingers.

Angela groaned.

"Shh, no sounds, we've only just started."

"Ahhh, please Mistress."

"Angela my sweet sub, your punishment will be the delay of your first orgasm." I planned to give the crowd a real show but now I would withhold her first release.

I used a deerskin flogger and concentrated on her breasts and upper thighs. I avoided her freshly shaved pussy knowing it was begging for pain and pleasure.

She began whimpering. I had no mercy. I didn't use vaginal or anal toys. I wanted her writhing from the feel of the soft leather strands striking her body. I stopped for a moment and approached. I took one hard nipple into my mouth, sucked, and then moved to the other.

I used the flogger again and she began moaning loudly. Without stopping, I looked to the side of the station at Kyle who placed a condom on his erect penis when I gave the signal.

Kyle told me earlier that he preferred giving pain. I wasn't sure why he said he would help me tonight but with a mysterious grin, he agreed.

Kyle walked to Angela and straddled her hips. I squeezed in between Kyle's outer thighs and Angel's upper body. She couldn't see what we were doing or who was doing it to her. I took a nipple between my lips and Kyle plunged inside her pussy in one smooth thrust.

Angela screamed, Kyle moaned, and I watched Angela jerk against the restraints. My pussy clenched and I wondered if I could resist Damian much longer.

My head turned and there he was with his hands on his cock. It was free of his pants and he stroked up and down. He turned to the sub at his feet and her mouth took over where his hands had been. I needed an ice cold shower for me, and, a baseball bat to knock out the little sub's teeth.

I snapped myself out of my less than pleasant thoughts. I owed my sub and the crowd a few more orgasms. It was time for my first toy.

After the scene and my time alone with Angela, Anna walked over and invited me to a private party in one of the suites after work. We quit work at two a.m. but first I went back to my room, changed, let Samson out, and then found my way to the party. It wasn't a D/s party, it was a good old fashioned let's get drunk and celebrate Saturday night party. I wore what Damian referred to as my hippie clothes. He had my closet stocked full of them. It actually made me smile.

I was getting tipsy and taking my first sip of my third margarita when the devil himself walked in. He was a flaming beacon in a room full of dazzling people but I slid my gaze away and spoke with one of the male El Diablo bartenders.

Steel fingers rested on my shoulders and hot breath passed over my bare neck then traveled to my ear. "I want you."

I turned on the stool and placed my thighs on the outside of his hips. My skirt pulled tight and his hands pulled the skirt up past my knees so he could move in closer. My lips traveled past his neck but I didn't touch. I gently bit his earlobe and then whispered, "No."

His hands slid under my bottom and brought the center of my thighs even with his hard erection. His mouth went back to my ear. "I have a bet for you."

Our voices were low but I'm sure everyone in the room was watching our sexual play. "Terms?"

"Two subs, blindfolded. Whips only, no toys, they won't know who's working who. First one to bring their sub to orgasm wins."

"And what is the wager?"

"One night of being the other's private sub."

I pulled back and looked into his shadowed sensual eyes. I was a little beyond tipsy but I knew what I heard."

"You would sub for me?"

Pure wickedness sparked in his eyes. "I have no intention of losing."

Chapter Nine

Our bet made the rounds like wildfire. It took place on Monday, usually the slowest night for the club. El Diablo was packed. Damian picked the subs. They were best girlfriends and enjoyed working together and partnering with one Dom. The rules made them smile. Neither would know who wielded their whip. No skin could be broken or the bet was forfeit. Damian had another St. Andrew's Cross moved into the largest station area. We blindfolded the women and then Damian gave me choice of Subs. I took the blonde.

My hand trembled slightly while I rotated my wrist. I inhaled deeply. I could win this. I refused to watch Damian prepare. I focused on my sub and managed to control my heartbeat.

The wager began.

I worked her slow with little pain allowing her to become accustomed to the feeling of the whip going around her arms and legs. Every four or five lashes and I would wrap the whip around her breasts or strike her pussy. The response was instantaneous and I backed off. I would then return to the arms, legs, belly, and upper thighs. All my focus was on my sub and her pending release.

It took twenty minutes but she was so close. I cast my first glance at Damian. He wasn't working his whip—he was staring at me. I looked at his sub. She hung limp in her restraints. With purposeful strides, he walked over, removed the whip from my hand, and handed it to another Dom. I didn't even see who it was. My eyes stayed glued to his devil's gaze.

I was hot, sweaty, and terrified.

He won.

Could I do it?

Looking around for an escape route was stupid but I did it anyway. My world tilted and I was over his shoulder like his promise from the first night we met. A round of applause broke out and I knew my ass was on display for everyone. It didn't matter—I lost the bet.

The blinking lights went by as he walked through the club straight to the back of office. His fingers punched in the access code for his private elevator. He was taking me to the penthouse.

"You can put me down now I'm not going anywhere."

A hard slap landed on my ass.

"You don't have permission to speak. You know the rules."

Another hard slap landed for emphasis but besides my quick suction of air, I remained quiet.

He carried me into the elevator and my stomach sank as we traveled upward. All I could see was the plush black carpeting.

Using quick strides, he carried me into his apartment. I tried to take in the surroundings but a moment later I found myself upended again and my butt hit a hard wooden chair. He left me there and walked away.

I expected the opulence but damn the room was beautiful and it was only a breakfast table for four. The walls displayed incredible artwork.

He came back carrying a yellow folder, two wine glasses, and a bottle… Borgogno something. I knew it was expensive because he would provide nothing less.

I kept my mouth shut giving him no reason to punish me again. For one night, I would play his sub and live out my nighttime fantasies. He would never know I wanted more than one night.

His eyebrow arched. Apparently, he was expecting a comment. I looked down and away like the good, little submissive he wanted.

His fingers tilted my chin up.

"If you can keep a civil tongue, you may speak. Your insolent mouth will only get you punished so be careful." He poured two glasses of wine.

"You know it's not a good idea to drink in this situation and I'd rather keep my wits about me."

"You only get one glass and you need to relax. We're going through your soft and hard limits and then you're signing the agreement."

"The deal was carte blanche. Why do you care what my limits are?"

"Good question but I'm not a complete sadist and I'd like you to get something out of this evening. It's not up for discussion—the wine, or the contract. If you come away with bruises, I don't want the cops at my door."

Embarrassingly enough, my hand shook as I reached for my glass. His eyes missed nothing but he didn't comment. He opened the folder and took out a contract. It was the same one used in the club. I could feel my face reddening which caused his dimples to show, damn him.

"Do you wish to go through this one by one or would you rather just tell me what I need to know. Understand, I will counter your demands with some of my own and we'll compromise on a few. Both our needs are being met tonight."

I wanted to scream but held it in. My screams would be ringing out soon enough.

"First hard limit; anal sex."

He didn't blink. "Okay but I will use anal toys."

"It's the same thing."

"No it isn't. My cock up your ass is anal sex. The toys are anal play. There's a big difference. Next item." His long fingers wrote in bold script across the white paper.

I swallowed the rest of my wine in one unladylike gulp. I hope it cost a thousand dollars.

He bit his lip, fighting his goddamn smile. This night was never going to end.

We went through it all, no animals, no fire play. He got hot wax, ouch but he promised no blisters if he decided to use it. It took the better part of an hour and by the end, I knew I was in deep trouble.

"I'll show you the bathroom. I want you showered, your hair washed, body shaved, and ready in twenty minutes. Everything you need is on the counter. There is a robe on the back of the door, and you will come out with nothing else on and the robe untied. Don't comb your hair only wrap it in a towel. When you approach me, you will kneel at my feet facing me in the sub position. Is there anything you are unclear about?"

"No."

He stood and led me through several rooms to the bathroom. It was magnificent; gray marble with black accents. He left the room leaving the door open a crack. I looked at the door but knew it wasn't worth the fight. I peed first and then got in the oversized shower. There were two showerheads and a bench seat on both sides.

I quickly washed and shaved. My cunt, legs, and arms were silky smooth when I finished. I couldn't help myself and ran my fingers through my hair getting out a few of the tangles. My time was up.

He was standing by the bed when I came out. His tie was gone and his shirt unbuttoned and hanging loose. His belt was still on but he had removed his shoes and his feet were bare. I didn't look him in the eye. I went into sub position while trying to control my breathing.

"Spread your knees further."

I obeyed.

The towel gently fell from my hair and the strands cascaded down in front of my eyes obscuring my face. His body folded in front of me and I could see his smooth chest without looking up. He ran a comb through the tangles. He never tugged just took his time. My pussy grew damp. Suddenly, I realized what this night would mean and tears began welling in my eyes.

One finger tilted my chin up. I didn't know the tear tracked down my face until he bent forward and licked it.

"None of that. Tonight is about pleasure. Forget our lives, the club, and your objections. Enjoy your incredible body that does nasty things to mine when I think about you. I won't take more than you can give.

"Bu…"

His finger covered my lips and he leaned in close. "You do not have permission to speak." The words were breathy soft in my ear and then he placed soft kisses on my hairline, the corner of my eye, and ended at my lips. The kiss was sensual and my hands gripped my thighs tightly so I could resist running them through his hair. I had to make him think I was playing the game. He couldn't know my true feelings.

His lips pulled away. "Tell me something about yourself that my investigators couldn't uncover. Something private."

I didn't hesitate, "No."

"That's your favorite word. You don't play the sub very well."

"I'm not a sub."

"But tonight you are." His dominant voice was back.

I remained silent but continued to look into his eyes.

"Another wager?"

I couldn't help it, I rolled my eyes."

His tsk, tsk almost made me smile. Knowing it was a wager that caused all my current problems I couldn't help myself. "Five orgasms?"

"Yours or mine?"

I did smile. "Mine."

"And your forfeit if I lose?"

"The same."

"Then we've reached a deal."

I expected him to shake my hand but instead his hands brushed aside the bathrobe and his palms covered my breasts.

"I knew they would be soft but they're pure silk and fit my hands perfectly." His thumb and forefinger not so gently pinched my nipples. "These first, it's time we get started. Eyes down."

He stood and walked away though he didn't leave the room. When he returned he knelt again. I could see the nipple clamps in his hand. He leaned forward and took one aching nipple into his mouth. He sucked and flicked it with his hot tongue. He pulled away and attached the first clamp. It hurt and I inhaled.

"You know the safe word. I won't remind you again and I expect you to know your limits and teach me about what your body needs."

He didn't wait for my reply just went to work on my other nipple. When he finished a small chain ran between my breasts. It had very small bells and when he plumped my breasts, they jingled slightly. I knew he was smiling but I didn't look up. He stood and moved behind me.

My heart stopped but he only divided my hair into three parts and deftly braided it down the back.

"Come." He walked from the room. Didn't he know I almost had?

Chapter Ten

I followed close behind keeping my eyes down as much as I could. I knew my role. I wasn't sure how many rooms we passed but we went through a large section of the house and then he opened a door and nodded his head for me to precede him down some stairs. There were eight. I counted each one. The smell of leather became stronger with every step.

I stopped at the bottom. We were in his private dungeon. My knees almost gave out.

His hands startled me when they landed on my shoulders and he placed a quick kiss on my bare neck. He took my hand and led me across the room to a bench. It had a bar overhead. He stepped behind me and slipped the bathrobe off my shoulders. It pooled at my feet. He turned me around so I was facing him and then his hands went to the backs of my thighs.

"Hold onto my neck."

He lifted me to the edge of the table, and then his large body stepped close, pushing my knees apart.

He backed away. "Don't move."

He walked over to a cabinet and took out several items before returning. He placed something behind my back on the bench and then took my right wrist and placed a leather cuff around it. He repeated the process with my other wrist. Next, he took first one arm and then the other and attached them to the bar above my head.

"This will allow you to hold the bar."

Fuck, my pussy tightened and I knew he wouldn't need to work hard for my first orgasm.

He moved the bar. It went back and locked into place forcing me to lay back with my hands over my head.

"I thought we would get this part out of the way."

I hadn't realized he'd picked up two objects behind my back before he lowered me. Lube and a medium sized butt plug now rested in his hand.

My legs came up and I tried to kick him. It was reflex.

"So you want to play like that?"

He grabbed my legs and removed a larger ankle cuff from his back pocket. Now I really started to fight.

A swift slap landed on my hip. It hurt and finally got through my panicked brain. He slapped me again and I stopped fighting completely.

He spread my legs wide and secured them. My butt was barely on the table. I tried bringing my knees inward but two inflexible hands held them apart. He released one and circled my pussy with his fingers. I was wet. I could look at what he was doing. I watched his face. So beautiful. He was always hot, but in full Dom mode, he was every woman's fantasy. His brown eyes lifted to mine and he brought his finger to his lips.

"I've wanted to taste you since the first night." He licked the glistening moisture. "Delicious."

The finger he licked went back to my pussy and entered, pushing deep. I gasped. It slid slowly in and then out. My hips were coming off the table and I wanted more. His other hand splayed over my stomach and held me down.

"Don't move." He rasped.

I lowered my head back to the bench taking deep breathes.

I could hear him opening the lube and squirting it onto the butt plug. My sphincter muscles tightened. I knew this was going to be uncomfortable. His finger came up and traveled between my butt cheeks seeking my ass. He lubricated the puckered circle but didn't try to enter. His hand continued to play gently and unexpectedly his mouth found the hot folds of my labia and his tongue laved my clit causing my hips to buck off the table.

His laugh was low and sexy. "The first thing I thought I would need was a gag for your mouth but you've been unexpectedly quiet. Unfortunately, you can't stay still but I can help with that. He pulled straps up from the sides of the table and secured them firmly over my hips. He didn't give me time to adjust; his sweet mouth went back to work. I then felt his finger slide into my pussy again and his lips found my clit and began to suck.

I thrashed against my bindings. His mouth was torturing me and there was nothing I could do but give in. The muscles of my pussy began to throb and a cry escaped my lips as the orgasm rolled over me. I felt pressure against my anus but I was too far gone to clench. The butt plug went past my sphincter and buried deeply inside my ass. My pussy clenched and continued pulsating. Teeth nibbled and sucked and my sob turned into a loud moan.

Finally, my orgasm tapered off and I managed to open my eyes.

He was watching me. "Your job is simple. You had better clench that butt plug tightly because if it falls out, there will be hell to pay and the next one I use won't be as small.

Argh, I screamed inside my head. He looked completely unaffected. His eyes hadn't softened with passion but they did sparkle with mirth.

"One down and four to go."

If I weren't tied down and at his mercy, I would have thrown something at him.

Chapter Eleven

He released me from the table though he left my wrist and ankle cuffs on. He also left the butt plug in. His hand grabbed mine and led me to a spanking bench. I could feel a trail of wet juices slide down my legs. I knew I was going to lose this bet and my pussy moistened more with anticipation.

He turned me toward the bench and pushed me down so my ass was in the air. He quickly secured my arms and legs. He squeezed my ass cheeks and he used his finger to follow along the crack, ending at the butt plug. I clenched my anus tight refusing to release the toy. He pulled slightly and a soft groan escaped my lips.

"I know you want my cock in here but it's too late to go back on the contract now." The plug slid slowly in and out. It hurt but if he touched my clit, he would have two orgasms in the bag. He must have known but for some reason he stopped.

"I've owed you your next punishment since the night we met. It's going to hurt, you're going to cry, but you're also going to love it.

Panic set in just like he knew it would. I'd be damned if I would cry no matter what he did but I couldn't help but wonder what that would be. My eyes followed him as he walked over to the wall and took down a blackleather, riding crop. He came back and placed the end under the front of my body running it across my breasts. He teased the nipple clamps causing sensual burning. My deep breaths grew erratic. He stopped and walked behind me out of my line of sight again.

"Do you remember the first night we met?"

The crop came down hard across my right butt cheek. I inhaled and a slight squeal escaped my mouth.

"I want an answer."

The crop came down again. I managed to hold in my groan but it hurt. "Yes."

"Did you really think I would harm you?"

Again, the crop struck and this time the pain was more intense.

"I didn't know you." I managed this sentence between clenched teeth.

"You were beautiful." The next strike landed on the back of my upper leg. "You sent me flying over your shoulder." The next one landed on my other leg. He striped my skin with deft perfection.

"I wanted to strangle you but more than anything, I wanted to fuck you."

The crop landed on the exposed part of my pussy and I screamed. I could no longer hold back my tears and they fell one after the other.

I felt his hand rub my lower back and then two fingers entered me ever so slowly. When they were finally as far as they could go the anal plug twisted.

"Damn you." I cried. I could no longer help myself.

"Oh baby, you played right into my hands."

He stepped away from my body and the riding crop again smacked my backside though this time it was lower on the back of my leg. I didn't have time to scream before the next strike landed. He systematically continued and I was sobbing in earnest now. His aim was perfection and he never hit the same place twice but my entire backside was a single burning sensation.

The last strike was between my legs and then his fingers took over. Slowly in and just as slowly out. When they came out the butt plug pushed in. I couldn't stop the explosion of my orgasm. It ripped through my body and I screamed with the burning intensity of pleasure.

When I came back and was aware of my surroundings, he released my arms and moved the bench down before assisting me to my knees. He came around in front of me.

"Unzip my pants and take my cock in your mouth. Use your hands on my balls. I like a small amount of pain so keep that in mind. You will drink me down and lick my cock clean."

My hands shook but I managed to get his pants apart. He was commando and his large luscious cock sprung free. I pushed his pants slightly past his hips so I could get to his balls. I took them in my hand and squeezed. His fingers went into my hair and though braided, he was able to weave them into the strands against my scalp. I took both his balls in one hand and took his cock with the other, levering it slightly so I could get my lips around it. My tongue swirled around the mushroom head but his hands pushed my head forward forcing me to take several inches into my mouth.

His sexy timbre of his voice traveled across my sensitive skin, "God, I've dreamed of this. Your mouth is so damn hot. Suck me baby, use your teeth."

Unless a man was submissive, I had never had anyone ask me to use my teeth. I pushed back and nibbled then licked when I thought I was being too rough. In this one moment, he was mine. I listened to the sounds he made as I assaulted his cock and gloried in my dominance. I would love to tie his hands and do this same thing to him without him having control of my head. I would drive him insane.

He finally let go. His hot semen filled my mouth and I let it slide down my throat. I never thought men tasted particularly good but he was delicious and I couldn't get enough. I licked and sucked him dry.

His hands were running soothingly over my hair and then my shoulders. Finally he stepped back and zipped himself carefully inside his pants. He raised the bench then placed me back in my original position. I didn't think I could take more pain against my tender flesh. I watched as he walked back to the cabinets, removed a dildo, and a small black box. He then went behind me.

"Do I need to restrain your hands?"

I would regret it but I answered no.

His fingers found the folds of my vagina. Spreading me, he pushed the dildo in with one smooth glide. The lubrication from my own juices made it slide easily. He placed a Velcro strap around my waist and then between my legs to secure the dildo in place.

"Remember the plug had better stay in."

I watched as he walked over to a desk. It was so non-assuming in this den of sin that it went unnoticeable until he sat down behind it. He opened the cover of a laptop and turned it on.

I know the look on my face must have been priceless. He had to be kidding. I was about to open my mouth and use a few choice words when his hand hit a button on the black box beside the laptop and the vibrator inside my cunt began humming.

My neck strained back as the pleasure centered deep inside my pussy where mind shattering bliss vibrated. My orgasm built, I gasped for air, and he shut off the power. My entire body sagged against the bench in overwhelming frustration.

When I could control myself, I looked across the room.

"How does it feel?" He leaned back in the chair. "My cock has been hard for you since day one but you remain unruffled and that tight little ass of yours keeps walking away."

"You basta…aweg." He turned the switch higher this time. My hips pumped against the bench. I couldn't think past the vibration in my pussy. I was panting and my release so close.

The vibration stopped.

I would kill him.

"What, nothing to say?"

My body was on fire. I wanted the son of a bitch and I needed his cock deep inside my pussy. I no longer wanted to play his dominance game but I wouldn't mind playing a few of my own. I closed my eyes and pictured him naked, tied to a bed, his long thick cock at attention waiting for my mouth. Slowly my tongue would run along the long veins on his cock ending at the mushroom head, circling, nibbling, and sucking. He wouldn't be able to touch me or control my movements and I would sit up, raise my body above him, and then I would impale myself.

The vibrations in my pussy started again and I went over the edge, screaming my release into the room. The orgasm went on and on. I received a hard slap to my already sore derriere.

"Shame on you. Bad little sub. What were you thinking about?"

It took a moment but then I was able to control myself enough to speak, "You. I was thinking of your neck between my fingers and pressure. Your face turning blue and your eyes rolling back in your head, and then I would let go and bury my knee deep in your groin. This time you wouldn't get up to chase me." I stared with cold intensity into his eyes. "At least not for a while."

His laughter was deep and full. His hand came up and touched my cheek in a caress. "You know you're mine don't you?"

His words—hot, sexy, and commanding quivered through my body into my brain. It couldn't happen but oh, I wanted it. Silence was the best answer at this point.

The vibrator turned back on.

"God, I'm going to kill you."

"You are such a bloodthirsty little sub but this time I won't make you wait. Come for me."

His fingers rubbed my clit and he slowly pulled out the butt plug and then plunged it back in. My ass was beyond sensitive. His lips touched my back and moist soft kisses followed by gentle nips traveled up to my neck. Suddenly my braid pulled and my head went to the side. His kiss took me over the edge and I groaned into his mouth. He continued to play my body like a musical instrument and jolts passed from my cunt to my toes. It went on and on.

I didn't realize he released my leg restraints or that he removed the toys until Damian's strong arms picked me up and carried me from the room. He took me out of the dungeon and placed me gently on a large bed. My eyes were barely open but I watched while he undressed and then those same strong arms brought me close to his chest. His fingers undid my braid and spread the damp strands around us.

He massaged my shoulders and back then softly ran his hands over my red ass and thighs. His voice was low, "My father started Pleas-her toys. He was rarely around when I was a child and he never married my mother. He had a different woman in almost every state. I still have no idea how many half brothers and sisters I have. He showed up once or twice a year. I would hear my mom's cries of pleasure coming from her bedroom. The few times my dad took me anywhere he would tell me all women were whores. He never used my mom's name but it was implied. I decked him when I was fifteen. I took over the company five years after I graduated from college. He died two years later. My mother still loves him."

The room was quiet with only our gentle breathing.

I was entirely out of my league. Damian was doing what I loved. This was the soothing time with a sub. My heart was a puddle at his feet.

"Why are you doing this Damian? You and I won't work. I'm leaving at the end of the month."

"You are so stubborn. Now it's your turn. Tell me something I don't know about you."

I giggled and looked at his face as his grin formed and his beautiful dimples appeared. He rolled our bodies until I was lying on top of him, our legs intertwined. His arms rose and then his hands grasped the brass rails of the headboard.

"This time is for you. I won't let go so do your worst."

How did he know my fantasy? "Can I tie you?"

"No baby but I won't let go."

It was enough. I sat up on his lower thighs and then moved back spreading his legs out on either side of me. Every muscle in his body was defined, the contours rippled and his hard abs begged for my lips. His erection was huge and beautiful. I wanted it inside me but I had a fantasy to play out first.

"If you need one there are condoms in the nightstand drawer."

"Oh, I'll eventually need one or two."

His cock jumped and I smiled. Looking up, his dark wicked eyes gazed back.

I fulfilled my fantasy and worshiped every inch of his body, every millimeter of his cock. He kept his hands tight on the rails but sweat dampened his skin. I licked my way up and then reached into the drawer to remove a condom. I slid it slowly over his cock and then straddled his waist.

His eyes were barely open and mine filled with need. I leaned forward and kissed him while my body sank down and my pussy surrounded his heat.

His body strained. I could feel his muscles bunch beneath my naked flesh but he held onto the bars. I stopped kissing him, placed my hands flat against his chest, and threw my head back finding my rhythm. It didn't take long and my body needed exactly the same thing as his. He went first, his groans filling the room. Hot semen filled the condom and I felt it deep inside my pussy. That was all it took. My muscles tightened and his groans became louder but my cries finally drowned out his.

Seconds, minutes, I don't know how long but then his arms came around me, holding me tight. My body was limp and satisfied. I didn't think I had ever felt this way. But, I was exhausted. His body disengaged from mine, he disposed of the condom, and then pulled a blanket over us but kept his arms around me.

I closed my eyes and slept through the night. Early morning sunlight shown through the sheer window coverings and woke me up. I was alone. There was a bathrobe at the foot of the bed. It wasn't the skimpy silk one from the night before. This one was soft plush terry cloth and when I put it on, it ended at my feet.

I went in search of my Dom.

Sitting at the table, drinking a cup of coffee and reading the paper, was the last person I expected to see. Carl looked up when I approached.

"Good morning, I've brought some clothes for you and then I'm to escort you back to your rooms. Samson has been walked and fed this morning and I was told to let you sleep and that you will not be working tonight."

"Where is he?"

"He left on a business trip and should be back in a few days."

My world collapsed. Carl didn't look at me just stood and carried his coffee cup into the kitchen. I glanced around and spotted my bag. Picking it up, I went in search of a bathroom. I wasn't going back into the bedroom. I couldn't.

The mirror showed my sleep tousled hair. The eyes reflecting back at me were devastated. Why didn't he tell me he was leaving? He could have left me a note, anything. The more I thought about it the less hurt I felt and the more anger took over. I jerked on my clothes and went out to Carl. We went through the front door and walked to a different set of elevator doors. We walked inside and Carl entered a code. The doors opened and we were in a bedroom. It looked familiar and then I heard Sam whine on the other side of the closed bedroom door. We were in one of the rooms of my apartment.

I looked at Carl. "Will my code work on this elevator and take me to Damian's suite?"

Carl glanced away. "I don't know. Damian would need to set the access code with your room code."

"I see, thank you for your escort, I'll see you tonight."

"Damian gave you the night off."

"When the rat's away the mice will play. I'll see you tonight."

Carl left. I tried the elevator but my room code didn't work.

Chapter Twelve

I opened the bedroom door and Sam gave me exuberant kisses. He missed me. I lay down on the floor and let him cuddle while I ran my hand through his short back fur. Then I cried.

I'm not sure how much time passed but a quiet knock sounded at my front door. I pulled myself off the floor and opened the door to find Raul. His arms came around me and I cried harder.

"Oh baby."

I felt myself lifted and my strong submissive friend carried me to the couch and sat down holding me on his lap. I felt gentle kisses on my head. I let everything out—our night, Damian's words, my hurt, and most of all my love. I loved the damn hell spawn.

Raul listened while offering comfort. "He loves you too. I don't know why he left without a word but he'll be back and you'll see. The man only has eyes for you. Even with his subs, his awareness is only for my red head blue-eyed girl. The man's crazy for you."

I was too mentally fucked up to believe him. I'd fought anorexia just as Damian accused me of. I feared my body returning to what it had been. Then, there was part of me that loved the way my body used to be. I wanted a man to love me, and every ounce of fat and muscle I possessed. I wanted to be cherished for the woman who screamed to get out of a world where perfection ruled. The little fat girl wanted to feel beautiful.

Raul held me and allowed me to cry through all the pain. Then, he fed me and put me to bed where I slept the better part of the day. I finally showered and dressed for work. The club was the same but I wasn't. I needed to finish my contract and get back home to my small apartment and the rest of my life.

I asked a shy cute guy named Luke to sub for me. He liked extreme pain. His type of need wasn't usually for me but tonight I tried. Halfway through the scene I felt my tears build until finally my arm dropped. I looked around and found Kyle standing to the side as he had when he joined me for a scene. I tossed the whip toward him and walked away letting Kyle finish.

Raul approached before I was out of the club but I shook my head no. I went back to my room. Sam and I needed to run. After I changed into sweats, I walked him out the front lobby and we took off. I found my pace and lost myself in my world of breathing, straining leg muscles, and feet pounding the pavement.

When I finally looked around, we were lost. I had no idea where I was. Headlights pulled up slowly next to us and my breath caught but then relaxed. The window slid down. It was Carl. "Get in."

"I'm walking but I need help with directions."

"You're not in the best area of town and Damian will kill me if something happens to you. Get in."

"I think you have me confused with a sub. I'm not. I can take care of myself and if not, Sam will protect me."

His sigh sounded loud and frustration showed on his face. "Okay but I'm armed and I won't hesitate to use my weapon if you get yourself into a bind. The death will be on you."

He wasn't joking but I was willing to accept the consequences for my actions. I still needed time to process what was going on in my head.

I was lucky and no one stopped us or bothered me. I got some strange looks. A woman with a Rottweiler followed by a limo could not be normal, but the walk home was uneventful. I went back to my room and fell into a deep sleep. I woke up and ate a light meal. My cell had multiple messages from Raul. I sent him a text telling him I would be back at the club that evening.

I felt bad about Luke because I failed to finish our scene the night before but he wasn't at the club. I worked with a new submissive, promising to be gentle as she explored the world of BDSM. I used the deerskin flogger on her thighs and ass. Though it was soft, it had a good pop. Next, I focused on her pussy and breasts knowing I wasn't causing pain. I wanted her to feel pleasure. I was back in control and had my feelings buried deep inside where they needed to stay for the next few weeks.

I wasn't watching the crowd only focusing on my sweet new sub. Hands came around me and a hard body pressed against my back. I couldn't move but I would know his smell and the feel of his arms anywhere. My body stiffened.

"Mistress Anna is taking over for you. I want you to come with me and not cause a scene."

He let me turn. "I don't want this. Please let me get back to work."

"No, this can be easy for you or hard."

Anna took the flogger from my hand. She grinned slightly but didn't say anything.

"Place your arms around my neck and then wrap your legs around my waist." He didn't give me time to reply just lifted me up.

I couldn't believe he was doing this but I complied. I expected him to walk to his office but he didn't. He walked past the carousel and took me to the bar. He placed my rear end on top of the long black marble surface. I let go and he took my hand.

"Stand up."

"What?"

"Stand up."

He was crazy, hell I was crazy. I stood. He lifted himself to the bar but instead of standing, he went to his knees and reached behind me, pulling my pelvis into his face. He rested his forehead against my stomach. I quickly inhaled and looked around. Everything had stopped even the carousel. Every member of the club focused on us.

"What are you doing?"

He leaned back and looked up at me. "I want you. I don't want you to wear my collar but I want you in my bed and in my life. You can tie me up and beat me if I can have the same privilege. I'll do anything it takes to keep you here. I love you."

My world stopped. The arrogant Dom was on his knees before me. My heart clenched and then melted. I sank to my knees and my trembling lips found his.

"Is that a yes?"

I gave a watery smile and wiped tears from my cheek. "Yes."

His dimples lit up his face. "My mother is upstairs and she wants to meet you."

"What?" I shook my head.

His grin grew wider. "I picked up my mom so she could talk some sense into you."

"You brought your mother here?"

"Well if waiting in my apartment is here then yes I did."

"You're insane."

"Yes I am so come on." He jumped down and placed his arms up to help me to the ground.

"I'm not going to see your mother dressed like this."

He laughed. "I told her I might be bringing you bound, gagged, and over my shoulder. She was in this lifestyle and probably still is but I don't want to picture it please. You'll love her and she will love you. She always wanted a daughter."

I couldn't believe what I was hearing. I couldn't meet his mother like this. Strong arms cradled me and he began striding to his office. Clapping broke out around us and I buried my head in his chest. "Please don't do this."

"She was my safety net if you said no and I told her I would bring you back within thirty minutes. I don't lie to my mother. She wants to tell you what an incredible little boy I was and what a great husband and father I'll make."

My face stayed buried.

Chapter Thirteen

His mother was everything he said and more. She made me feel like she already cared for me and it was obvious she loved her son. She was nothing like the devil's mother should be but I was wrapped around her finger within minutes of meeting her.

She had darker skin than her son and brown hair but wore a loose flowing gauzy dress just like the ones I preferred. She was plump, her eyes showed laugh lines, and she had the same dimples.

After an hour, she turned to her son. "Take her to bed and celebrate life. I'm tired and need my beauty sleep. We can go shopping tomorrow Lydia and enjoy some private female time. I have so many stories to tell you about my rascal." Her voice was slightly accented.

His mother was perfect.

He took me to his bedroom. I almost expected the dungeon.

"What do you want?" His intense eyes looked into mine.

"I want you."

"Are you up for a little vanilla or do you want to tie me to the bed this time? I'm all yours."

My panties dampened at the thought. "You really don't want me tying you up do you?"

"No, but I trust you and if it turns you on I'll do it."

"The thought turns me on but maybe we'll give it a try some other time."

"What else turns you on?"

"Having you for my Dom in the bedroom. You whipping me and punishing me. I guarantee there will be many punishments. I want your cock buried deep in my pussy and soon I want it buried in my ass if it pleases you Master."

He actually growled from deep in his throat and kissed me. It was carnal and everything a good submissive could ask for.

The sex wasn't quite vanilla but it held a promise. We had a lifetime to explore each other's body. We celebrated pure love.

Much later, I lay curled in his arms, his hand on my breast. "You owe me a secret. You never paid up on your lost bet and fell asleep before I could claim my reward."

I took a moment to gather my thoughts. He didn't rush me.

"I'm sure you know my father was a jockey. He was short and thin. I think it would have been better if my mom was alive but I grew up with little people surrounding me and I felt huge. I was plump and my father said that's what attracted him to my mother. Even the rich horse owner's daughters were thin and gorgeous. I was the fat girl until I finally decided to stop eating. It was after my father died and eventually I found myself in the hospital. By then I was both anorexic and bulimic." I took several slow deep breaths before continuing. "I found a balance and use exercise to keep my demons at bay. I'm borderline now and I would give anything to eat chocolate cake until my blood went on sugar overload but I can't. I'm afraid I would force myself to throw it up and I don't want to go backwards. I want to be loved regardless of my weight."

I couldn't look at him. I was telling him I could lose the battle either way and be back in the hospital or fat again. I struggled with both.

His hand traveled from my breast to my stomach and his voice whispered in the deep Dom way he had. "I want my child here. I want you plump before and after the baby's arrival. You're too skinny but it really doesn't matter to me. I love what's in here." His other hand went to my forehead and gently smoothed his thumb across it. "I love what's in here." His hand moved down traveling over my body and stopped between my legs, one finger going inside my moist pussy. He then brought his hand up, trailing moisture along my body, and stopping over my heart. "And I love what's in here."

He kissed me.

I finally came up for air and whispered, "I love you."

His dimples showed with his laugh. "I know and you better because once my mother knows you need her she will never leave you alone. She won't stop until we have ten babies in ten years. You've been warned."

"Do you know how fat I'll be after ten babies?"

"I can only imagine and now I'm turned on. No more condoms from here on out. I want to make love to you when you're fat and mushy beneath my fingers."

"Please shut up and fuck me."

His dark eyes promised retribution for my smart mouth and I couldn't wait.

The beginning...

Book II

Piercing a Dom's Heart

Chapter One

He walked into the suite and looked around. It hadn't changed since his last visit a year ago. The bell hop dropped his luggage into the master bedroom before taking the offered tip and closing the door gently behind him. Brandon made his way to the bar, picked up the note lying next to the bottle of Ardbeg, and smiled.

Bran, I looked forward to sharing a glass but something unexpected has come up so please start the party without me. I'll see you at the club tonight. Damian.

This was what he needed. Filling a tumbler, he walked over to the wall to wall glass window looking out over the Houston skyline. His nose inhaled the rich smoky aroma before bringing the liquid to his lips and tasting the single malt scotch. Damian knew his whisky and the Ardbeg was perfection.

Exhaustion weighed heavily but nothing would keep him away from the club tonight. This wasn't about his need for sex or his desire to escape a clingy, mentally taxing relationship that had continued for far too long. This was about his inner demon and the need to dominate and allow his kinky side to lead his cock for a while.

When his father, Brandon Edward Sterling III died suddenly, it stopped Bran's playboy lifestyle and threw him into the world of corporate finance before he was ready. A desire for companionship also made a strong push for him to settle down and live the boring structured life of his parents. The same parents he loathed and wanted to be nothing like. In only one year he went back on all the promises he and his college buddies made when they swore to never live by the rules of their ultra-wealthy parents which landed them at Harvard to begin with.

Damian was the only friend who turned his nose at the acceptable and didn't play the game but then, the majority of Bran's college buddies never accepted Damian because of his money's roots. It was one thing to hate the disgustingly rich echelon you were born into but quite another to have a father who gained his wealth by designing sex toys. When Damian picked a fight and broke Bran's nose their first year in college, it was either take the other down or become friends. It could have gone either way but friendship won.

Accepting Damian's lifestyle was a little harder but once Bran let his conservative barriers down, visiting the club became his sin-filled pleasure. Before he became the head of Sterling International, the strict club privacy policies kept this side of his life from the press. During the previous year, he had denied his darker side, kept his nose clean, and rejected what his mind and body craved. His engagement to Elizabeth and the consequential end to the engagement made him realize he needed to let loose and fuck a sweet little sub's brains out. After that, he would make a decision. But he didn't know if he could wholeheartedly throw himself into running his father's— no *his* billion dollar corporation and give up completely on his desire for a D/s relationship. It filled a need from deep within and he was tired of rejecting it.

The clock showed two p.m. and he decided to live on the edge and do something he hadn't done in years. His clothes hit the floor and the soft bed called. He crawled naked between the luxurious cotton sheets and then Brandon Edward Sterling IV took a nap.

***

He was awake at seven after enjoying the first solid sleep he'd had in months. Feeling refreshed and energized, he looked forward to an evening of play. After ordering dinner, he took a shower. It was hard not to check his phone and email messages but he let his cock override the mental pull of business. Once he started on work, it could be days before he came up for air. He was taking one week for himself and playing hooky from the real world. No one but his secretary knew of his location including his nosey mother. She wasn't happy when he told her about his leave of absence and he wouldn't be surprised if she tried to track his movements. Too bad she never gave a shit about him when he was young. He knew his control of the money was all that guided her now.

After dinner, he poured another scotch and dressed for the evening. He knew Damian rented the suite out in his absence but his leathers were hanging in the closet. The only normal routine he managed over the past year was his daily trip to a private gym to relieve the stress from his life. He was glad for it now because everything fit like a glove. He pulled the black leather vest over his bare chest and felt control slide over his tall frame. It wasn't that he didn't have control of his business life but this was different. There, he went through the motions hating each second he spent behind a desk.

This was a discipline that required give and take; a power exchange that would end each night with the ultimate dominant sexual encounter his body craved.

He entered the private access code at the end of the hallway, outside his rooms, and walked onto the elevator, which took him to another world. The lighting, sound, and smells hadn't changed. Here he was Sir with no pressed white shirt or tie required. He bypassed the large carousel, which was the center attraction. The naked to half-naked men and women were provocatively posed with some straddling the colorful horses waiting for their master's return. He smiled on his way to the bar where he requested water.

Bran looked around the club and absorbed the sights and sounds. Several stations to the side of the enormous room were being used which was normal for this time of the evening. There was a large group standing at the second alcove and he decided to have a look.

The scene was sexy as hell. A red headed Domme wielded a bullwhip with a master's precision. It was one of the most provocative things Bran had ever seen. She looked to be six months pregnant and her tight black tank top only accented her curves and the roundness of her belly. She wore leather shorts that formed a v under her protruding stomach.

"Beautiful isn't she?"

Bran would know that voice anywhere.

"Damn sexy if you asked me. Topping that could be the highlight of my trip but maybe we can hold off on the baby until we've known each other for a while."

"She isn't for you because that's my baby in her belly and I don't share."

Bran's eyes didn't leave the scene. "I wouldn't be sharing either but then again I don't see my future wife with a whip in her hand. Are you being topped these days?"

Deep laughter was his answer. He turned and looked at his good friend placing his hand out. Damian bypassed the handshake and gave Bran a strong hug. "I'm sorry I didn't make it to the funeral. I knew it would piss your mother off if I came and I felt this was one time I should leave well enough alone."

"The flowers did the trick. She had trouble holding on to her polite visage when she read your card. It gave me a chuckle so thank you."

"I'm also sorry to hear about your broken engagement. I'm a happily married man now and I can highly recommend the state of matrimony."

Bran looked back at the woman who was now kissing a dark haired female sub on the lips. "With that to come home to I can see why."

"You have no idea." Damian's grin was self-satisfied. "Lydia requests your presence at dinner tomorrow night. You can come to the club afterwards if you like."

"I'd love to. I could also use a recommendation for tonight's play if you don't mind suggesting someone amiable to my tastes."

An angry voice sounded above the subtle background music. "Get the hell away from me or I'll put a stick of dynamite up your ass."

"Well fuck." said Damian, "This night just keeps getting better and better. Come on and meet my sister, unfortunately she'll probably be at dinner tomorrow night too."

Bran followed Damian to the angry voice. An older Dom looked at them when they approached and began apologizing to Damian. "Master D, I only asked her if she would like to do a scene with me on one of her days off. I didn't mean to cause a problem."

"Understood Paul, I'll handle things. Have a drink at the bar, it's on me."

Paul practically ran to the bar. Damian reached forward and tried to button his sister's black shirt but her hands came up and angrily brushed his aside.

Her voice was angry, frustrated, and bitchy, "You are such a prude brother dear. My breasts aren't even showing.

If you don't like seeing the exposed parts then don't have your employees wear such provocative uniforms."

"You are my sister so yours don't count as a pair of breasts I want to see. And, you my dear are the prude. This is a BDSM club. Asking to join a scene is almost a requirement and I told you this would happen."

"That man's idea of a scene included a butt plug and nipple clamps."

Bran stood to the side fighting a grin. Damian's sister was at least five foot eight. She had thick black hair in a high ponytail, garish makeup, and more piercings than he'd ever seen on a human body. She was your typical Goth chick. Piercings were highly fashionable among the fetish crowd but they had never done anything for him. Bran took a second look at the curves in front of him and admired her luscious figure. The black lacy bra she wore covered her nipples, which was a shame even if Damian didn't think so. Her black leather skirt hugged her hips and barely covered her upper thighs. Long legs meant to wrap around a man's waist made his cock hard. In deference to her Goth persona, sparkling metallic gold polish covered her long fingernails. While the other female employees wore slinky heeled shoes, Damian's sister wore black combat boots. His cock stiffened even more.

He snapped out of his thoughts when Damian introduced them. Bran's eyes traveled up and met the sky blue orbs on a very unhappy face.

"Never seen a pair of boobs before or do you also want to stick something up my ass?"

"Will!" Damian's voice rose.

Bran couldn't help raising his eyebrows at the name "Will" but it didn't stop his reply, "I've seen plenty of boobs but yours are exceptional. I don't think I'll put something up your ass unless it's my cock but I'll be sure to put a nice ball gag in your mouth before I do it."

"You fucking pervert."

"Willow, my office now." Damian used his Master "you'll be punished if I'm disobeyed" voice and turned on his heel. He looked at Bran and gave a sharp tilt of his head. Bran followed.

Once they were safely away from club ears, Damian let his sister have it and didn't seem to mind that Bran was listening."

"I told you to expect that kind of behavior and to politely refuse anything you weren't interested in. I also told you to work at the downstairs bar but your ass insisted on being up here. If you upset my wife I will ship you to a third world country where they circumcise their women and then cover them from head to toe."

The office door opened and Lydia entered. Damian stopped his tirade but his face remained red.

Lydia's voice was soft but direct, "You must be Brandon. Damian has told me very naughty things about your college adventures. I'm sorry you arrived during a time of family turmoil." Her eyes left Bran's for a moment and she gave her husband a tight smile before focusing on their guest again. "But, we're happy to have you. I hope your stay is relaxing and pleasing."

He took her hand and kissed her palm, "Call me Bran."

She gave him a sexy smile before turning her attention back to her husband.

"She's not upsetting me Damian, but she is upsetting you." Lydia's eyes traveled to her sister-in-law. "He won't ship you anywhere because that would make me angry. I heard Master P wanted to use you in a scene?"

"He wanted to put a plug up my ass and told me he would make it feel good."

"Well, if you've never tried it how do you know it won't?"

Willow plopped down on the couch in exasperation and Lydia sat beside her. The two men made their escape.

Chapter Two

Bran followed Damian to his private elevator and they disembarked at the penthouse. Damian stalked straight to the bar.

"This was the unexpected problem I referred to in my note. She's only been here five days" He looked at his watch. "And six hours and forty minutes. Please shoot me. I learned she existed six years ago, paid for her college, and then lined up several jobs. She's been fired, or quit because she refuses to remove her piercings or dress for the normal business world. She also finds dipshit guys who use her, chew her up, and spit her out. To top it off my pregnant wife has a soft spot when it comes to that hellion."

"I hate to ask but who's her mother?"

"A retired stripper in Vegas. She was a beauty back in her day but now alcohol and drugs have turned her into a nut case. I've provided money for years though I established a separate account for Willow. I couldn't trust her mother to take care of her properly."

"What's she doing here?"

"Hell if I know. She arrived at the hotel unannounced and said she wanted to work at the El Diablo Club. She knew exactly what it was and I've tried for days to talk her out of it. Lydia finally took her side and insists I give her a chance. I need help, and I hate to ask, but while you're here, could you keep an eye on her if I'm not around? If you need to gag and bind her to a sub bench be my guest, but please make sure Lydia doesn't see you get down and dirty. Shit, I don't want to see it either. I'm at a loss; she didn't have boobs when she was fifteen and the last thing I want to see are her breasts or someone putting a plug up her ass. A bullet to my head is sounding better and better."

Bran smiled. Damian was always in complete control of his world. He remembered the shock he felt when Damian called and said he was married with a baby on the way. His friend's strong Dom voice had even sounded dreamy. Now that Bran saw Lydia in person, he had a slight inkling about what drew his friend to the fiery redhead. She was damned appealing and exactly opposite of Willow the terrible. But… he would help out his friend. Right now though, he just wanted a sweet little sub to play with in the club and then take back to his room for a night of hard fucking.

"I'd be happy to take your sister in hand when you're not around but please don't leave me for long or world war three might start. I want to remain on your good side so I can meet the new addition to your family when he or she gets here."

"It's a she and I most certainly pissed off the Gods because I don't think I can handle another female right now. Lydia cries at the drop of a hat and I do everything in my power to keep her happy. You and I are taking a guy's night while you're here. No women."

"My how the mighty have fallen. No women would have been the worst night of your life two years ago."

"I won't argue but seriously, Lydia doesn't stop me from enjoying a submissive at a station or delivering discipline if a sub gets out of hand at the club. She's the most popular Domme we've ever had and my cock stays hard the entire time I see her work someone over. She remains on the payroll, the club stays happy, and I get the rewards after work."

"As long as you don't mind if I get turned on by your wife too."

"Be my guest but keep your hands off." Damian's smile was wicked.

Bran smiled back at his friend, "No problem but I need to work off a bit of tension. Do you have a sub you think I would like?"

"Let's go, I have just the submissive beauty to get you started on your week of sin."

Damian hadn't lied, Penny was perfect. They sat talking while he explained what he was looking for. This included a continued liaison throughout the night alone in his hotel room after some public play. She also didn't have a problem with a one-sub stand when he made it clear he would look for someone else the following evening.

They spoke about her limits and safe words. He then took her hand, and led her to station three securing her to the St. Andrews Cross. At one time, he was quite good with a whip but it had been awhile and he felt safer with something he could control a little more. If Lydia had some spare time he might ask her to run him through some exercises to bring his comfort level back up, but tonight, he would use a crop to place nice pink stripes on Penny's gorgeous body if she misbehaved.

Her mouth tasted of mint and cherries when he took her lips in a sensuous kiss. He checked her bonds and ran a hand down her chest stopping and paying homage to each of her nipples before clamping them. He smiled, remembering Miss Willow's disgust at the request to clamp her nipples. She had no idea of the heightened sensations they caused. Or, that they intensified her pleasure. Looking at Penny's extended nipples, his cock stiffened. They didn't hurt his pleasure either.

Bran liked performing for the club crowd but when it came to sex, he preferred the privacy of his room. He could punish a particularly misbehaving sub with a little personal public display but he liked them pliant and willing when he took them to bed. Their hands and legs bound wasn't a requirement once he had their body primed and he received their complete submission.

His goal was to have Penny submit to his will and fight her body's need for gratification until they were in his room. He explained very clearly what his expectations were.

"Yes Sir."

Bran preferred "Sir" to master. BDSM was all about personal tastes. He began placing moist kisses down her soft skin. He kissed and nipped along her jawline, down her neck, traveling to the curve of her shoulder. His tongue slid over her nipple circling the clamp giving a slight pull. Her moan made his erection swell. She was incredibly responsive and he was glad he asked Damian for a suggestion.

He played with both breasts and her body arched as she made the sweet sounds he loved. His lips and tongue went to her other nipple and his hands went to her ass. He massaged and played along the crevice never touching her precisely where she wanted, leaving her anticipating what came next.

He loved the play and the calculated skim of his hands over a subs body. The smell of arousal and bringing a woman to a fevered pitch turned him on. He took his time and mentally blocked out the growing crowd as Penny's cries grew louder.

Slowly he used a finger to delve along her feminine folds swirling in the growing wetness she provided. Her thighs tensed and her muscles flexed as his knowing fingers continued to explore. Her breathing grew harsher as his finger slowly slid inside her pussy ringing a strangled cry from her lips.

He stopped the movement of his finger and stood to whisper in her ear, "Oh baby, slow down and control your body. Remember my rules." He kissed her again and began the slow movement of his finger while using his mouth on one of her nipples.

Penny's entire body began to squirm and her hips bucked against his hand. He removed his fingers.

"Shh, my sweet, I want you yearning for release but you will hold back."

He kissed slowly down her body ending at the juncture of her thighs. Using two fingers, he spread her labia so his tongue could lick across her clit.

"Awe, I can't take it." Her cry was desperate.

"Yes you can. Hold on." He demanded.

"No master no, I can't." Penny went over the edge. Bran could feel her vaginal walls pulse against his finger and he allowed her orgasm to finish before backing away.

"You my dear have been a naughty sub."

"I'm sorry Sir." Her head was down and her breathing uneven.

"We will try again, but first you will be punished."

Brand removed a leather-braided crop from the wall and Penny whimpered when he walked toward her. First, he ran the cowhide flap down the side of her face continuing over her body, down her chest, over her pelvic bone and between her legs. She let out another whimper as the tip passed over her highly sensitized pussy. Stepping back, he let the first strike land against the front of her thigh.

"Augg." Her body jumped.

"Don't lock your muscles or the pain is more intense." The second strike took her across the stomach. He used the crop in a steady rhythm along her torso but avoided her pussy and breasts. This was a penalty for not obeying his commands. He wanted her to control her orgasm and hold back.

"We are going to start again Penny but this time you will fight your release. It should be easier now that your sweet pussy has been satisfied. What do I want Penny?"

"My pleasure, sir."

"Yes, Penny, I want all your pleasure and I don't wish to share with the people watching.

"Yes sir."

This time he began by kissing her red striped stomach and thighs using his moist tongue to ease the sting. If she disobeyed again, he would turn her around and stripe her bottom along with the backs of her thighs. He wanted her to fight her body no matter how far he pushed. The thought made his dick throb painfully.

Penny held on for thirty minutes and he finally let up.

"Oh my sweet you have been so good and your body is beautiful at this moment. Your pussy is swollen and dripping just waiting for me. Hang on a little longer and I'll give your body what it needs."

He removed Penny from the cross and carried her to the alcove set up behind the station. She sobbed in his arms, her mind and body completely his. He kissed her forehead and cheek before settling on her mouth. From a side table he leaned over and picked up a sub blanket wrapping it around her quivering body. Her trembling finally slowed as he massaged her arm and leg muscles to relieve the strain from the cross.

"We're going to my suite where I will lick your pussy until you go over the edge and then I plan to fuck you for hours."

She was too overwhelmed to respond and he picked her up and began walking out of the club. Before he reached the exit doors, which led to the elevators, he felt eyes following him. He turned and looked into Willow's cold glare. His gaze traveled to her breasts and he admired their perfection before moving slowly upwards. Anger, doubt, and an edge of desire showed on her face causing his mouth to quirk slightly. He pulled Penny tighter against his body and placed a soft kiss to the top of her head. He then looked back at Damian's sister.

"Does it make you feel strong when you beat a woman?"

He inhaled sharply at her startling question but humor won out, "There seems to be something you don't understand about this lifestyle." He fought to keep his laughter under control. "Everything that takes place here is consensual. There is no difference in Lydia whipping a sub or me doing it. If you want to continue working at El Diablo you have a choice."

Her eyes sparked, "And what would that be?"

I winked. "Hold a whip or submit."

A giggle came from his chest where Penny's head lay buried.

"You actually enjoy torturing women?" Disgust dripped from every fiber of her being.

"I know I would love to take you over my knee and redden your bottom. It might be torture for you but it would definitely be pleasurable on my end. I'm sure Penny would enjoy your company in my bedroom if you care to join us?" Every bit of his dominant persuasive voice went into the words and his erection pressed tighter against his pants at the thought.

Unfortunately, Willow didn't wish to play and she practically ran in the opposite direction.

He whispered in Penny's ear, "I'm glad you enjoyed that. I'm sure I can find a suitable punishment for giggles."

A slight giggle sounded again and Bran smiled. This was the world he needed to relieve the stress of his day to day life. Why did he stay away so long? And why did thoughts of the over made up Goth chick send his erection soaring?

Chapter Three

Penny was gone when Brandon woke up in the morning. He told her she could stay but she said she wanted to get back to her home. He understood. The deal was for one night. That was another reason BDSM appealed to him; if you wanted a lasting D/s relationship you could find one. If you liked to play the field, there were always enthusiastic takers. Though he knew she was over twenty-one, Penny probably continued to live with her rich parents and they didn't need to know their baby girl liked kinky sex.

He decided to visit the gym before breakfast. He grabbed a banana from the fruit bowl and headed out the door. It was five thirty a.m. on a Sunday morning and the gym was silent. He hit the weights and put his body through the grind. It felt good to stretch his muscles after a full night of sex. Sweat dripped down his chest and soaked his t-shirt. Finally, he moved to the treadmill and set it at a steady heart-pumping pace.

"Are you following me?"

He looked over and saw Willow, clearly disgruntled, standing beside the adjoining treadmill. She was wearing baggie black sweatpants and a short black top that showed off her belly button ring. He wondered if she owned another color of clothing.

Brandon couldn't help his grin, "I believe I was here first and the thought of you following me is downright scary. But if you show a little nipple, I'll probably get over it."

"So you can attach a torture device to it?"

His grin stayed in place, "I think you're too afraid to admit that the idea turns you on."

"Argh, you must be kidding. You are the most egotistical ass I've ever been unfortunate enough to meet."

He hit the button and his treadmill stopped. He was hot, sweaty, and aroused. He was also tired of playing this game.

She backed up as he moved forward. She wasn't as dominant as she liked to act.

"What do you think you're doing?"

"I'm planning to paddle your ass and give you something to complain about."

"This is a public place and you'll be arrested if you even try."

"By who?"

She glanced around and he saw the calculating look on her face. A split second later, she ran for the door.

Once outside the gym, she gained speed down the long hallway. He managed to grab her before she reached the elevator and bring her around facing him. He used his body to push her back into the wall and then he grabbed her hands forcing them above her head. She was breathing hard and he saw desire spark in her eyes. Damian's little sister was submissive and without tons of black makeup, she was sexy as hell. He didn't hesitate. His mouth crushed hers. He expected a knee to his groin or a loud scream but what he got was one long leg wrapping around his waist and an aching cry when her pelvis ground into his erection. She had a tongue ring and the sexy feel of it drove him wild.

The kiss grew in intensity and his hand went down to the bottom of her cropped top and slid beneath the material. She was wearing a sport's bra and his fingers delved underneath closing around her soft breast. Her pierced nipple was hard and erect. Thank god his sweatpants allowed his erection to grow unencumbered. He pressed his cock against her pussy. Even covered he could feel her wetness seep into the material of his pants.

The elevator door beside them binged. Bran released her mouth but rested his forehead against the top of her head as her leg slid to the floor. There was no way he was releasing her at this point no matter who came through the doors.

Damian walked out of the elevator his displeasure apparent. "There I was, on a Sunday morning, in the process of tying my wife's hands to the headboard and having very appropriate sex with the woman I married. The phone rings at a crucial moment, and my security staff tells me two very inappropriate hotel guests are getting hot and heavy in the hallway outside the main gym. Now here I am and I find my sister playing hot lip Lucy with my best friend while entertaining the guards monitoring the security feed."

Bran looked into Damian's lethal stare; the same stare that gave him the reputation as a down and dirty fighter when they were in college.

"I couldn't help myself and she needs a spanking."

Willow pushed out of his arms. "Why you..."

"That's enough sister mine. I think the two of you need to find a private room and get whatever this is out of your system. You've been caught on the security tapes and I'm sure Mr. Uptight here would rather not have this video on the evening news."

Bran laughed. "I don't know about that, my mother would have apoplexy."

"You bastard, you forced me."

Bran burst out laughing and then fought for control in order to speak, "Your pussy ground into my cock and your tongue snaked down my throat. I think the cameras will tell the real story if you care to go watch. You can rub my cock while we enjoy vanilla porn."

Willow turned on her heel and tried to walk away. Bran's large hand on the back of her neck stopped her. He brought her backward to his body and not caring if her brother was standing there, he whispered hotly into her ear, "You're wet. I can smell you. We will finish this and I will fuck you so hard you won't be walking away for a few days."

She turned and lifted her hand but he grabbed it in a tight hold. "I owe you a spanking across my knee but I can change that to a whip if it rocks your boat."

"If the rock is tied around your neck and you fall overboard my pussy will cream from here to next Sunday." She turned and entered the elevator without a backward glance.

"Well Romeo you sure know how to attract the chicks. I don't think my sister is sub enough for you."

"I'm not sure she's sub enough for anyone but I plan to find out. God, she pierced her nipples and they drive me wild. I wonder what other body ornaments she has hidden."

"You did not just tell me that. I'm her brother for god sake."

"Go back to your room and finish tying up your wife. I'm heading to my room for a cold shower."

Chapter Four

After his shower, Bran couldn't help but check phone and email messages. He had several voicemails from his mother along with one from his secretary telling him to stop checking his messages. She went on to say that nothing had fallen apart while he was gone.

One of the reasons he hired Jenny Mack was to infuriate his mother but it was the best move he ever made. Jenny weighed three hundred plus pounds, was smart as a whip, and refused to put up with anyone's shit including his. She most definitely didn't fit the corporate world's administrative assistant stereotype but she was perfect for him. She kept his schedule tight but made sure he was eating and exercising. To top it off, the woman could cook and she took better care of him than his long parade of nannies ever had.

He deleted his mother's messages only hearing the angry tone of her voice and not the words. He then called Jen.

"What would I do without you?" He greeted.

"You would turn into a frog, waste away to nothing, murder your mother, and lose your fortune. Have I mentioned a raise recently?"

"For putting up with Mrs. Sterling you deserve one."

"I'm hoping you find the real Mrs. Sterling on your trip. One who can handle your mother, carry a teacup in one hand and an AK-47 in the other."

Jen knew about his fascination with weapons. He possessed a private collection that was the envy of the Unites States' Secretary of Defense.

"Hmm, I hadn't thought of the tea cup angle."

"While you're at it, get some relief for your blue balls. I'm tired of your crabby mood."

He laughed. "I wasn't aware you inspected my balls before I left."

"If that cold bitch you were engaged to was putting out, your dick would have frozen off, and you would be in the hospital getting it reattached."

"This is exactly why I hired you. You not only keep my office running smoothly but you keep my personal life under control."

"We'll talk about my raise when you get back but for now stop calling and checking your messages."

"Understood. Are you sure you're not available for a week of vivacious fornication and carefree copulation?"

"I'm fanning myself over such big bad words but I'm not sure if it's a hot flash or the beginnings of my first female ejaculation."

"Goodbye Jenny."

Her boisterous laugh sounded and then the line went dead.

He called the hotel lobby, "Could you connect me to Ms. Willow Collins' room please?"

The phone rang and Willow answered. "This is Bran. I'm heading to the firing range for some target shooting and thought you might like a chance to fire a few rounds. No sex, no D/s, just a place to let off some steam."

"Is this for real?"

"Can you shoot?"

"When are you leaving?"

"Thirty minutes."

"I'll meet you in the lobby."

She was waiting when he got there. Her camouflage green toned shirt was tight and showed off her breasts. Safety pins adorned her black cargo pants. She now had a large gold barbell above her eyebrow with various gold hoops displayed on various parts of her face. A pair of huge black military boots added another three inches to her height. She had toned down her makeup but that was the only concession she made to their outing.

"Are we preparing for war?" Humor laced his voice.

"With you in the mix, I thought it best."

"Then let's get out of here."

They walked outside the main lobby and Carl; Damian's driver, waited beside a limousine. "Good morning Mr. Sterling, Miss Collins." He nodded his head and held the door as they entered the back of the luxurious vehicle.

They didn't speak on the drive to the range but he noticed her furtive glances at his body. He decided to let her look her fill. He leaned his head back and closed his eyes. If Goth chick wanted to look, he would give her the chance.

They went to Top Gun, one of Houston's most popular indoor shooting ranges. Bless Jenny for giving him the idea. He needed to blow off some sexual frustration and there was nothing like the cold grip of a firearm in his hands to focus his energy.

When they arrived, he told Willow to pick a handgun.

She looked at the clerk, "Do you have a Glock 35 .40 caliber available?"

"Yes ma'am we do, I'll get you set up."

Bran turned and watched as she admired the guns in the glass case beneath her sparkling gold fingernails. "Is there a reason you want that particular model?"

"Yes, it's used for competition shooting and I like the feel. I have one back home with a custom grip but that's because Damian spoils me."

"You can shoot?"

"Do you care to make a wager?"

"I never wager on the unknown. I'm quite conservative."

Her laughter was deep and sexy. He felt his cock stir beneath his jeans.

"I must see if the use of nipple clamps is in the definition of conservative."

"You are too stuck on nipple clamps and I don't understand. Isn't having them pierced a lifelong clamp?"

"No, I don't usually notice them but my nipples are always hard."

She was doing this on purpose but he was willing to play along.

"There's hard and then there's a pair of nipples slick with saliva and begging to be sucked."

"I could say the same thing about your cock but I won't."

The cock in question jerked. He knew when to cut and run. If they were in private, he would win this match but not here. He gave her a wicked promising smile.

They made their way to a private shooting lane.

Damian loaded his .45 caliber rounds into two magazines. His gun of choice was a Kimber Pro TLE II. It was lightweight but packed a nice punch. He liked the look and feel of the Kimber.

They both put on eye and ear protection provided by the range.

Willow looked like she knew what she was doing and had no trouble loading her magazines. They stood in side by side cubicles and emptied their first rounds at fifteen feet. They lay down their weapons after the last shot and pressed the button bringing the targets in close. His were a tight grouping of shots to the head while hers were to the body primarily in the chest though one went high and into the neck.

"Now that we're warmed up are you ready for the twenty-five?"

"Bring it on business man."

He had to smile. There were a lot of things she could call him and "business man" was tame in comparison.

They spent the next hour going through rounds. Willow was more than good.

"Who taught you to shoot?"

"Back before my mom let drugs and alcohol get the best of her she was married to a cop for a short time."

"I had no idea cops married strippers."

"In Vegas it's a fairly common practice though strippers prefer to be known as show girls."

"Duly noted. This cop taught you to shoot?"

"Yes, when my mom went on a drinking binge he would take me to the range."

He almost didn't ask but he had to. "Can you shoot an AK?"

"Now you're talking but I don't think this range is set up for a high powered rifle."

"No, it isn't, I just wanted to know."

"Yes, but I prefer a Bushmaster AR-15."

His dick became uncomfortably hard. This was a woman Jenny would like. He didn't ask about the tea. It was too much for his cock to handle.

Chapter Five

He was relaxed when they climbed into the back of the limo and Carl drove them toward the hotel. Bran hit a button and the smoky privacy window rose cutting off Carl's view of the backseat.

Willow's triple pierced brow arched as she looked at him.

"I thought we should talk."

"And what would you like to talk about?"

"Besides the objections you've brought up, I'd like to know your feelings about BDSM and why you insist on working at your brother's club."

"I'm not sure I know you well enough to share my feelings on those issues."

"Our tongues have been down the other's throat and my hand skin to skin on your breast. I'm willing to fuck you right now if it will help you feel more comfortable."

"Is fucking the only way you know to communicate with woman?"

"I just spent the past two hours shooting, talking, and doing everything but fucking. I'm asking because you turn me on and I'm wondering if there is a way we can meet somewhere in the middle and both enjoy a day or two having dirty sweaty sex. D/s is about communication. It takes out the guesswork on both sides. I want to know what turns you on, why you pierce your body, and if there's anything kinky you like. Not wanting to scare you away, I started with easy questions."

"You make yourself sound so reasonable."

"A simple, I'm not interested will work."

He didn't think she would answer but after several moments, she gave a long sigh.

"My last boyfriend beat me up. It's not the first time it's happened and he's not the only one."

Bran's hands tightened into fists but then he forced them to relax. He didn't want her to stop talking and she might if she noticed his angry.

"A friend of mine attended fetish parties and she spent some time talking about the give and take relationships that didn't involve anything both sides aren't willing to do. It just so happens, my brother owns one of the most prominent BDSM clubs in the US and I decided to check it out."

"So besides nipple clamps and butt plugs, is there something else you like?"

She gave him a chagrined smile, knowing he was needling her. "I'm not comfortable with the whole voyeurism thing. I don't get it. There doesn't seem to be any jealousy but at the same time I don't think I want a group of people watching me have an orgasm."

"Funny, because that was one of my hang ups too," he answered honestly. "Having a sub completely focused on me is a turn on. The first time one forgot everything going on around her, became totally immersed in the sound of my voice, and what I was doing to her body, I finally understood. At the same time, I like to finish playing in the privacy of my room. It's the public warm up and desire for control to make a sub withhold her pleasure that places me in my sexual zone." His eyes didn't leave hers. "What puts you in that zone?"

She looked down. He leaned over and lifted her chin with his fingers. The kiss was tender and at the same time deeply sensual. His voice was husky when he pulled back but he didn't let go of her chin, "Tell me Willow."

"I don't know. I've never been there."

"You're not a virgin." It was a statement.

She laughed softly, "No, I'm not a virgin but I don't think a guy has ever cared enough to show me the 'zone' as you call it."

"Are you willing to trust me?"

"Will you put a plug up my ass?"

"You are so hung up on your ass. I should just get it out of the way but no, I won't if it's a hard limit for you."

"I think it is but is it really something you like?"

"The pleasure for a woman is intense when a cock is deep in her pussy and a plug is deep in her anus. The man can feel it too and the sensation is stimulating. Having my cock buried balls deep in a subs ass is also erotic as hell but I'm fine without anal play and I have a lot more tricks in my bag that can take you into the zone if you're willing."

"Why me?"

The hand not holding her chin traveled under her shirt and took hold of her breast above her bra. "This is one reason. Your breasts are beautiful and they turn me on. I want to slide my cock between them and then watch my cum release over your nipples." His hand moved down to her waist and skimmed over the outside of her pants down to the juncture of her thighs. "I also want to know if you're pierced here, but don't tell me. I want to discover it with my mouth. I want your legs locked around my back as I push slowly into you with my cock. Then I want you on your hands and knees when I take you from behind."

"Yes." It was a sigh.

"That's what I wanted to hear. Somehow we need to get through dinner at your brother's without ripping each other's clothes off."

"Those words are ice cold water on my hot body."

They both laughed.

"Will you trust me tonight and let me take you to the club?"

"I…I."

"We can stop at any time. I will display only your breasts and use a deerskin flogger that will be intense but you will feel little more than a slight sting. You can stop everything with your safe word."

"I don't have a safe word."

"Choose one."

"I know red is normal but I'd like to use something different."

"You have until tonight to think about it."

The car pulled up in front of the hotel and they stepped out.

"Well, umm, thank you for the afternoon, I'll see you tonight." It was obvious she was uncomfortable and wasn't sure what to say.

He pulled her into his arms and covered her mouth in a short hot kiss. "Tonight." He walked away.

Chapter Six

Lydia cooked a delicious dinner. Damian and Bran talked about business ventures they partnered in until the conversation rolled around to Harvard and their escapades that were now past the statute of limitations.

"See sister dear, I was never the hero you thought I was." He said to Willow.

"I never thought you a hero. I thought you were a scoundrel and I dreamed that I gave up your location to the FBI and they placed me in the witness protection program." Her face was solemn.

"Would you really give me up?"

"I told all my friends in high school that you were a double agent and wanted internationally."

"Why."

"Because I needed an excuse when you didn't come to see me." She took his hand when she saw his hurt look. "After Jeff left mom, things got really bad. I needed to have fantasy dreams about your life to keep mine going. Mom told me I had brothers and sisters when I was small but you were the only one who ever came looking for me. I needed those dreams."

"I have more money than sense and I should have come for you much sooner."

"Yes you should have but I'll forgive you if you name the baby after me."

Lydia laughed but she had tears in her eyes.

Willow jumped up and embraced her sister in law. "Don't cry. I'm sorry. This should have been a private conversation and I didn't mean to upset you."

"I cry over everything right now but I'm so sorry you had to make your way to us."

"Don't be. If you would have known me a few years ago we wouldn't be friends now. I was not the easiest person to get along with and I destroyed everything I touched. Come on, let's go wipe our eyes. I need some advice for tonight."

"Okay." Lydia gave Damian a questioning look but he just shrugged his shoulders. Her eyes turned to Bran and then burned when he stared back without flinching. She followed Willow from the room.

Damian's eyes took up where Lydia's left off. "You know I'll kill you if you hurt her."

Bran gazed back with no remorse, "I plan on tying her up, teaching her about her desires, and showing her the real reason she's here. If that bothers you, you shouldn't come to the club tonight."

"Fuck, this is my sister you're talking about."

"Really Damian. You own a BDSM club. You talked me into experiencing the lifestyle. I never judged you and I learned about my needs and my unfulfilled kinks. Do you want some asshole who likes to beat women with their fists getting ahold of her again?"

"No. And just so you're aware, the assholes you speak of spent lengthy stays at neighborhood hospitals and will never be back around."

"She needs to understand what her body wants. It may not be a full BDSM lifestyle and those needs may not accent mine but I'd like to try."

"I won't be at the club tonight and I'll find something to keep my wife distracted."

"Fair enough."

***

She was waiting at the bar. He had given her no instructions about clothing and figured she asked Lydia for advice. Her body was in profile and her breasts covered in a black leather bra. She had on a short skirt but he couldn't see what was under it. Her hair was in its usual disarray; partially braided, short in some places and long in others. He would love to feel it glide through his fingers dripping wet and just combed after a shower but that would wait. He finished his perusal down her body and noticed her bare feet. Her lack of boots was hot, who knew?

He promised only her breasts would be on public display but he planned for some private time before they got started at a station. She was drinking water. Strict rules prohibited anyone from getting drunk at the club but it had been a while since the wine at dinner and she might need to loosen up a bit.

There were several Doms around and he wondered if any had approached her. Her response to Paul the evening before might be keeping them away. His hands went to either side of her body and rested on the bar. His mouth came in close to her multi-pierced ear. "May I buy you a drink or would you like to get started?" It was a deep husky whisper."

"I'm trying to talk myself into this."

"Let's go to a private room first and I'll convince you to stay."

"Must we?"

"You have a lot to learn about submissive behavior." He held back a grin and then took her hand. They walked past the full-length bar and the appreciative looks on the other Dom's faces to a back hallway monitored by one of the El Diablo bouncers.

"Room two is open."

He walked her through the door and turned up the lighting using the mood controller. He planned to have a long look at her body and he wanted to see each curve clearly. Walking to a leather couch facing the bed he didn't release her hand but pulled her into his lap when he sat down. His mouth took hers in a penetrating kiss and his hands went to her shoulders where he gently massaged her tense muscles.

When he ended the kiss, he gazed at her face. She hadn't overdone her makeup but coal black accented her large eyes, which stared into his.

"We're taking this slow but I need to know your safe word or if you would rather have two. The first means slow down the intensity and the second means stop."

"Just one. I want to use purple."

He couldn't hide his smile. He expected something unique, not a color but purple would do. "If you use your safe word everything stops. You can walk away at that time or go somewhere private with me and talk about what went wrong if that's what you want. That's the only hard and fast rule here."

"Do I look down and not in your eyes?"

"When we go to the station, I want your eyes on me focusing on what I'm doing. Tonight is about learning and exploring your limits. We can go over a few things now. First, I want you to kneel in front of me with your head down."

"Now?"

"Yes."

She disengaged from his lap and went to her knees in front of him. His hand went through her half braided hair. It always looked messy but was actually incredibly soft. He reached down and placed his hand on her inner thigh. "Spread your legs a little more."

She complied without comment.

"This is how I want you if I nod down at the floor. In this room, you may ask questions. I won't deny answers tonight even after we go to the station but here is the more appropriate place."

"Can another Dom punish me?"

"Not without my permission so please don't worry about it."

"Are you going to hurt me?"

"I thought I would get that over with so you're more comfortable when we walk out."

"You're going to hurt me now?"

"This is about trust. You have a safe word and I trust you to use it. You need to trust me to keep you from wanting to."

"What are you going to do?"

"I plan to give you the spanking I've promised for the past two days."

"You're kidding, why?"

"One because you need it, two because I want my handprint on your ass, and three I want you to know the level of pain I won't cross tonight."

"Your handprint on my ass turns you on?"

"You have no idea." He placed his hand in front of her and when her fingers touched his, he tightened his grasp and gave her a short pull facedown onto his lap. "Rest your head on the couch. I want to see what's under your skirt." Just having her in this position made his cock ache.

"I'm sure it's the normal parts found under a woman's skirt."

His hand came down with a resounding slap. "I planned to explore first but your mouth has a way of getting you in trouble."

"That hurt."

"It was meant to, now be quiet for a minute while I satisfy my curiosity."

Thin black lace covered her rounded bottom. His fingers feathered over her silky curves. He wanted more than anything to delve inside her pussy but he was delaying that final moment to discover if she was pierced. He knew she was wet and the scent of her spicy arousal traveled straight to his cock causing his erection to press against his black jeans.

His hand came down harder and then he soothed his fingers over her heated flesh. "You're beautiful. Your ass is perfect and I so want to taste your pussy and suck your clit between my lips." His hand came down again and this time she made a small noise. He rubbed and soothed before giving her opposite ass cheek a burning slap. Her indrawn breath and soft "oh" let him know she was feeling more than pain.

"BDSM is about kinky sex and fetish behavior. Most people in the lifestyle learned early on to hide what they desired because it's not acceptable in normal everyday society. But, the number of people with sexual hang ups in this world is growing. Then we have you come along with your toxic tongue and make Master Paul uncomfortable because you turned him on. That was quite naughty." His hand came down.

"It won't happen again."

His voice dropped even more, "Tell me if you're wet."

"Why?"

The slap was harder this time and her entire body flinched.

"I didn't ask you to question me. I asked if your pussy was wet."

"God yes."

"Thank you. I'm not touching you where you need it most. I'm waiting until we're in my room but I need to know if you're turned on."

"Yes, but I don't know why."

His hand landed on her ass again but this time in the center and lower where she felt it on her pussy.

"Ahh, I can't do this."

"Yes you can. There is so much you can do and take. I'll show you." His hand came down in rapid succession. She squirmed to get away but he kept a tight hold on her.

"Please stop." She finally cried.

He stopped and his hand soothed over her hot flesh. You didn't use your safe word but I'm giving you the benefit of the doubt. Do I need to stop?"

"Yes…no. Oh god, I don't know."

"Then the answer is no but I'll stop. That's it. No pain will be greater than that but the intensity and desire for fulfillment will be much harder to bear." He brought her up from his lap and kissed her again placing his hands over her breasts. "These I want to play with." He said between nibbling kisses.

"Umm, they're sensitive and I like your hands covering them."

"Good because it's time and I want them completely naked just for me."

"And the entire club?"

"Your job is to think about me."

"I'll try."

"You will. I promise."

He nodded to the floor when they arrived at the station and she went to her knees. "Spread them a little more for me baby." He only said it to push her submission but she obeyed his command.

He walked further into the station and prepared the items he wanted to use placing them on a side tray out of her sight. He adjusted the overhead bar so her arms could be suspended over her head but her feet would be on solid ground. He wanted access around her entire body and this was the best apparatus for his needs. He walked over and placed his hand in front of her. "Come."

She stood and followed his lead.

He stopped beside the bar and turned her back to curious eyes that were gathering to see his station play. He released the front clasp of her bra and slowly drew it over her shoulders and down her arms. He took it entirely off her body, turned her sideways, and placed her bra on a table. Her hands came up and covered her breasts. He moved to her back, reaching around to remove her hands but replaced them with his own. He cupped her breasts and his fingers played with the nipple rings. His breath was hot in her ear. "Look at my hands. You are not allowed to use yours. For tonight, these breasts are mine. I want everyone to see your beauty uncovered. I want your breasts to burn with desire knowing the Doms watching can't touch their softness." He placed long slow kisses down the side of her neck to her shoulder and then stepped back. "Place your right arm behind you."

He buckled a black leather cuff around her wrist and then asked for her other arm and repeated the process. He turned her body so she was facing the front of the station and also the eyes of the club members. He quickly walked around and placed a kiss on her brow. "Bring your hands up and grasp the bar above your head."

Her hands trembled but she complied. He secured the heavy metal clips on the bar to her cuffs. "Your job is to hold tightly to the bar, understood?"

"Yes Sir." It sounded so incredibly sweet coming from her.

"Close your eyes."

She didn't hesitate. He walked away and picked up a spreader bar then returned and dropped to his knees at her feet.

"Keep your eyes closed. I'm securing your legs." He kissed her thigh as he placed the straps around her ankle and then repeated the process. Once her thighs were spread, he ran slow wet kisses up her legs ending just under her skirt. He stood in front of her again and grabbed nipple clamps off the side table.

Leaning in, he touched the side of her face, "Open." Her expression was halfway between terrified and sensual but he planned on changing that.

"I want your eyes on me and following my movements." He ran his fingers down the side of her cheek, neck and over her breasts. Showing her the nipple clamps in his hand he explained, "These will be tight but your body will adjust quickly. I'm not taking them off until we're in my room." He clipped the first one on behind her piercing.

"Ahh."

"Give it a minute." She stopped squirming and he placed the other one on. A chain dropped between the two and he gave it a gentle tug, which got the desired response from between her lips. "Follow me with your eyes." He walked to the tray beside them and picked up the flogger before bringing it in front of her. "This is deer skin. It's soft but, with a little extra wrist action, it can cause a slight sting. We'll work up to that but first I want you to feel it across your body."

He started at her cheek running the soft strands over the curve of her shoulder, down her arms, and across her pierced bellybutton before moving it upward again. He never took his eyes from hers. When he ran the flogger back down and circled it over her hip and then under her skirt to the inside of her thighs, her eyes closed.

"Open, I want you following the movements of my hands, understood?"

"Yes Sir." Her voice was dreamy.

He brought his head forward and using his tongue he circled her nipple going around the piercing and moistening the tight skin. He felt her body tense making him smile. "Oh baby, we've only just begun. I want you wet for me." His mouth went to her other nipple. When he released it, he walked around behind her and began slowly torturing her with the flogger covering the skin of her back and then her bottom beneath her skirt. He brought his left hand around and squeezed first one breast and then the other.

He brought his hips in close to her back grinding his erection into her body. "This is what you do to me. Now close your eyes sweetheart." He took her earlobe between his teeth and bit down softly then suckled for a moment before stepping back. He let the flogger go with a snap of his wrist. It hit her back curling around her side with the knotted ends landing across her breast. Her body bucked against the restraints and he let the flogger fly again. He began systematically striking her back so the knots hit the front of her.

Her sighs grew louder but he never let up just continued the slow steady rhythm. She arched and she tried to twist as he moved to her ass and allowed the knots to hit her pussy using more arm strength because of her skirt.

"Please, I can't stop, I'm going to come."

He stopped and didn't move or say a word. He waited until her breathing calmed and then he stepped around to the front of her and began again. It didn't take as long this time before her moans became pleas for release. He stilled his hand and waited.

"I can't take anymore, please." Her voice was breathless and her body undulated trying to get relief.

He stepped forward and pressed the entire front of his body to hers. His bare chest rubbed against her nipples and his cock ground against her pussy. Using his hands, he clasped her ass cheeks and with steady movements rubbed against her. His mouth took her hers in a brutal kiss. He could feel her body grinding into his crotch and the tremors running through her arms and legs. He ended the kiss suddenly and stepped away. It took three strikes of the flogger before she screamed and her orgasm rippled through her body. Before she gained control of herself, he released her legs and then her hands and picked her up in his arms. With quick strides, he left the club and carried her to his room.

Chapter Seven

He used one hand to pull back the duvet and then he placed her on the bed in the shadowed bedroom. She was a trembling mass of heightened nerve endings and this was exactly what his internal demon screamed for.

Reaching just below her waist he pulled her skirt and underwear from her body bringing them slowly down her legs but he never took his eyes from hers. He placed his legs on either side of her hips then took her wrists and fastened them to the brass bars of the headboard. Her eyes grew larger.

"Later I'll release your arms and let you use your hands but right now. I want you focused on your own desire."

"Please, I'm burning up." Her voice was breathy and filled with need.

"We're almost there." He poured his desire into a soul-shattering kiss as his lips and tongue savaged her mouth. His lips left hers and he pulled back slightly and released one of her nipple clamps.

"Arrrh, oh god."

His lips surrounded her nipple and sucked greedily enhancing the sweet torturous ecstasy. Her hips tried to pump off the bed but he leaned into her body keeping her from moving. When she was back in control, he removed the other clamp continuing to suck and lick.

At last, he sat back on her thighs.

"I dreamed of you here, like this. Last night I fucked another sub but imagined you in this bed. I don't know if I'll ever get enough of the sweet sounds you make, the smell of your body, or your beautiful breasts." He shifted backwards and positioned himself between her thighs. "I also dreamed of tasting you."

He moved down the bed using his hands to hold her legs apart. He slid his tongue along her inner thighs and zeroed in on her pussy. He found what his brain fantasized about. It wasn't just one piercing; her labia had several along the outer folds and a round ball above her clit. He backed off the bed and reached for the bedside light. It blinked on.

"What the hell are you doing, god please just fuck me."

"I want to look first. I expected a piercing but you're full of surprises."

She twisted but his hands and body stopped her movements. He went between her legs and using his hands, examined the metal rings on either side of her slit. His tongue ran over the outer labia rings and then the two tiny twin metal balls, one below and one above her clit.

"You taste sweet and spicy at the same time. I don't know why you torture your body but it's sexy as hell. I want to slide between these rings and feel them run along the nerves of my cock."

"Then fucking do it."

"Awe my sweet little sub. All things in good time." Two fingers entered her moist heat and her body arched off the bed. His lips went around her clit and sucked it into his mouth."

Her cries caused more blood to pound through his erection. He wouldn't last much longer but he wanted her to go over the edge and lose control again before he satisfied himself. They had all night. He brought his wet fingers out and pulled gently on the gold rings in her labia, stretching her skin. The rough texture of his tongue ran along the folds and then his fingers slid inside once more.

Her orgasm was beautiful. Her pussy contracted against his fingers and his tongue continued to lick the juices her body released. He used his teeth to nip and then suck while she cried out again and again.

He sat back watching her face as her orgasm slowly subsided. He placed a condom on his throbbing cock and ran his hand up and down the length.

When she could breathe, her liquid blue eyes opened. She gave a beautifully sensual smile mixed with satisfaction as she stared at his cock.

"This is what I call being in the zone." He said.

"Do you plan on taking me there again?" She whispered.

"You have no idea."

He quickly moved his body over hers and with one thrust buried his cock deep inside her pussy. It was heaven. Her burning heat surrounded him as her muscles clenched tightly. She rocked with an upward thrust and the angle caused his cock to glide over her clit and piercing.

"Please release my hands." She practically screamed.

His voice was strained, "Not this time but soon, I promise."

"Please."

He found a slow steady rhythm. He could feel the metal piercings against his cock, and the lower ball under her clit stimulated him almost to the point of releasing his seed before he was ready. He never considered what an incredible sensual experience having sex with a Goth chick would entail and he wanted this first time to drive them both wild.

She stopped begging and pressed her pelvis into his when he made a downward stroke. He could feel his desire build and his entire body became focused on reaching his peak and taking her with him.

Their bodies' trembled and low groans became desperate cries. The heat built until lava ruptured from deep inside. His hands held her hips using a bruising grip as he pumped into her while his orgasm erupted.

Unhurriedly, he unfastened her hands and then massaged her arm and shoulder muscles. He continued the steady pressure until her breathing slowed.

Her lips begged for his kiss and his tongue explored her mouth and ended by stroking her tongue ring. The unique honey blend of her mouth caused his cock to harden again. He didn't stop and their sexual dance started once more.

Several hours later, he led her to the shower and washed the makeup from her eyes. He tipped her head up and looked at her gorgeous complexion and the natural beauty of her face. Her large blue eyes stared back.

"Tell me about the piercings."

"You want to know why my pussy is pierced?"

"No, I want to know about your face."

"I'd rather tell you about the other ones."

"I know, but these are more important."

She smiled sensually.

"Yes, the others turn me on but these," His fingers pulled on the individual loops and barbells including the ones on the sides of her nose and mouth, "These are the better story."

She dropped her eyes and he waited. His hands smoothed over the curves of her body, which fit perfectly to his. After several long moments, she began talking.

"My mother was beautiful before drugs and alcohol took over completely. When I was young, she brought men to our house and I could hear them throughout the night. Some were friendly, some never gave me any attention, and some paid me too much attention." She took another deep breath, "My mother had a thing about body perfection. When I was twelve, a friend of mine pierced my eyebrow and my mom flipped out. I guess she always thought her baby girl would grow up in her illustrious footsteps and become a stripper. She told me mutilating my body would ruin any chance I had of making it in Vegas. Every week I came home with new holes in my face and ears. I did it to hurt my mother but I also enjoyed the pain and feel of the needle. I have holes in my face that I allowed to close over so I could have them pierced again." She tilted her head back and looked into his eyes. "I'm totally fucked up."

He moved his body around and pulled her slick wet back to his chest. He took her hands and placed them flat on the wall pushing her upper body down so she bent slightly at the waist. In one fluid thrust, he buried his cock deep inside her pussy. "No, this is fucked and I want to fuck you again and again."

His hands grasped her hips as his cock slid in and out. When both their bodies trembled and pulsed with release, he turned her around and slowly kissed each of her facial piercings. "These are sexy as hell and I want to see a needle enter your skin. Then I want to fuck you hard. God my bitch of a mother would loath you."

"That's funny because my mother would love you."

Chapter Eight

The next day they argued about where her piercing would go.

"I want another one on my lip."

"And I want to kiss you and not worry about you being in pain or possible infection."

"You want to take a whip to my body but you're worried about a little pain when we kiss?"

"Come on, indulge me." His voice was low and sexy.

"I'm letting my brother's limo driver take us to the piercer so when we're done you can throw me in the back and fuck me hard. I think I'm being generous enough."

He kissed her, his tongue playing with her tongue ring. Pulling back, he grinned wickedly. "Do I need to paddle you into submission?"

"Hmm, that might help."

***

They adjusted their clothing after he pounded her body into the leather upholstery in the back of the limo. Her eyebrow was red and slightly swollen. He placed a gentle kiss on the gold ring he bought her.

"My ass is red too."

"Oh baby, I'll kiss your ass but you have no idea how bad I want to do naughty things to it too."

"You almost have me convinced I should let you."

"Tomorrow night, I'll have you tied up in my room thinking only of pleasure. We'll get a little kinkier and I'll show you a few ways to prepare your ass for my cock."

"I don't know if anything's kinkier than getting turned on while I'm being pierced. Hmm, maybe watching you get your cock pierced would do it for me."

"As much as I love your cunt rings, no one is getting near my cock with a needle."

Her laughter made him smile. "I can't believe you're going out with my brother tonight and getting drunk."

"Neither can I. My dick will be hard the entire time but the poor man needs a break."

"Call me in the morning and I'll give you a blowjob to help you with your hangover."

He nuzzled her ear. "How about one for my pre-hangover?"

"We'll be at the hotel in a minute."

Bran hit the intercom, "Carl can you drive us around until I tell you otherwise?"

"Yes Sir, I'd be happy to."

Willow slid off the seat and went to her knees. Her fingers slowly lowered his zipper inch by inch. The rasp of the metal teeth sounded loudly in the luxurious space. He breathed deeply watching her face as she removed his cock from the confines of his pants. Her tongue came out and the large round ball traveled along the underside of his cock. He didn't breathe until she took the head into her mouth. His hips lifted from the seat when she used her tongue and then suction to drive him wild. He leaned his head back against the seat and closed his eyes while his hands went into her hair."

"You don't want to watch?"

He didn't open his eyes, "God yes, but I'll last thirty seconds. You have no idea what your tongue ring does for me."

"I love your kinky side."

"I love your mouth. Now use it baby."

Her laugh vibrated over his cock as she took him back into her mouth. She swirled her tongue and teased. When he could take no more he grabbed her hair and bucked his hips so she took him deeper against the back of her throat. He fucked her mouth until his cum shot hotly down her throat. He groaned loudly while she used her tongue to lick him clean.

His mother might hate her but he was falling hard.

***

Damian took him to one of the best strip clubs in Houston.

"Does your wife know we're here?"

"Yes, and I need to be good and drunk because she made me promise she could tie me to the bed the next time I'm conscious."

Bran couldn't hold back his laughter. "That's what you get for marrying a dominatrix. I'll help you get so blistering drunk that even if you wake up you won't remember."

"That'll work. So how's my baby sister?"

"I know you use the word 'baby' to make me squirm but it won't work. She's coming over in the morning to help me with my hangover."

"Okay I'm sorry I asked. I don't want to know any more about tomorrow morning but how does she seem otherwise."

"She's fucked up like the rest of us but I think working at the club is the best thing for her. You may need to find her a permanent position. Just what did she major in during college?"

"She has her Master's in accounting."

Bran almost spit out his drink. "You're kidding me?"

"Nope, baby sister is brilliant with numbers. She's promised to look over my books and make sure my accountant is doing everything he should be. She can also count cards so never play blackjack with her."

"Goth chick has quite a few hidden secrets."

"You call her Goth chick?"

"I'm pretty sure that's what she is but right now she's my Goth chick."

"You never have a sub more than one night. Do you think this wise?"

"There's nothing wise about it but she's still learning and I'm enjoying the lessons."

"That's it; I'm buying another round and changing the subject."

They talked about college, business, and then anything that popped into their befuddled brains. Carl helped them both to their rooms when they finally got back to the hotel. Bran didn't remember removing his shoes but when he woke up the following morning with his head pounding, they were by his bed. He needed a Carl in his life but oh god he needed Willow more.

Fingers feathering through his hair woke him a second time. He squinted into the morning light and took the offered pills and glass of water.

"Thank you."

"You're welcome. Breakfast is in the other room if you think you can make it. If not I'll bring a tray in here."

"What about my morning blowjob."

"It's on hold until you've eaten and showered but if you're good I'll join you and help wash the smell of booze from your pores."

"That bad?"

"Yep, if I licked your skin right now I would probably get high."

"I'll eat and bathe first but no talking about licking my skin or I'll tie you to the bed."

She stood up and took his hand. "Come on drunken business man. Eat some food and I promise you'll feel better."

"I'm holding you to that promise Goth chick."

Chapter Nine

They spent the day being lazy and Bran realized how much work consumed his life during the past year. It wasn't a bad thing but at the same time, he had to find a way to mix pleasure into his busy life. Maybe he could open an office in Houston and become a regular visitor to El Diablo again. He had enough business interests with Damian that it would make sense.

He enjoyed Willow's company and for the first time thought about a permanent D/s relationship. The club and Willow's delicious body didn't need to encroach on the work he did. He could visit a few times a month and teach her more about her body and the ways he could please it. Finding out about her past, and what made her tick was another bonus.

Her sweet mouth was the perfect antidote for too much alcohol and he would get drunk nightly if this was his reward. A blowjob without a pierced tongue would never quite do it for him again.

One hour led to another and they spent the day together. When their bodies were overly satisfied they watched two movies in the afternoon. He chose a new action flick and she chose a chick flick. He loved watching her facial expressions while the movie played and then wiping her eyes when it ended. His movie was not nearly as fun until she fell asleep with her head on his lap. His hand traveled inside the white dress shirt of his that she donned after their shower. It never looked this good on him. Soft blue sleepy eyes opened and gazed upward.

"I'm getting you prepared for tonight. I want you needy." His husky voice whispered over the sound of car crashes coming from the television.

"Have you been watching the movie or me?"

"Hmm, it's a tossup; I'm not sure what's happened during the past ten minutes."

She stretched and he almost lost his resolve to wait until they were inside the club to taste her again.

"This is what I want you wearing tonight but nothing underneath."

"This doesn't cover my ass."

"Exactly and it won't cover anything after I get you into a station."

"I don't know if I'm ready."

"I'm not asking." He felt her flinch at his dominant voice. "Trust me Willow and I'll give you what you need."

"What do you need?"

"Hmm, this is nice but tonight will be better."

Her hands circled his neck and pulled him down. He ended the kiss quickly, and pulled her arms from around him and stretched them over her head using one hand to hold them in place. His other brushed the sides of the shirt away to play with her piercings and the silky skin surrounding them. He never considered himself exclusively a breast man but hers drove him wild. Maybe it was because he hadn't taken her softly rounded ass yet. He would find out tonight.

***

She followed him into the club with the front of his shirt unbuttoned and the tails slapping against her naked ass. He went to the bar and ordered them a drink. He could feel her tension but surprisingly she kept quiet. He needed her relaxed. Walking to a group of chairs close to the slowly spinning carousel, he nodded for her to get on her knees beside him and he handed her a drink.

A pair of shiny black latex covered legs appeared next to them and Lydia took a seat.

"Damian will have trouble with this."

Bran couldn't help his grin or noticing how beautiful she was, with her rounded tummy bare, and a matching black latex bra covering her swollen breasts. He wondered how Damian ever let her out of bed.

"He knows she's submissive."

"Permission to speak to your sub?"

"Granted."

"Are you okay with this Willow?"

"Yes, I think I am."

"Yes what?" Bran wanted her complete submission tonight and it included recognizing other Doms and Dommes.

"Yes Mistress Lydia." Her eyes remained down but he knew she was biting her lip.

He lifted her chin and hot fire sparked in her eyes.

"Here comes trouble." Lydia stood up and partially blocked her husband's path.

He didn't look at his sister just his friend.

"I would prefer her not be naked in here." His words were hard.

"Then you need to stay away from my station later. This isn't about you, and, your squeamish behavior is getting on my nerves."

"I think you forget who decked who back in college."

"You sucker punched me while I was drinking. I'm not drunk now."

Lydia's hand went to her husband's arm. "He's right Damian this isn't about you or me. You're being a hypocrite. It's Willow's choice and you will butt out."

Damian took a deep breath. "Christ, when our baby girl gets here I'm closing down the club and practicing vanilla sex for the rest of my life."

"And who are you going to practice with?" Lydia held back her laughter.

Bran saw his friend's face soften and the tension leave his shoulders. He couldn't help himself, "I think station three is open."

"You're killing me. I drank too much last night but I think I need another good drunk to get me through this."

"No, you're not drinking. You promised Angela she could sub for you tonight and I don't want you hurting her. I need to see if anyone is signed up for me and if not, I'm looking for a guy that knows how a submissive should behave."

"You're doing this because I let you tie me up and then broke the headboard."

"You ruined my fantasy."

"Oh but I doubled mine." Damian grabbed his wife and gave her a very public kiss, which was rare when they were both in Dom mode. Her dreamy smile said she didn't mind.

"If you two will excuse us, my giggling sub and I have some kinky sex to work on."

Damian groaned and Willow immediately went quiet. Bran stood up and took her hand striding toward the empty station. It beckoned for a Dom and his sub.

He gave a nod to the floor when they walked into the softly lit alcove and she knelt. He took his time preparing what he needed but kept everything out of her sight. Taking a black scarf, he walked over and commanded her to stand. He wrapped her eyes and adjusted the material so she saw nothing. He then picked her up in his arms and carried her to the St Andrews Cross.

"Trust me." He whispered softly as he let her body slide down the front of his. He placed her back to the cross and secured her arms and legs. The white shirt gaped open exposing her breasts and a glimpse of her smoothly shaved bejeweled pussy. He walked away and then rolled the cart closer to the cross. "Don't move at all. I need you completely still." There was nothing soft about his command.

"Yes Sir." There was a tremor in her voice.

He took a razor sharp knife and cut the sleeves of her shirt from shoulder to wrist. She flinched but didn't move. The material barely hung over her frame when he grabbed the sides, shimmied it down her back, over her hips, and stopped when it rested across her bottom. Kneeling in front of her, he used the shirt to pull her pussy closer to his mouth. His tongue came out and licked.

"Ahhre, what are you doing?"

"You, my stubborn sub are to keep your mouth closed unless I tell you to open it." He gave a gentle nip to her soft flesh.

He continued nipping and sucking, using his tongue against her piercings. By holding the shirt tight, he kept her from wiggling. Her sighs grew wild but he didn't reprimand her for the noise. The sounds she made while he continued playing with her wet slit turned him on and forced his cock to full attention. Her sighs slowed and it became apparent she was more worried about the people talking in low voices around the station than finding fulfillment and letting her body go. This was exactly what he didn't want. He stood and let the shirt drop to the floor at her feet. He leaned in close and whispered in her ear, "Willow, you need to think of me. You will have several orgasms out here tonight. Do you understand?"

"But I thought you didn't want your subs to have orgasms out here?" Her choked voice was questioning.

"This is about getting past some of your inhibitions. Your body belongs to your Dom and tonight that's me. I won't let you see anyone watching and you'll never know who they are. So trust me."

"Yes Sir."

"We are going to try a little pain to get you in the proper mind set."

"But."

"No, that's enough. I'll gag you if you speak again. Only your soft little sex sounds are acceptable."

Using a braided high intensity flogger, he started slow and gently. He knew she felt the sting but she managed to hold on. When the nerve endings of her cunt and breasts were sexually stimulated, he added nipple clamps with weighted bells. "You're doing wonderful sweetness, do you want me?"

"Yes." The one word held incredible need.

Two of his fingers entered her at the same time he took one of her nipples between his lips and applied hard suction. It was enough to take her over the top. Her pussy pulsated over his fingers and her body shivered as the orgasm consumed her. He took her cries into his mouth and kissed her deeply for being a good little sub.

Breaking away, he placed his hands in her hair and tugged until her ear tilted to his warm breath, "Shh, you're beautiful and every person here is envious of what you just gave me. Now I want more." He walked away and picked up one of his favorite toys. He wouldn't need lube because her juice was trailing between her legs. He didn't turn it on but used the tip of the vibrator to play against the folds of skin of her pussy. He smiled at the sound of the metal gently clanging against her vaginal piercings. Ever so slowly, he inserted the long cool steel. "Clamp your muscles tight and don't let go." He said as he seated the vibrator fully inside her.

Stepping back, he picked up the flogger again. Using more force, he brought the leather braids against her upper thighs just avoiding her swollen cunt. Her cry was louder and he ran his hand over her hip before checking the location of the vibrator. "You're doing wonderful baby." The next strike was to her breasts, and he let her feel more of the sting and then in rapid succession he struck down her stomach and finally on the front of her pussy where her need was greatest. As the last lash came down, he hit the control and turned on the vibrator.

"Ahh, god, I can't take it." She screamed and her pelvis thrust forward and back as her orgasm exploded throughout her body.

He couldn't feel the pulses of her pussy this time but he could see her body shake as the release went on and on. His hand went between her legs and he inserted the tip of the heavily lubed butt plug into the tight rosette of her ass. He pushed it in place before she knew what he was doing. Her body began bucking at the strange invasion.

"Relax; it's only a small one."

"Take it out please."

"No, and you don't have permission to speak only to feel." He turned up the speed of the vibrator and pulled the plug slightly out before pushing it back in.

She no longer had control and this was what he'd been waiting for all night. Her unrestrained cries of pleasure made his cock swell. He wanted to bury his face in her pussy and continue to draw cries from her throat. This last orgasm was all the club patrons were getting from Willow. He'd given them more than he'd ever allowed but he wanted her to understand her body, realize why she objected to certain sexual acts, and know what her body craved without fighting it. He removed the toys but didn't remove the blindfold. He then unfastened the straps securing her to the cross. "I don't want you to see who's around so keep the blindfold on."

She didn't answer just breathed heavily while tremors continued to run through her body.

He wanted nothing more than to carry her to his room but he knew she needed care before he allowed his cock to take her sweet pussy. Picking her up, he went to the alcove behind the station taking a bottle of water from a side bar with him. Standing her on her feet, he quickly grabbed a sub blanket and wrapped her tight before sitting and gathering her onto his lap. Her mouth beckoned and he placed a soft kiss to the small wire ring passing through her lip. He smoothed the damp hair that fell over the blindfold and continued to place gentle kisses on her brow tasting the delicious salted honey flavor of her skin. Her trembling slowly subsided and he lifted her head and placed the bottled water to her lips. "Drink."

She took a long pull. "Permission to speak Sir."

"You were so good tonight and I would love nothing more than to hear what you have to say."

"Next time you're too drunk to know what's happening, I'm sticking a butt plug up your ass."

His laughter rang out and he tightened his hold kissing her deeply. Finally, he managed to come up for air. "I'm told it's as erotic as hell but I've never had the honors of being the recipient. I don't think I'll ever be that drunk but be my guest and try. Your punishment will be exceptional and you've been warned."

His voice trailed away because he started thinking about the next two nights being the last he spent with her. Even if she was interested in a semi-permanent D/s relationship, she needed to spread her wings and discover more from different Doms.

"You're squeezing too tight and I'm having trouble breathing Sir."

He loosened his hold. "Are you ready to go to my room?"

"Are you leading me or carrying me?"

"It's my pleasure to carry you."

"You will have back problems in a few years if you keep this up."

"That's enough sub. I want absolute quiet until we get to the room."

She was becoming good at taking orders.

Chapter Ten

Laying her on the bed, Bran left the blindfold secured, and quickly removed his clothes. Peeling the sub blanket from her body was like unwrapping candy. For the first time in years, he waited only long enough to cover himself in a condom. He allowed her hands to remain free covering her body and pushing his cock in to the hilt. Her fingers slid over his back and she dug her nails into his skin as his pace increased. He couldn't get enough and seeing her orgasm again and again at the club made it impossible for him to go slow. He absorbed the sensation of her tight hot sheath wrapped around his cock and the metal in her pussy sliding against him.

His hand went between their bodies and he used his fingers to uncover the swollen hood covering her clit. Repositioning himself, he slid against her clit and the genital piercings that drove him crazy. The need to explode was building in his balls and tightening up through his cock. She felt so incredibly perfect. At last, his balls contracted and he ejaculated into the condom. Her muscles clenched around him over and over nursing every drop of semen from his testicles.

His hand went to the blindfold and removed it looking deep into her eyes. They were incredible even when they squinted against the sudden light from the lamp by the bed. He grabbed her hair and pulled her lips to his. The kiss began tenderly but grew more demanding. It was his goodbye kiss, and he put all his pent up emotions into it, absorbing her taste and hoping he never forgot what her mouth and pussy felt like when they surrounded his cock.

Finally, he ended the kiss and rolled to her side bringing his arm up over his eyes. "You can stay the night but I want you to try a new Dom tomorrow evening."

He didn't receive an answer and chanced a glance at her upturned face. She was staring at the ceiling with no expression. He turned slightly toward her and rested his hand on her breast absently playing with the nipple ring he couldn't resist. "It's important that you learn what your body needs and wants. I gave you tonight so you could understand your desires but I told you before I'm not into exhibitionism like most Doms. I'm thinking of opening an office here in the city and when I get things settled, I would love to top you again if you're available."

Her hand came to his and stopped the movement on her breast. She rolled over and then stood by the bed looking down at him. "Thank you for everything. I'm not staying the night. I need some sleep. I work at the club tomorrow at noon and have an eight-hour shift. I'll see you then."

Her voice was steady and he rolled to his back again when she walked into the bathroom and gently shut the door. He didn't know what he expected but it wasn't the lack of emotion she displayed. He kept assuring himself he would hook up with her when he came back for a visit.

A few minutes later, she walked out of the bathroom naked. She walked over to the closet and removed another of his white shirts. He didn't object. She buttoned it from hem to neck and then walked toward the bed. She sat and bending forward kissed his cheek. She pulled away when he turned his lips to take her mouth.

"No, this is it. Thank you Bran, I'll never forget our time together."

She walked away and he refused to admit the hurt deep in his soul. "Fuck." The word sounded in the room but it was only for his ears.

***

He expected Damian to visit the following day but he never came. Willow obviously didn't go running to her brother. He hadn't meant to hurt her and the lack of communication from his friend made him feel like he might be the only one with the emptiness inside. He hoped he was.

Not being able to get her out of his mind, he broke the vacation rule and answered emails along with returning a few phone calls. He also called Jenny Mack.

"Why are you bothering me again? I've only lost a few million dollars of your money but you have a few billion left. Nothing to worry about."

"I just needed to hear the sound of your sexy voice."

"What's wrong?"

He laughed, "What makes you think anything is wrong?"

"I can hear it in your voice, something's happened."

"You worry too much. I've had a wonderful time and given my blue balls the workout they needed."

"With one woman or several?"

"One the first night and then another for the past three."

"That's what I thought. Who is she?"

"Damian's sister."

"Are you bringing her back with you?"

"No, she's staying here. Last night was the end though I might come see her in a few months."

"You are a stupid man."

"I'm afraid you're right."

"So fix it."

"I don't know if I can."

"Oh I see, the mega stud, billion dollar Dom has met a woman he's unsure about."

"Yes, I have."

"You're a dumbass."

The line went dead.

He was a dumbass. He looked at the time and decided to get ready. He didn't wear his Dom clothes but chose a soft pair of jeans and a black silk shirt. He wasn't looking for a sub tonight. He was planning to watch one.

He arrived at nine and Damian immediately herded him into his office. "What the hell is going on?"

"I don't know, why don't you tell me?"

"My sister is being topped by Kyle tonight and she asked me for a Dom who liked to inflict pain."

"You suggested Kyle?"

"He likes subs that can take a lash but he won't hurt her permanently. He actually came to me to make sure you were out of the picture before he took her on."

"I am out of the picture."

"You spent the entire day with her yesterday and the day before. You've never done that and I thought maybe this would be a lasting relationship."

"I don't do lasting D/s relationships."

"Ah hell, fine. It was hard knowing you were fucking my sister anyway. Maybe it will be easier with Kyle."

"He doesn't stay around either."

"I know but I won't feel badly if I need to knock out a few of his teeth."

"Do you mind if I get back to the club now?"

"No, let's check out what's going on." Damian's phone rang and after a minute he waved Bran out.

Bran looked around but didn't see her at first. Then the carousel came around and he found her perched on one of the brightly colored horses. This meant she was claimed and he couldn't approach her. The flaps of his white shirt rose and fell gently with the up and down movement of the horse. She was at least wearing a pair of lacy black underwear. His dick ached but he had no plans to give it relief. He wasn't in the mood but he didn't think he would survive the night with his sub under someone else's control.

He walked to the bar and ordered a shot of whiskey while gazing into the mirror behind the bar, and watching the carousel turn. It was ten minutes before Kyle arrived and took Willow down. He ordered another whisky.

He waited fifteen minutes and drank a third whisky before going to the station.

Tied to the overhead bar, she had her back to the audience and wore nothing but her black panties. Kyle was a wimp for not making her take them off and Bran was a fool for feeling jealousy that it wasn't him wielding the whip. He walked closer. Her back, bottom, and thighs had thick red welts. Kyle's hand came up and his wrist let loose. He was barely holding back and he heard Willow sob. Fuck.

He was quick and before the next slash of the whip his hand came out and stopped Kyle. "That's enough."

Sweat was dripping down Kyle's face but his look was calm and controlled. "This is none of your affair, she has a safe word, and she hasn't used it."

"I said that's enough." The words came out through gritted teeth. He could hear her gentle even cries even though the whip wasn't making contact with her skin. He strode forward and his hand went to the strap holding her right leg.

"Well fuck, if she was yours why didn't you claim her."

Bran ignored Kyle and continued releasing the restraints.

"Why are you doing this?" The words came between her pain-filled gasps for breath.

"This isn't what you want."

"Like hell, it's exactly what I want. I want pain and humiliation. I want to be fucked by a different man each night and I want you to leave me alone."

He finally released the last strap and even with his arms partially holding her up, her knees gave out and he brought her fully within his embrace. He carried her out of the station to the back alcove.

Sitting on the couch, he pulled her head to his chest and let her cry. He couldn't rub her back, butt or legs because it would cause her more pain. This was part of the lifestyle but he didn't understand the need for extremes. He knew it made him abnormal to feel this way, but what else was new?

He looked up when a shadow feel across Willow. It was Lydia and she handed him a bottle. "It's my own special lotion and will help with the burn."

"Thank you, after it's on, I'm taking her back to my room."

"Oh hell no." Her sob was loud.

A hellcat began struggling in his arms. Unless he hurt her he had no way keep her secured.

"I am not going back to your room. Lydia please get me out of here."

Lydia grabbed a sub blanket and placed it softly around Willow's shoulders.

"What the hell are you doing?" He stood, but before he could step in the women's direction Damian's fist connected with his jaw and he fell back against the couch.

He looked into the angry eyes of his friend. "Do you feel better?" He touched his mouth and his hand came away covered in blood.

"Yes actually, I do. Stay away from my sister. If she wants to see you or speak with you, she'll be in contact. If you get near her again without her permission I'll ban you from the club."

"Did you see what he was doing to her?"

"You seem to have no trouble reminding me this is a BDSM club. I'd be happy to use my fist and remind you. Again."

Bran's eyes followed as Lydia led Willow into Damian's office. He looked up at his friend and then placed his head in his hands and sank back against the couch cushions. "I've really fucked this up."

"Yes, you have." Damian followed the women.

Bran went back to his room, threw his clothing into his bag, and left for the airport. He had no plans to return.

Chapter Eleven

"Your mother called three times this morning while you were in your meeting. I won't repeat the names she used but I'm not a fan of the "c" word."

"My mother did not use the "c" word unless she said cuckoo."

"Well, she was thinking it. That woman says more with her silence than anyone I've ever met."

"I'm busy this afternoon but I'll try and call her back tonight."

"You know the raise you gave me is now a month old and I need another one."

Bran had rarely smiled during the past month but his lip quirked.

"I knew you still had a grin or two somewhere in that thick head of yours."

"Why don't I just place your name on my checking account and you can decide how much money you make each week. If you deal with my mother more than normal just write yourself a bonus."

"That works for me. Now I need to get back to work so I can earn the raise I just gave myself. You know I'd be happy to arrange a flight to Houston so you can work off a little extra steam?"

"It's not going to happen. She's moved on, I've moved on."

"If you call burying yourself in work moving on, you've forgotten how babies are made."

"Why? Are you interested in having my baby?"

"I'm past child baring age. You know you need to release your seed somewhere. I'm sure your shower is getting very lonely."

"You're fired."

"What, the big bad Dom doesn't want to talk about masturbation."

"You are no longer here because I fired you."

"Okay I'll get back to work. Do you want me to order you a blow up doll?"

His glare did the trick and she left his office. He smiled again when the door closed behind her. He remembered the night over a year ago that she drank him under the table and he told her about his BDSM fetish. She didn't laugh or run away in horror she just asked why one of the richest men in the U.S. couldn't have it all. It was a good question and it eventually convinced him to take his vacation. Now he needed a vacation from his memories of vaginal jewelry, nipple piercings, beautiful breasts, laugher, sighs of pleasure, and blue eyes that reminded him of the vast ocean water. He was completely screwed.

A few minutes later life got worse.

He heard the commotion first then recognized the grating superior sound of his mother's voice. His office door opened and she strode in looking like she had a glass butt plug up her ass.

"In order to see my own son you force me to go through the Grand Canyon of secretaries." Her tone was bitter like always.

"I hired her to keep you out. I'll order Jenny more food so she has better luck the next time you visit without an appointment."

Jenny slammed his door shut from the outside. She'd heard every bigoted "fat" insult his mother had ever come up with, handled them like a pro, and once told Mrs.

Sterling she would sit on her face after eating a can of beans. Unfortunately, his mother didn't have a heart attack and he guessed overall he was glad because that was one bonus he didn't have enough ready cash to pay.

"Are you going to tell me why you're here or do I need to call security and have you removed?"

"You are just like your father."

"I am nothing like that man except for the fact neither of us could stand being around you for more than two minutes." He looked at his watch. "The clock is ticking."

"You are no different, he ran around with every slut he could find." Her face was growing red.

Now he was getting angry. "I do not run around with sluts but if I thought it would keep you away, I would behave exactly like my father."

"You need to get married and after ruining things with Elizabeth because of your kinky sex habits, I think a slut would be the only female your money could buy."

His clenched jaw turned into a wicked smile. "If you have a slut in mind who doesn't mind being tied to the bed post please send her to my house tonight." He wasn't surprised Elizabeth confided in his mother. It was actually funny because Elizabeth had no idea how kinky he could be. Unfortunately, his mother wasn't giving up or leaving. She was the queen of ignoring what she didn't want to hear.

"A friend of mine has a daughter that you will escort to the hospital benefit on Saturday night. I'm told you do not have a date."

"If I can bring handcuffs to the ball and find a place to have a little kinky sex, I'll think about it."

Her face grew redder but she held her ground. "No, this one will make the perfect mother for my grandchildren and I'm sure she could force herself into being restrained if you are generous enough in the prenup."

"We do not live in the middle ages where it takes an heir to inherit a fortune. I plan to go to my grave childless and leave my money to charity. And besides, your grandchildren will run and hide when they see you coming."

"Why are you so hateful?"

"I learned from the best Mommy Dearest."

"If I hadn't suffered through twelve hours of labor bringing you into the world, I would swear you didn't belong to me. The only good thing you've ever done was keep your father away after I produced his prodigal son."

"That may be the nicest thing you've ever said to me. I would hate to think of the torture you would have put a sister or brother through if given the chance."

Her eyes filled with hatred. She was normally able to hide her feelings but today she was more on edge than usual.

Early in Bran's life, his father explained that his mother fell in love with a man that painted her parent's summer home. Bran's grandparents paid him off and the man immediately dumped her without a backwards glance. She was heartbroken. On the rebound, she became pregnant with Bran and was forced to marry Brandon Edward Sterling III much to her parent's delight. Bran often wondered if she would be such a bitter woman if she ran off with her painter. He shook his head to clear any feelings of sympathy for the mother who spent years abroad, never called or gave a damn what happened to her son, and that was when he was little more than a toddler. When he was five, she slapped him in the face when she overheard him call his nanny mommy and then fired the distraught woman. Bran learned early on that if he showed any type of feelings for one of his caregivers they never returned. His father wouldn't interfere because he was too busy working to keep his wealth and fucking every secretary in his office. That was one of the reasons Bran hired Jenny Mack. He was determined to have brains and beauty working for him. He was not like his father.

"The answer is no. I have a date for the benefit and would never consider escorting someone you suggested."

"I can only imagine what type of female you found to attend with you."

"You may leave now mother. Unlike you, I have work to do. Please see yourself out."

The door shut quietly, his mother would never be caught dead doing something as common as slamming a door.

Jenny stepped in. "Do you really have a date for the event on Saturday?"

"Do you enjoy listening to my private conversations through the intercom?"

"How on earth would I finish writing my book of insults if I didn't? Date, Saturday?"

"No, I lied. I'm going alone unless I can talk you into attending with me."

"Sorry, my calendar is full on Saturday. I downloaded a good murder mystery to my Kindle and we're sharing a bottle of wine."

"I'm wounded."

"Yes, I know. A woman the size of the Grand Canyon can do a lot with a man when he's lost between her thighs."

"Stop or I'll need to take advantage of my private shower here."

"Be my guest but I'm sure it won't be my luscious thighs that get you off. It'll be the picture of the sweet little sub you left behind in Houston."

"You know me too well."

"Have you at least contacted Damian and asked about her?"

"My best friend is not speaking to me but his wife has been nice enough to give short clipped replies to the enquiries I've make."

"And?"

"She continues to work at the club and has a steady Dom. Lydia won't tell me who but I don't think that's something I need to know anyway. Lydia doesn't pass on any personal information just that Willow is content."

"That sucks."

"Yes it does."

Chapter Twelve

He hated formal dinners but he was a major contributor to the hospital and had no choice but to attend. He stood next to his mother in the receiving line and shook hands hoping the boring evening would somehow end sooner than later.

"Mr. and Mrs. Damian Collins and guest Miss Collins."

His eyes turned from the man he was greeting.

The woman invading his nightly dreams was here and she was breathtaking. Brandon smiled and then began laughing. Everyone around looked at him curiously and he noticed his mother's grimace over the names announced. He wasn't close enough to take in every detail but he would recognize her gown anywhere. It was the exact replica of the red evening gown worn by Julia Roberts in the movie Pretty Woman. The same movie they watched over a month ago in his hotel room on one of the best days of his life. She even wore the long white gloves with her hair styled in the same manner though it was brown and not red.

He didn't wait for her to make her way down the line. His long strides quickly carried him forward. Willow turned and they stared at each other. Most of her facial piercings were gone with two concessions. She wore the delicate gold wire through her eyebrow that he bought for her and a small diamond in her nose. Her blue eyes were huge and she all but gobbled him up while he stood watching her.

Finally, he took the last few steps barely noticing Damian and Lydia. His eyes were for one woman. He lifted her gloved hand and very deliberately peeled the cloth from her fingers and brought them to his lips.

Her voice was breathy but also held humor, "Do you know how difficult it was to put that glove on?"

He pulled her close. "It doesn't matter because the dress and other glove are coming off in less than five minutes."

"No, they are not." It was Damian's irritated Dom voice.

Bran could match him Dom for Dom. "I owe you a bruised jaw. Don't push your luck."

"Both of you behave." Lydia's voice was an irritated whisper. "We are going to enjoy our evening." She looked directly at Bran, "And you will keep your cock in your pants for the next two hours. If you're lucky, I'll let you dance with my sub."

"Your sub?"

"Yes, she didn't want another man touching her so I had the honors."

"Stop it. I wanted him jealous and wondering what I've been doing for the last month."

"And you don't think I'm jealous over Lydia putting her hands on you? I want no one but me touching your body."

"That's enough, we're holding up the line." Damian's voice reflected his lack of patience.

Bran took her ungloved hand and pulled her away from the greeting line. He walked quickly past his frowning mother not caring if he caused a scene. Approaching a waiter, he requested a change to his table seating and the Collins party seating. He handed the waiter a large tip and then looked around the ballroom. Keeping a tight grip on her hand, he strode between tables and then across the dance floor. He walked to where the orchestra was playing and took her into a section behind the stage. As soon as they were out of sight he pressed her back to the wall and kissed her with every bit of pent up frustration he possessed. The kiss went on and on as he sucked, nipped, and fenced with her tongue. When at last they came up for air, he rested his chin on her head and took deep breaths. His stomach unclenched for the first time in over a month and his body relaxed.

"This will be the longest two hours of my life but I'm not letting you out of my sight."

"Yes Sir." Her seductive voice made his cock throb.

His thumb went to her lips where he'd messed up her red lipstick. He wiped it gently fixing the damage. Her hand came up and returned the favor. He bit her thumb and then laved it with his tongue.

"Come." His fingers tightened on hers and he walked them back into the ballroom. She protested but he refused to acknowledge her complaint. If he was alone with her for one more minute, the sexy red dress would be over her head and he would be buried balls deep in her pussy. Many curious eyes followed but he zeroed in on Damian and Lydia, paying no attention to their stunned audience. They took their seats and he placed her hand in his lap against his hard cock. If he couldn't get her naked he would damn sure keep her occupied.

"How are you feeling Lydia?" He would be polite even if it killed him.

"As big as a house and wondering if I'm carrying twins."

"No twins, only a pudgy little baby girl like her mother." Damian's hand went to the large rounded tummy in question.

"Did you just call me pudgy?"

"I did and I'm hoping you'll punish me for it later." Damian whispered in his wife's ear but Bran heard the comment and smiled. He wanted Willow pudgy with his child and he planned to begin working on it when they got home. Determined fingers wrapped around his dick and slid back and forth. His eyes met her wicked grin.

They ate dinner and then listened to far too many speeches. Eventually, he was able to escort her to the dance floor.

"I don't dance very well."

"I'll show you. It's like making love with a Dom. I'll lead."

And he did. Her smell; spicy, floral, and sensual filled his senses. "You have no idea how much I missed you."

"I think I do." She rebuked.

"I'm sorry. I didn't want to hurt you."

"But you did."

"I hurt us both. Will you forgive me?"

"Will you get your dick pierced?"

He flinched but answered honestly, "If that's what it takes."

"No, I just wanted to see how far you would go."

"I'll go to my knees."

"I want that privilege Sir."

"Granted. We must get you out of her so I can fuck you."

Damian cut in. Bran burned with need but turned and took Lydia into his arms.

"Are you sure you don't mind dancing with a pudgy lady?"

"You are the second most beautiful woman here and you would have Willow beat if you added a few piercings."

"I'm not sure she'll fit into your world but you'll be happy."

"She doesn't need to fit she just needs to be herself."

"She loves you."

"I'm glad to hear that because we're flying to Vegas tomorrow for our wedding."

"Does she know?"

"No, but her answer will be yes Sir."

Lydia laughed, "I believe you may be right."

Finally, the evening ended. They said their goodbyes to Damian and Lydia but as he turned he found his mother waiting to pounce.

"Half the people in this ballroom recognized your whore's dress."

"Mother." Bran's tone threatened murder.

"You cannot be serious. You only want her because she came in with your slimy friend and his slut of a wife."

A hand went to Bran's arm and cut off his reply.

"My sister-in-law is a far more beautiful slut than you. We are here tonight because Damian thought this benefit would have possible clientele for his club and we were happy to hand out business cards."

For the first time, Mrs. Brandon Edward Sterling III had no reply. She turned on her heel and walked away like she had a fireball up her ass.

"Bravo my dear, anyone who can leave my mother speechless turns me on." He nipped her earlobe gently. "That was the sexiest thing I've ever seen and I can't wait any longer. Don't stop walking or talk to anyone."

And they didn't.

The drive to his house was interminable. He grasped her fingers within his hand not releasing them even when he changed gears.

When they arrived at his home, he took her straight to his bedroom and grabbed handcuffs from a drawer next to his bed.

She raised her eyebrows.

"I am locking you to my bed and have no intention of letting you go until the plane takes off tomorrow." He unzipped her dress and slid it down her body to the floor and then made quick work of her bra but left her panties, garters, and stockings on. He picked her up and laid her on the bed. He secured the handcuffs with a resounding ratchet. His dreams did no justice to having her body spread before him in that moment.

She shivered. "Where are we going?"

"To Vegas. We will be married by this time tomorrow. What do you have to say?"

"Oh god my mother."

"That's not what I wanted to hear and I'll delight in punishing you for not giving me the correct answer."

"If you think your mother is bad, wait until you meet mine."

He ran his hands into her hair and took out the pins. It fell gloriously around her shoulders.

"I like the braids but I love being able to run my hands through it like this. His fingers threaded the soft strands and massaged her scalp.

"Are you ever going to fuck me?"

"In a moment but I want to look at you and let it sink it that you're actually in my bed. Kneeling beside her his hands went to her panties and tore the crotch. At the same time, his fingers entered her pussy and his other hand went to her chin making her look into his eyes. "Your answer?"

"Yes Sir."

"Perfect, but I think you still require more sub training." He took his clothing off in between torturing her with his hands and mouth. At last, he released the handcuffs from the headboard but reattached them to her wrists. He placed her arms over his head. Sitting up on the bed, he brought her pussy even with his cock and adjusted her legs around his back. He took ahold of both her breasts and twirled the rings on her nipples. She rubbed her pussy against him but he didn't yet enter her hot sheath. His kiss held promise but still he kept his cock from her opening.

She pried her mouth from his. "Fuck me Bran, please."

His hands traveled down her chest and waist, to her hips, then around to her ass and he dug fingers into her soft flesh. With one forward thrust, he buried his cock deeply inside her hot moist heat. He took her scream into his mouth and pulled his cock out without making another forward thrust.

"What are you doing?" She breathed raggedly.

"Loving you."

"But I want you to fuck me."

"That too." His hips plunged, his cock driving deep into her depths but this time he didn't stop his movements until they both felt the hot rush of their orgasms.

Taking her once wasn't enough and it was after three a.m. when he called Jenny. Her voice was alert even though he knew she had been asleep.

"I'm flying to Vegas tomorrow and I need you to call and schedule my plane. Clear your calendar too because you're going with us."

"Who is 'us'?"

"My future wife."

"So she accepted the invitations I sent for last night's event?"

"Yes, you may write yourself a hefty bonus."

"I thought so. I can't wait to meet her and get the kinky lowdown on your sexy body."

"I may be able to talk her into a threesome." He received a not so gentle pinch to his arm and grinned. "Or maybe not."

"You know what they say; once you go cow you continue to plow."

He shook his head and laughed again. "I'll be sure to let her know that before she makes a final decision."

"Tell her my bellybutton is pierced."

He received a soft click in his ear before he could reply.

Turning to the woman beside him, he pulled her tightly into his arms. "Jenny Mack will make the perfect grandmother for our children." He kissed her brow. "I love you."

She snuggled closer and softly whispered the words back.

***

The following day Bran met Willow's mother. She wore a gold jumpsuit to the ceremony. He could tell she was once beautiful but she would never hold a candle to Willow. She also touched him every chance she got. His mother-in-law enjoyed rubbing her body against his and it was hard not to cringe. Jenny Mack pulled her off him continually.

"Jenny will make a wonderful grandmother." Willow whispered in his ear though he could hear the laughter caused by watching him avoid her octopus of a mother.

"Your mother is all hands, I'm actually afraid to be alone with her."

"We'll just change Jenny's job description to include bodyguard."

Willow's kiss made him forget his mother-in-law.

After carrying his bride over the threshold of the honeymoon suite Jenny booked for them, he took Willow straight to the shower so he could get rid of the strong odor of her mother's cloying perfume.

"Do you think we should introduce our mothers?" She was giggling while she washed his body from head to toe.

"I'm thinking we'll force them to live together. They're perfect for each other."

"No, you Mr. Business Man are perfect for me."

He turned her so she was facing the wall and ran his hand down the crevice of her ass and then sank his fingers into her hot pussy. "Yes I am Goth chick and don't ever forget it."

"Yes Sir."

The Beginning...

Book III

Touched By a Dom

Chapter One

Her friend Gloria put the membership code into the elevator's discreet electronic box and Trisha watched the lobby grow smaller through the glass. She continued to kick herself for allowing Gloria to talk her into this. Though they were going up, she couldn't help but think hell would be waiting on the other side of the doors. Glancing down, she shook her head at her risqué clothes and felt sweat beading between her breasts. El Diablo might be one of the most exclusive BDSM clubs in the country but "B" stood for bondage, "D" stood for dominance, "S" stood for sadism, and "M" stood for masochism. This entire idea was insane.

"Gloria, I can't do this. I'll lose my job if anyone finds out."

"You can't lose your job because you aren't doing anything illegal and everyone signs the same nondisclosure agreement. Most of these people are wealthy and the last thing they want is media attention."

"Well that only proves I don't fit in. I'm not wealthy."

"You're here to watch. You told me you've never had the big "O" with a man and you need to find out what's holding you back. It's not your fault if your past lovers weren't fulfilling your needs and your vibrator was."

Trisha's face flamed and she so regretted relaying that bit of personal information to her friend. "There's only been one past lover and his problem was trying to fill the needs of too many women that I didn't know about."

Before Gloria could snap back with a cutting remark, the doors opened and they found themselves in a normal, everyday, run of the mill office. Trisha relaxed slightly.

"Hi Gloria" A pretty woman in her mid-twenties said from behind a large oak desk. She was wearing a pink bustier with black lace accents.

Trisha expected black leather and metal spiked studs for some reason and not the sexy Dallas cheerleader version of kink. Since Gloria mentioned inviting her to the club, Trisha read everything she could find on BDSM. The dominance and submission side of the lifestyle actually turned her on but she would die before telling Gloria that.

"Hi Michelle, I've brought a friend and she has her paperwork in order."

Gloria nudged Trisha's arm.

The arm in question came out and a shaking hand offered the manila envelope.

Michelle began looking through the information.

Trisha could feel her face redden and her heartbeat pick up. Her entire medical history was in there with her good bill of health, a nondisclosure agreement, and a copy of her driver's license. She wasn't even inside the doors and her nerves were about to cause a heart attack.

Michelle glanced up and smiled softly. "By the look on your face I'm assuming you're being forced into this?"

Gloria snickered.

"Yes I am." She gave Michelle a grimace.

"We have strict rules in place and you will find things inside quite different from visiting a nightclub. Here… no, means no. You will not be harassed if you use that one simple word. Voyeurism is acceptable on your first few visits but eventually participation is required or we would be happy to connect you with a suitable voyeur group elsewhere. If you decide to try El Diablo's other features, come back into this office and I'll see if we can schedule you with a regular. There will be another batch of paperwork but you fill those out with a Dom, Domme, or submissive." Michelle glanced down at her paperwork and marked a little box next to each item she mentioned. "Breaking our rules causes immediate and possibly permanent removal from the club. No interrupting scenes, no approaching another Dom's sub on the carousel, and no cell phones or any device that can take pictures. This is about exploring sexuality in a safe private environment. We promote SSC; Safe, Sane, and Consensual behavior here." She pointed toward the door behind her. "That will be the door you enter and exit. There are private elevators inside the club for guests staying in the hotel. You will not have the correct access code to enter unless you are with a hotel guest. If you decide to return at a later date you may use Gloria's membership for one month before you need to see an employee in this office and set up your own."

Michelle checked off the last items.

"If you need any help, employees are dressed in black shirts with a black bow tie. As much as you think you might need alcohol for courage in the beginning, we don't recommend that you have more than two drinks. Drunkenness will get you removed quickly. Personally, on your first visit, I would stop at one. You may find some things that go on here objectionable but everything is consensual. Be aware if you stop a scene or step between a Dom and his or her sub, you open yourself to punishment or banishment from the premises. Do you have any questions?"

A million. "No, I don't think so."

"Would you like a wristband to designate you as being new to this lifestyle?"

"What would that do?"

"Some of the offers you receive will be toned down a bit and there are plenty of Doms who will stay away entirely though there are always a few who like to prey on newbies. We try to weed the bad ones out but it's not always possible. Most Doms and subs want experience and prefer to avoid beginners."

Trisha's eyes went to Gloria who shook her head no.

"No thank you."

Michelle noticed Gloria's prompt and frowned. "You only need to come back through that door and I can provide you with a bracelet at any time tonight or in the future. It's relatively quiet tonight so it shouldn't make a big difference."

"Thank you."

"Sign here and you may enter."

Her hand continued to shake but she scrawled her signature at the bottom of the document.

"There are dressing rooms on the other side of the door."

Trisha glanced down at herself and then back up. "I wasn't sure what to wear but I didn't bring anything else."

Michelle smiled, "What you're wearing is fine and you can have on as many or as little clothing as you like. Naked is acceptable. Please remember there are no perfect bodies here only desired ones. Everyone has different tastes."

"Come on Trisha, stop thinking about this, and let's go. I have something in my bag for you." Gloria took her arm. They passed through the door entering a large mirrored dressing room. There were cabinets on one wall and after Gloria changed into a tight black shiny vinyl short skirt and bra, she placed her clothes inside.

"I bought you this." Gloria pulled out a lacy baby doll black teddy. "You can keep your bra and panties on."

Trisha looked at the swath of delicate lace designed to cover very little. "I thought the clothes I had on were skimpy enough."

"You are gorgeous and what you're wearing is fine for a normal nightclub but trust me you will feel more comfortable in this."

"It's almost transparent and my ass will hang out?"

"Your panties will cover your ass but most of the subs here will have bare cheeks. Trust me. Please?" It was almost a whine.

"How do you know I'm not Dom material?"

Gloria laughed and held out the black piece of nothing.

Trisha knew from her reading that she wasn't Dom material either but it irritated her that her friend wouldn't even consider it. She was surprised when Gloria admitted to being a sub. She was always strong, outgoing, and bossy; which was why Trisha found herself here tonight.

Trisha took the lace and then removed her low cut red bejeweled shirt and black skirt with the thigh slit. It was the most risqué ensemble she owned. Slipping the gauzy material over her head, she looked in horror at her black panties peeking out from under the bottom ruffle.

"I'll be arrested for indecent exposure."

"Trust me you'll feel more at home dressed like this."

"What do I do with my clothes?"

"Place your shoes and clothes in the cabinet with mine."

"My shoes?"

"Yes."

"Okay but what if they're stolen?"

"We are being monitored on camera and no one steals from here."

"Someone just watched me strip?"

"You didn't strip, now stop stalling, and let's go."

Chapter Two

Trisha expected many things, but not what she walked into. The lighting was low with sexy subtle music playing in the background. The steady thumping bass went straight to her erogenous zones. She had attended a friend's bachelorette party a week ago and her ears rang three days later because of the volume of the music. This mix was incredibly erotic and just the right level. She heard a scream from somewhere and her back stiffened.

"What was that?" She whispered.

"Someone having a good time. Come on and let's get you that one drink."

Trisha couldn't help but stare as they walked further into the gigantic room. There was a large carousel in the middle of the floor. It spun slowly and Trisha's jaw dropped at the sight of several naked men and women moving up and down on the colorful brightly painted horses.

"Oh my God."

"I told you about this silly."

"I know but seeing it is much different."

"Come on. You so need a drink."

They walked to the bar and Gloria ordered a Cosmo and turned to her friend.

"A shot of tequila and a lime please."

Trisha glanced at Gloria's raised eyebrows.

"If I only get one I'm making it count."

Trisha appreciated that the bartender didn't check out her breasts when he returned with their drinks. It really was different from a nightclub.

"Bottoms up."

Both women downed the liquid.

Trisha couldn't believe the quality of the alcohol. She figured it would be cheap but it was smooth and slid down her throat. She only used the lime because she liked the mixed flavor.

"Come on, I brought you tonight because Lydia was scheduled and I wanted you to watch her work."

The alcohol did help a wee bit with her courage. "Lead the way."

They walked into yet another world. Twenty by twenty foot stations lined one entire wall and from what she could see, each had different lighting, décor, and purpose. At the station Gloria took her closest to, Trisha glued her eyes on a five and a half foot tall redheaded woman using a leather strap on another woman bound to a metal frame. The redhead's stomach protruded and it was apparent she was incredibly pregnant. She suddenly stopped striking her captive and walked up to the bound woman. She kissed her cheek and whispered something in her ear.

Trisha liked men and never considered a woman as a sexual partner but the display sent vibes through her pussy. "Is she a lesbian?"

Gloria grinned and rolled her eyes, "No, she's married to the owner of the club. In the vanilla world, she would be considered bisexual because she works with men and women. She'll perform a little sexual play during a scene but I've never seen her have intercourse; a little oral sex and definitely toy play but never intercourse."

"She has oral sex during a scene?" Trisha couldn't hide the shock in her voice.

"Yes, and believe me if you're with a guy who's not doing it for you, it wouldn't hurt to fantasize about what you see here."

"Oh God, she just put her hand between that woman's thighs."

Gloria only laughed. "She was checking the positioning of the vibrator she must have put there before we showed up."

"I'm so glad the lighting is low. I can feel my face flaming."

"Gloria, introduce me to your friend please." A deep male voice rumbled at their side.

"Raul! When did you get back?" Gloria's smile was huge.

"A week ago and I was hoping you would show up soon. I have a new man in my life and I wanted to bend your ear, but right now, there are several club members asking about your friend and I've been sent over to get the down low."

"Raul, this is Trisha. She's new to the lifestyle and just checking things out."

Raul took her hand, "Very nice to meet you my dear." He kissed the backs of her fingers.

Trisha couldn't remember anyone ever kissing her hand. "Nice to meet you Raul." She kept her eyes on his after her first foray down his nearly naked body. He was gorgeous but dressed only in two-inch leather straps that crisscrossed down his chest, barely covered his genitals, and then traveled down his legs. She noticed scars on his hip and upper leg but they only made him more attractive.

Raul glanced back at Gloria, "I'm subbing for Anna in a while and you might both enjoy watching. She's using hot wax and promises I'll love it. My last experience was not exactly pleasant but if I trust anyone as much as Lydia it's Anna."

"If I'm not busy we'll come by. I'm keeping Trisha close."

"It was nice to meet you Trisha and I hope to see you again." He hugged Gloria, "Stay in touch babe. Now I need to help Lydia." He walked away with his bare ass cheeks displayed for everyone to see. Raul and his leather straps walked to Lydia's scene and began helping her with the now shaking sub.

Trisha's eyes followed, "He's a sub?"

"Yes and gay."

"But he subs for a woman?"

"One of the things I love about this lifestyle is the gender openness. Lydia and Anna aren't gay but they know what makes women tick and have no problem showing sexual affection. Male subs, even gay ones, appreciate woman on occasion. Unfortunately, there are not enough good, strong, male Dominants to go around. You, like most people, think of BDSM as weird kinky sex but it's so much more and often sex isn't involved. The club is about testing limits, acknowledging our fetishes, and fulfilling our desires in a safe environment where we're not judged by a vanilla crowd."

Trisha turned her gaze back to Gloria just as a man walked up behind her friend. His presence practically took the oxygen from the air and Trisha's heart stalled. He was tall and lean with a bare tanned chest displaying six pack abs like those of a professional tennis player. His skin was smooth and beads of sweat stood out as if he just finished a long jog. He stood five feet away but she could smell his musky man-sweat with a hint of amaretto of all things. Trisha gaze traveled upward and met a pair of incredibly sexy dark brown eyes. His stunned expression startled her.

Gloria turned to see who had her attention. "Master Kyle." Gloria's eyes went down.

"Gloria." He said but didn't take his burning gaze from Trisha's.

She wasn't sure what to do but she'd be damned if she would look down. He finally glanced at Gloria and used his hand to lift her chin so she was looking at him. He kissed her gently on the lips.

"Are you looking for a Dom tonight?" His voice was like melted chocolate—thick, deep, and smooth but commanding in its intensity.

"Yes Sir."

"I believe Master Jordan is looking for a partner."

"I only wish to sub in a scene Sir. My friend Trisha is new and I don't want to leave her."

His dark penetrating stare returned to Trisha. "Do you enjoy pain?"

"What?" It was almost a squeak; did he really just ask that?

"I'll take that as a 'no' or an 'I'm not sure yet.'"

"Umm no, I don't think I do."

"If you decide to find out please see Michelle in scheduling and request me." He turned on his heel and walked away.

Trisha stared after his lithe body and tight ass covered in a pair of black leather that looked painted on.

Gloria whispered, "Stay away from him Trish. He's known for extremes even among the fetish crowd. I'm really surprised he gave you the time of day. He's quite set in the type of female he prefers and frankly, you're not it. But god, he drips sex."

"What kind of pain?"

Gloria laughed and came out of her submissive role, which Kyle so quickly brought her to. "More than you can take. He'd have you screaming with an orgasm in seconds but you wouldn't sit down for a week because your ass would be black and blue."

"He gets off on pain?"

"Yes but the subs he uses don't complain. Quite frankly, he scares the shit out of me. He's entirely too intense and when he takes on a sub he expects absolute obedience. I saw him punish a woman physically and sexually for hours and then walked away without letting her have an orgasm. He never topped her again due to some unknown transgression. He attracts the subs that need hard pain to be satisfied."

Trisha shivered. "I'm sorry Gloria, I don't know if any of this is for me."

"You are supposed to hold back making a decision until the night is over. You promised not to judge."

"I'm not judging I just don't see how a relationship here could work."

"It's called a wet pussy, learning about what turns you on, and having a man focused on your needs."

A picture of Kyle holding a whip flashed in her brain and Trisha groaned, "Okay, okay—open mind here." Why did being with him instantly become her fantasy?

"Let's go see if I can get into a scene with someone."

Trisha followed Gloria as she walked back to the front office and scheduled to work with Master Stephen in an hour.

"What do you want me to do while you're with this Master Stephen?"

"Watch."

"That has a certain amount of ick factor and I don't know if I can."

"Come on, you've seen me naked, we've been friends for years and you might learn something about your orgasm problems. Now let's go talk to a few of the other subs."

Chapter Three

Josie, a rather plain looking woman in her early forties was in a permanent D/s relationship with Master Kevin. This evening he was at home with his wife and Josie was on her own though not available to other Doms as designated by her collar. Trisha had questions and Josie had no problem answering.

"Kevin is married and has three children. His wife isn't into this lifestyle. She knows about me and Kevin pays my expenses so I can live here at the hotel. It's great because I work in the city. I had two lousy marriages and Kevin and I have been together for eight years. I love him but have no problem sending him off to his wife."

"What do you do for a living?"

Josie laughed. "I'm a detective with Houston PD."

Trisha's jaw dropped again, "But, but you…"

Josie only laughed harder. "I know, not what you expected but I work long hours and enjoy playing hard. I'm strong and independent though it's probably hard for you to believe. My relationship with Master Kevin works. If you find something in this world that works honey, don't let it go."

"You're right and thank you for answering my nosy questions. What do you usually do here when Master Kevin isn't available?"

"I talk to other subs about anything that takes my mind away from work. Cops tend to spend all their time with other cops and talk shop. I just couldn't do it anymore. In here, I wear my collar and it's respected. I don't need to worry about dirty old men trying to pick me up in bars or playing touchy-feely. So who's catching your eye tonight?"

"Umm, well."

"Master Kyle gave her the once over and invited her to do a scene with him." This information came from Gloria.

"Really? He's yummy and dangerous which is part of his attraction. If he has his eye on you, there's a reason. This could be interesting."

"Don't encourage her. Master Kyle will chew her up and spit her out."

"Oh but the teeth marks might be worth it."

"I'm sitting right here listening to you two talk over me and seriously I'm not interested in having Kyle master me."

Both women turned to stare and then their laughter joined together.

"There isn't a sub here who wouldn't want to be mastered by him." Gloria said between continued giggles.

"But I thought you said he liked extreme pain and to stay away?" She looked at her friend in consternation.

"I did but we need our fantasies and he's way up there for me. Just thinking of his intense look is enough to give me a double. Come on it's time to get to the station."

Trisha was even more confused but followed along like a good little puppy dog.

Master Stephen was a surprise. He was short and stalky, but muscular with a few extra pounds that said he liked to eat. Gloria went to her knees at the front of the station and waited for his commands. He ran his hand gently down her cheek in a feather light caress.

"So my little sub has been bad?"

"No Master."

"Oh, I think my little sub has been bad."

"Yes Master, I've been bad." Gloria's voice sounded anything but contrite.

"I want you to stand up and remove your clothing and fold them neatly then lay them on the side table."

His voice was nowhere near as commanding as Kyle's but Gloria did as told.

Trisha had trouble keeping her eyes on her naked friend as the scene progressed. Her cheeks burned and she wasn't sure she could handle watching what came next. She turned her head and glances around the club. There were several people standing next to her but she refused to look directly at anyone. Something drew her eyes to a dark corner across the room. When her pupils adjusted, Kyle's hot gaze stared into hers. He didn't look away. Trisha's pulse sped up and dampness seeped into her panties. It took everything she had to force herself to turn back to the scene but she could feel his continued stare sizzling on the almost bare skin of her back. She ran her fingers nervously through her hair and tried to concentrate on Gloria who was now ass up over a bench with her legs spread and secured. No, she couldn't do this.

She refused to look in Kyle's direction but decided to return to the dressing room, change her clothes, and wait for her friend in the office. This entire evening was a mistake. She walked quickly toward her destination but firm fingers grabbed her arm startling her. She flowed backward into a solid bare chest. His unique scent kept her from being afraid though her mind was telling her to run like hell.

"Going somewhere?" His voice held the same deep vibration from earlier and the words passed by her ear on a brush of warm air.

"I...I'm just." She couldn't think.

"Are you leaving?"

"Yes."

"Is this too much kink for you?"

She tried to twist but he held tight. She really wasn't afraid but the firm control of his hold was causing her pussy to repeatedly gush then clench tight.

"Would you please release me?"

Instantly his arms dropped and he stepped away. She swayed and he put a gentle hand on her shoulder to steady her but let it go after a few seconds.

She turned.

His eyes seared into hers and she took another step away from him.

"I won't hurt you."

"But isn't that what you do?"

His eyes grew cloudy and his voice huskier. "Pleasure and pain are an erotic combination. Would you care for a demonstration?"

"What, umm, I don't know."

"By the time you decide it will be over." And with that he stepped forward and pulled her into his body as his hot mouth came down on hers. His lips demanded entrance and then his tongue went deep. His breath smelled and tasted of amaretto. It was the sexiest thing she'd ever experienced and this was only a kiss.

Her head was spinning and she felt his hands slide under the bottom lace at her hips and then his fingers pushed the cups of her bra upward and his hands closed around her breasts. She could barely breathe and suddenly his fingers pinched her nipples at the same time his leg slid between hers and his hard thigh rubbed across her pussy. The pressure on her nipples intensified; it was painful but more. She rode his leg and he increased the pinch, relaxed his fingers, and then tightened again. She didn't know what happened when her body convulsed and her pussy pulsated with an orgasm.

Yes, his fingers caused pain but god she never wanted it to end; the pain, the pleasure, the kiss; they were amazing. He was able to do this in a few minutes when her vibrator took twenty.

He pulled back but gently rubbed her breasts sliding his hands over her sensitive nipples. Slowly they traveled down to her waist and then up the outside of the lace over her curves to her face before threading his fingers through her hair. He pulled, lifting her face so she looked into his eyes. His leg continued the pressure against her wet pussy and his mouth came down and punished her lips, holding her head so she had no choice but to accept his brutal kiss.

Without loosening the hold on her hair or the hard torture of his leg, he separated his mouth from hers. "Come to my room with me and I'll teach you about pain and ecstasy." Her body was still trembling with her orgasm and his words and touch almost took her over again.

She knew her eyes were huge and she wanted to say yes so bad. "No, I can't." She barely held back a groan.

"Can't or won't?"

She inhaled, while trying to control her need to submit. "Both."

"Will you come to the club tomorrow?"

"I don't know. I don't think so."

His hands fell away. He kissed her on the forehead and then turned. She watched, stunned, as his gorgeous ass walk away again.

Chapter Four

She barely remembered changing her clothes and leaving the club. She took the elevator downstairs and asked the concierge to call her a cab. She also left Gloria a note saying she went home and to call her the following day.

She lay in bed tossing and turning. Her hand went to the wetness between her thighs. It was the first time she didn't need lube with her vibrator but nothing she tried completely stopped the hot ache. She wanted her nipples squeezed by large hands and a hint of amaretto on her lips.

She wouldn't go back to the club, she just couldn't.

The next day she found herself at the mall shopping. She hated the mall but subconsciously knew what she was there for. It wasn't leather but velvet; a black velvet corset. She bought black thigh highs and combination short skirt garter belt. She couldn't believe she was doing this. She returned home with her purchases hidden in a small bag, thinking she would hide the items in her closet and forget they were there. The ringing of her cell phone stopped her as she walked to the back of her apartment.

It was Gloria.

"So the BDSM lifestyle isn't for you?"

"Oh Gloria, I'm sorry about last night. I couldn't stay." She purposely didn't answer her friend's question because she didn't want to lie. She thought the lifestyle might be exactly what her body craved. The need for that small bit of pain was driving her mad.

"Are we still friends?"

"Yes, don't be ridiculous. You will always be my goofy friend. What are you doing this evening?"

"I'm dining with my parents and then we're having a family game night with my brother and his wife. Do you want to come?"

"Not this time though it's hard to resist the pull of your 'win at all costs' father and brother."

"They love you and you know us women cheat like hell just to drive them crazy. We've become good at it through the years."

"Your dad is just so sweet; millionaire tycoon having family night with his grown kids."

"That's why I'm the luckiest daughter on the planet. Sure you can't come over?"

She declined again and then arranged to meet for coffee later in the week. Gloria didn't need a job but she had a degree in liberal arts and worked at a university press as an editor. Her father owned an extremely prominent law firm and the last thing Gloria swore she would ever do was go into the legal profession.

Trisha disconnected and then looked at the bag sitting on the floor. It was four p.m. and she decided to take a long soothing bath. She shaved her legs and then her pussy, which she had never completely bared before. Her hands slid over her smooth skin rubbing in expensive lotion. She knew her face had turned bright red when she asked the sales assistant for a lotion that smelled and tasted good. The woman got a twinkle in her eyes and found the perfect combination. It felt like silk and she realized her panties would be wet before she ever got to the club.

Her stomach clenched again while the elevator flew past each floor. She wore designer jeans and a tight t-shirt. Her bag with her club attire was in her hand. Michelle was sitting at her desk and showed a blink of surprise at seeing Trisha but quickly recovered and gave a welcoming smile.

"I'm sorry Michelle but I think I need some help with my clothes."

"No problem at all. Let me call for someone to watch the office and I'd be glad to help."

"Thank you, I really appreciate it."

A few minutes later Lydia walked into the room and smiled at Trisha.

"You're Gloria's friend right?"

"Yes." She put her hand out not quite sure how to properly greet a Domme.

Lydia's fingers closed around hers and her smile became softer. "So you've decided to brave the club on your own without backup?"

"Yes, I think so."

"I would love to work with you and I'm quite gentle with new subs if you decide to give me a try?"

"Well, actually I'm meeting a Dom here."

"Someone you met last night?"

"Umm yes."

"I see."

Trisha didn't think so. She wondered what they would say if they knew it was Kyle. Michelle followed her into the dressing room and helped her change.

"You look beautiful. Let me know if you need anything." Michelle went back to the office.

Trisha's hands trembled when she gained enough courage to open the door and enter the main room of the club. She decided to get a drink at the bar and sat waiting for one of the bartenders to take her order. She felt a warm presence at her back and then the voice that haunted her dreams.

"She'll have a shot of tequila with lime and I'll have my usual." He said when the bartender asked for her order.

"How did you know my drink?"

"It's my job to know everything about you." His warm breath flowed softly over her ear. "You smell wonderful."

How did she tell him he smelled better? The scent of amaretto teased her senses again. It became stronger when their drinks arrived.

"Would you like a taste?"

He must have noticed her looking at his glass. "Please." If she went to all the trouble to shave her pussy she decided she needed to live dangerously.

He didn't hand her the small glass, he placed it to her lips. It tasted delicious, like him. She stared down at her tequila wondering what it tasted like when he kissed her.

"Drink, it was wonderful on your breath."

How did he know what she was thinking?

He put down his glass and picked up hers bringing it to her lips. "All the way down, tip your head back. We have paperwork to complete, and I've reserved a private room for the evening." He tipped the liquid into her throat and then placed the lime to her mouth and squeezed. Every move he made was a sexual turn on.

"The evening?"

"Yes, we can handle the paperwork there and then work on a few basics."

She knew her face was red and her eyes huge. He turned her bar stool around and gently placed pressure on the inside of her thighs, spreading them apart so he could move between them. His cock nestled against her pussy and he rubbed himself slowly across her moist heat making her gasp.

"It's been years since I've worked with a novice sub but I thought about you all night. Did you think about me while you pleasured yourself?"

"You knew I would be here and you knew I pleasured myself last night?" Her voice sounded slightly disgruntled.

"That's something we need to talk about. You will not be touching your sweet pussy again for a while. This," His hand went to her damp panties, "Will feel so much better when I give you what you need."

She was ready to burst and wanted to scream aloud and press herself harder against his hot palm.

He gently kissed the tip of her nose. "Unfortunately, we must complete the paperwork or you will have me in trouble with Mistress Lydia. Come." He stepped back and pulled her hand guiding her toward the office.

Lydia and Michelle were talking when Kyle led her in. Their voices stopped suddenly when they saw Trisha behind him.

"I need a D/s contract."

Lydia didn't look happy and her voice held censor. "Do you think this is a good idea Kyle?"

"I think that my D/s relationship is my business and you need to stay out of it."

Lydia stubbornly looked at Trisha, "Honesty, communication, and trust are the foundations of BDSM. If you need to speak with someone please just ask Michelle to get in touch with me or you may approach me on the floor."

"Umm, thank you. I will."

Kyle's hand took hold of her hair and pulled it slightly so his mouth was a breath away from her ear. "The proper way to answer a Domme is yes ma'am or yes mistress."

Trisha looked at Lydia and spoke the words softly lowering her eyes, "Yes Mistress."

Kyle's teeth closed around her earlobe and he bit it gently then licked the slight sting he left behind. Even more liquid pooled between her quivering thighs. He took the papers from Michelle, and released Trisha's hair taking her hand and pulling her behind him as he walked from the room.

In only a few minutes, she was jelly in his hands. She barely had a mind of her own.

He led her down a long hallway monitored by an employee in a black shirt and bow tie. He opened a door and pulled her through.

She stopped.

It was a torture chamber. She tugged on his hand when he tried to draw her further into the room.

"Don't let this scare you. I want you to grow accustomed to different items and I'll answer any questions you have. Tonight is about getting to know each other. Come over here."

He picked up a pen and clipboard from a shelf next to the door and then walked to a leather couch and sat down. His eyes drilled into hers but he didn't say another word. She knew he expected her to obey his command. Her feet carried her forward; she was little more than a moth drawn to his bright hot flame.

"Lydia told you this is about trust and honesty. You will answer every question I ask. There is a reason for each one though you might not understand. When we're finished I'll teach you about the toys and equipment in the room."

She didn't think she could speak.

"You will answer, yes Sir or yes Master though it's not established that I'm your master."

She inhaled quickly, "Yes Sir."

"I want you to tell me what your friend Gloria explained about BDSM."

She gave a quick embarrassed overview of what she knew.

"Gloria comes here and plays in a scene and spends a few hours with a Dom. She doesn't do much more than play out her sexual fantasies. What I'm offering you is more. During your training, I don't want you with another man. Is that understood?"

Yes Sir, I'm no longer with my ex-boyfriend and haven't been for several months.

"Good. When you're at the club, you belong to me and defer to what I say. I will make sure my instructions are clear."

"Yes Sir."

"Excellent, now, when was your last menstrual cycle?"

Her face reddened. "About ten days ago."

"Are you regular?"

"Yes, for the most part."

"Do you have cramps?"

"Mild ones." Her brain was buzzing. Pat had never asked her about her period. He treated it like an inconvenience.

"You will tell me when your cycle begins." It wasn't a question.

"Okay." Again her head reeled. He was talking as if their relationship would last for a while. She noticed he was looking at her with stern displeasure. "Yes Sir."

He gave a brief nod, "What type of contraception do you use?"

"An IUD."

His large hand scrawled across the paper and her eyes followed wanting that hand on her.

"We need to discuss your hard and soft limits. Those are the things you are worried about or are completely opposed to."

"Yes Sir."

His smile sent a thrill through her body.

"First, is there anything you've done with a sexual partner in the past that you didn't like?"

"I'm not sure."

His eyes were intense, "Explain."

"Umm, my boyfriend Pat didn't umm do a whole lot just him on top or me on top. Nothing was really displeasing I guess."

"What about before Pat?"

"There was no before Pat."

"I see. So you practiced vanilla sex with Pat. What about oral sex?"

"A couple of times but it wasn't something I cared for."

His lips quirked, "My job is to make sure you really care for it."

She gulped. "Okay, umm that sounds fine Sir."

His smile deepened but he didn't laugh at her. She knew she was making a complete fool of herself.

"What about toys?"

She looked away from him in mortification. "I have a vibrator."

His fingers found her chin and turned her face back. "Did Pat ever use the vibrator on you?"

"No."

"I will."

"Okay."

"Okay?"

"Yes Sir."

He continued asking her questions and on several items, he had to explain before she could answer. Flogger, whip, and paddle were pretty obvious but her mind refused to acknowledge what they could do to her. Pinwheel, electro stimulation, and harness needed explanations no matter how embarrassing it was to ask. He explained patiently assuring her he wasn't into everything mentioned but needed to understand her likes and dislikes. The fact he was into anything he mentioned should have made her run like hell. She didn't move.

"What about anal sex."

She was ashamed but answered honestly. "Okay."

"Have you had anal sex?"

"No."

"Have you thought about it?"

She tried to look away but his fingers stopped her. "Yes."

"Okay, if it's done right and you are properly prepared it's extremely stimulating and erotic."

He continued with the paperwork writing down her answers. "What is your most erotic fantasy?"

"My fantasy?"

"Yes."

"I don't know. I guess I thought about you last night."

"What were you thinking?"

She hesitated but then realized this was no more embarrassing than anything else they discussed. "I thought about you tying me up."

"Good, just a few more questions, and then we'll start there."

"There?"

"I will tie you up."

"Yes sir."

His smile was back. "You need a safe word."

This she knew about. "Isn't the normal red?"

"Yes, do you want to use red?"

"Yes. Yes Sir."

He stood and carried the paperwork back to the shelf and lay down the clipboard and then turned to face her. "Stand up and walk over here."

She stood and made her way to his side.

"I like what you're wearing but I want to see what's under it too."

His hands turned her, and then went to the back ties of the corset and slowly loosened the strings. When he was finished he peeled it from her body, turned her to face him and then sat it on the shelf next to the clipboard. His hands took her voluptuous breasts and kneaded them gently causing her eyelids to lower.

"Beautiful and perfect, there is so much I can do with these." Bending his head, he took one nipple into his mouth. His tongue teased with fluttering twirls before sucking with slow firm pressure. Her nipple was tight and aching when he moved to her other breast.

His mouth had a direct line to her pussy and a low moan sounded from between her lips. Her entire pelvic region ached and throbbed.

His head came up. "Come." He walked across the room.

She practically groaned out, "Yes Sir."

She couldn't see his face but knew he lips quirked slightly in that sexy way. He had to know what she was thinking about the word "come" and how she wanted it used in another context. She looked around and a touch of apprehension tensed her shoulders. Thankfully, he led her past the equipment and stopped before a wall to wall mirror. He waited patiently for her to stop in front of him and then bent his head and continued the slow torture of her breasts.

"You taste so good." He licked her skin sliding his roughened tongue over her flesh, leaving a cooling trail of saliva.

She couldn't stay still and squirmed.

He finally stopped and turned her body so she was facing the mirror. His hands came up and he palmed the underside of her breasts. He kissed her ear, gently sucked her earlobe. She felt her knees collapsing but he pulled her further into his hard chest.

His breath was hot against her cheek. "This." His hands traveled down over the curve of her waist. "Is my body when we're together. When we're apart and you think about what we do together, you will not touch yourself. I trust you to hold back your pleasure."

One of his hands traveled down and slipped inside her skirt beneath her underwear. His fingers found her clit and then glided over the slit of her pussy gathering the wetness on his fingers and bringing the dampness up to her clit. He only used one finger as he softly rubbed, making her body tense, and her hips thrust forward.

"I will give you this to relieve the ache and help you control when and how you have orgasms."

Her breathing grew heavy and short gasps escaped her lips.

"Come for me sweet Trisha, I want to feel your cunt pulse."

And it did. His words, his hands, and his hot breath drove her over the edge with seemingly little effort.

Chapter Five

When her eyes opened, his gazed back through the mirror. "That was beautiful. I want you comfortable in your body. This is all about trust. I need your focus on what we talk about tonight and not on your aching pussy. Do you understand?"

"Umm, I'm not sure."

"Your body needed release. You have been in a state of sexual anticipation since last night. Not just from me, but by what your virgin eyes saw for the first time. It can be overpowering. This lifestyle is not for everyone. We will take it slow so you're absolutely sure this is what you want. I like pain, a lot of pain, but that's something each individual sub needs to find out about their self. It's also not something that you go immediately into when you're new."

"I don't think I can take a lot of pain, maybe not even a little pain."

"Many people feel that way in the beginning but this lifestyle has a way of rearranging and pushing boundaries. We'll start exploring more of your needs after tonight."

"Yes Sir."

"Now, I want to teach you about some of the items in here."

She looked down at herself. "May I have my top back please?"

"No, your breasts are beautiful and it pleases me to look at them."

"Yes Sir." She had no doubt he desired her and it was an intoxicating feeling.

"Let's talk about restraints." He walked a few feet away and opened a drawer. There were leather straps inside with metal clips. Some had buckles and some were Velcro. "Give me your wrists."

She knew her eyes grew bigger.

He laughed gently. "I just want you to see that they won't hurt. Remember, you have control and your safe word stops everything even cuffs on your wrist."

Her hands came out in front of her and he secured the leather straps. "Now for your ankles, place your foot up here."

She raised her right foot onto a low bench. His hand without the cuff went to the back of her calf and gently kneaded the muscle through her stocking before placing the cuff around her ankle. Just seeing him strapping on the leather was erotic.

"Other foot."

She switched feet and he repeated the process.

He stood and his eyes traveled her body.

"Lovely."

"What are you going to do now?"

"First you need to relax. We are going to talk about the other items in the room and then we will have some very gentle play."

He took her arm and led her to an item made out of black metal with padding and straps.

"This is a spanking bench. It's pretty self-explanatory and you can see by the design; once you're secured, your delectable ass will be at my mercy. Go ahead touch it."

She held back. It was one thing to think about being restrained and spanked and quite another to see how vulnerable she would be.

His hand took hers and guided it to the cold metal.

"I want you to climb on."

Her eyes closed.

His voice was gentle and coaxing, "For only a few minutes and I won't secure the restraints...this time."

He helped her onto the bench. His fingers skimmed over her flesh as he walked around her body. He pressed her head so her cheek was resting more comfortably against the leather.

"It's very hard to see you like this and not take advantage, but not tonight." He moved her hair out of her eyes and kissed her lips. "I so want my hand on your ass."

Her sigh brought that sexy as hell quirk to his lips.

"Let me help you up."

She stood but she was becoming frustrated and her pussy was aching again.

"I don't understand."

He pulled her in close to his body his voice husky and sexy as hell, "You have apprehension written all over your expressive face. I'm finding out what turns you on because when the fear changes to desire, your blue eyes become deep pools of need. Tonight is about the little things and as a Dom, it's important for me to learn every nuance that affects your body.

"What about you?"

He pulled away slightly. "I already know what I like and don't like. I will be very clear on what pleases me. There will be no guessing. Now let me show you the rest and answer the questions I know you have."

They went to each piece of apparatus in the room. He knew every mechanism; how it twisted or turned, worked and moved. His self-assurance and precision caused her insides to quake and her pussy to throb. He answered each of her questions with explicit decisiveness. His focus intensified and she knew he was taking in every bit of her arousal while he spoke. It was unsettling but also alluring.

Pat never asked her about her sexual desires, he never seemed to care.

Kyle had her try a few of the positions the equipment required but never restrained or touched her after assisting her to get her situated.

Last, he took her to the wall of whips, floggers, and canes.

"Each of these has a purpose too. Some are for pain, some for pleasure, and some for both. Stay here for a moment."

He walked away and she followed him with her eyes. He pulled out a piece of long black material and then a large silver clip of some sort before walking back over.

"I'm going to secure your hands behind you. This is a carabiner and long enough that it shouldn't hurt your shoulders. This will take a while; I want you to feel the touch of each item. I don't want you becoming uncomfortable. Just tell me if you begin feeling the strain. Now turn for me and place your hands behind your back."

He attached her cuffs together with the clip and then placed the cloth over her eyes completely cutting off her sight.

Her senses intensified and she felt his warm breath on her cheek and then a kiss to her neck.

"Stay still."

She could hear him remove an item from the wall.

A hard cool object ran over her belly and up to her breasts. "This is a cane. It's meant for pain though today I just want you to feel its texture."

The cane continued to run over parts of her body; along her arms, over her trembling hands secured behind her back and then up and around feathering across her face and neck. The touch stopped and she heard him take down another instrument.

He explained each item in sensual detail before he touched her. His lesson was the most erotic thing she ever encountered. She wanted him to use them, even the cane. She knew this was wrong, that something was wrong with her, but she couldn't stop her longing.

He slowly and methodically fine-tuned her senses. Her breathing accelerated and she was having trouble holding still.

Suddenly, his hands came from behind and grasped her breasts.

"I can smell your arousal and your need for more than what I'm giving you. Take these memories with you tonight and meet me here again tomorrow at eight p.m. When I enter, I want you completely naked and waiting on your knees in front of the mirror. Leave your hair loose. You are not to touch yourself intimately or give yourself pleasure before I see you tomorrow. Do you understand?"

"Yes Sir," she groaned.

She felt him unclasping her hands and then he massaged her shoulders, kneading deeply into her muscles. Last, he removed the blindfold and took her hand leading her to the couch. He sat and pulled her against him, running his hands soothingly through her hair.

"Now tell me what you enjoyed tonight."

Their time was coming to an end and she wanted more. Her body ached with the need for sexual release.

"I enjoyed everything…but." She didn't continue.

"But?"

"I want more."

His husky laugh whispered across her skin. "I know but that's part of the thrill. I want more too but not tonight. Never have sex on your first encounter with a new Dom. If the Dom insists then you need to look elsewhere. Doing a scene in the club is different but you aren't ready for that yet. I will take you to a station when you are. After your training is over, you will request Lydia make a recommendation. And then, you will clearly define what you want. They monitor everything on camera but not inside these private rooms. You are safer out there. Check with staff about different Doms that request you in one of these rooms. They deny access to unknown Doms but you need a great deal of trust before coming in here. Understood?"

"I'm not safe in here with you?"

His slight smile was wicked. "No you aren't and you should run like hell. But I want you back tomorrow night." He nuzzled, and placed small kisses on her neck and shoulder.

"I don't think I can stay away."

He sighed, his warm breath caressing her sensitive skin. His arms tightened momentarily before he continued speaking. "Club El Diablo has a better clientele than most but from time to time someone unscrupulous makes it past the safeguards. If something happens that makes you feel uncomfortable and you need to talk to someone, go to the front office immediately."

"Last night you invited me to your room."

"I'm sorry but that was a mistake." He paused before continuing, "I wasn't thinking and quite frankly my cock was overruling my brain." He took her hand and placed it on his hard erection. "This is what you do to me."

Her hand tightened but she couldn't see the look on his face only the quick intake of breath before he exhaled slowly.

Her voice was breathy, "I want you to feel pleasure too?" She wanted to know everything about his body exactly as he was learning hers.

"You will and just sitting with you like this gives me pleasure. Before I came to the club, I masturbated so I wouldn't be tempted to break my own rules. This first time is about reading your body and learning about your wants and needs. It's hard to think with a throbbing cock and beautiful sub at my mercy." He kissed the top of her head and then removed her fingers from the front of his pants. Do you have more questions?"

She tilted her head toward him, "Will you kiss me?"

There was that grin of his she liked so much but his words disappointed and frustrated her, "No, because I want you thinking about the kiss I'll give you tomorrow."

"Is this to ensure I come back tomorrow?"

"If that's what you want to think." He began unbuckling the cuffs on her wrists and then turned her sideways on the couch so he could reach her ankles. "Do you want to watch me in a scene tonight? It'll be intense and may scare you away for good."

His fingers circled her ankle and rubbed across the sensitive skin. Watching his movements caused a shiver to run up her leg and zing directly into her pussy.

He knew the effect he was having on her but continued speaking in his controlled voice, "My focus will be on the sub, and I won't be able to answer your questions."

She had to concentrate through her lust-filled brain to get her next words out though her voice practically croaked. Her tone told him exactly what his touch was doing to her. "You are allowed other subs but I can't be with another man?"

"Not while I'm training you. I don't want anyone screwing up my hard work. I'm enjoying your instruction with soft play but I plan to push you to fulfill more of your needs. I enjoy inflicting pain. That won't change but your body's desire and tolerance for pain will."

Yes, she should run like hell. At that moment, he could tie her up and strip the skin from her back but she knew her moans would be more from pleasure than pain. She managed to focus on his earlier question. "I want to watch."

"Then let's get you dressed."

Chapter Six

He walked to the bar and ordered her another shot of tequila. "I'll be in station three. Finish your drink and then come over. I don't want you staying here late, you need rest. I'll see you tomorrow night."

He gave her a kiss but it was only a frustratingly brief touch of his lips. She wanted to sigh aloud and it only made things worse to watch his tight ass stroll away.

"So you haven't run from the club kicking and screaming yet?"

Trisha turned to see Lydia sit down in the seat beside her.

"No Ma'am."

"Kyle hasn't taken on a beginning sub while I've been here and that's been a year. I spoke with my husband Damian and he said it's been over five years since Kyle's seen someone privately."

There was no censor in her voice and it wasn't a question but Trisha could hear the curiosity. She chose to ignore it.

"When is your baby due?"

"In the next six weeks. Damian thinks he can keep me out of the club but he's been known to be wrong."

She couldn't help her laugh. "Aren't most husbands?"

"Have you been married before?"

"No, but I have married friends. They love to complain about their husbands' needing control."

"Having a Dom is similar but so much more. Are you going to watch Kyle's scene?"

"Yes and I'm terrified."

"You should be. He's the most intense Dom here. He knows what he's doing and only uses subs who want the extreme pain he likes to inflict."

"I don't think I could handle it."

"Well that's what training is about. You must discover for yourself what part of this world works for you, and what doesn't.

"That's what Kyle said. You don't like him do you?"

"I wouldn't quite word it that way. He makes me nervous and I'm not sure what makes him tick. He's helped me out on a few scenes when I needed someone but what he really likes is to use pain to wrestle demons; his and his subs. He does care but his limits go past what I can comprehend. I like giving small amounts of pain mixed with pleasure. Kyle prefers to push his subs past every limit they have. I think he has Simone tonight. I won't work with her because I can't dish out what she really needs. This is your chance to see what Kyle is all about."

Trisha downed her drink, sucked the lime, and then followed Lydia who was absolutely beautiful with black silky thin ropes crisscrossing her stomach. She waddled slightly when she walked.

Kyle had just finished securing a naked Simone. She was facing a stone wall located at the back of the semi empty scene area.

The wall had to be uncomfortable and cold.

Grabbing her hair, he pulled her head to the side and placed a hard punishing kiss on her lips. Her arms were over her head slightly apart and she had her fingers wrapped around the chains. Spread wide, with her legs secured too.

Kyle released her mouth and his hand landed solidly on her ass.

The slap startled Trisha and made her feel uncomfortably aware of what was about to happen.

He walked away and retrieved a silver cat-o-nine tailed flogger. Trisha cringed and remembered Kyle explaining this particular flogger and running it over her body. The metal studs at the end were ice cold and made her feel apprehension over the intensity of what it could do.

This was what he wanted from his subs and what he would eventually want from her. There was no love involved in this world only sexual lust and gratification. She glanced over when a gorgeous man approached. It was easy to figure out he was Damian the club's owner. His arms went around his wife and pulled her close pressing a soft kiss to the top of her head. His hands went to her belly and lovingly rested there.

Ultimately, that was what Trisha wanted but she knew she probably wouldn't find it at Club El Diablo and it would never come from Kyle. Why did he ask her to his room the night before? He said it was a mistake.

She was startled out of her thoughts when the first strike hit the sub's back and Simone cried out. Trisha could see the welts begin to form before the metal studs found their target again. She wanted to bolt as she had the night before but she remained frozen; her eyes glued to Kyle and his sub.

His face was a hard mask. There didn't seem to be any anger but his intensity was frightening. Why would he want a new sub to train when this was his desire?

The beating continued; Trisha didn't see anything sensual about it and she couldn't describe it as anything less than torture. Kyle was a sadist and he methodically painted Simone's body with stark red welts and didn't seem to care when her cries grew painfully louder. Finally, she was begging and sucking in air, hanging by her arms because her legs would no longer hold her. Sweat ran down Kyle's face and chest. His hand went back but then stopped. He threw the flogger to the floor and quickly walked up to Simone releasing her legs and then arms. She collapsed crying into his embrace and he picked her up.

He whispered something in the crying woman's ear but Trisha had no idea what he said. Swiftly, he carried her out of the station and behind a grouping of plants, which obscured most of a long couch.

"You need to go watch. Kyle may like pain but he's good with after care." Lydia was staring at her.

"I can watch?"

"You should. Kyle won't be your only Dom if you continue in this lifestyle, and you need to know the difference between a good Dom and a bad one."

"How could Kyle be a good Dom? That woman almost passed out."

"Yes, and she should have used her safe word but she didn't. A good Dom knows when someone is going past their limit. Kyle stopped, though I always think he could stop sooner. He works with Simone regularly and knows what she needs though you and I may not understand."

Trisha didn't understand and she was so terribly confused. Her legs trembled when she made her way over to Kyle and peered out from behind the plants. He was on his knees and rubbing oil into Simone's body while she lay on the couch and cried softly.

"God Simone, what the hell were you thinking?" He leaned over and kissed her softly on the cheek. His voice was chiding almost like that of a parent. "I told you the last time that you were pushing too far."

"Please don't leave me Master Kyle." Her voice was almost frantic.

"You know you need a fulltime Master and I can't do that for you. I've spoken to Leroy and he is taking you on. He will be here tomorrow at four and I want you here waiting for him. This doesn't mean I will never do another scene with you but you don't need physical punishment for a while and I'll let him know. Now sit up and drink some water. I have fruit here for you too."

He helped her lean onto the side of the couch and covered her with a blanket. He sat down and partially pulled her in his direction placing the water bottle to her lips. "Drink."

After she complied, he placed small bites of apple between her lips and waited for her to swallow before giving her more.

"What are you doing for the rest of the evening Simone?"

"I'm going home because I need sleep."

"Yes. What are you doing tomorrow?"

"I'm sleeping in and then eating a large breakfast. Then I'm going to the salon to get my hair fixed and I'll be back here at four to see Master Leroy." This was obviously a question he asked often because she recited her answers by rote.

"Good. If you aren't here, Leroy will be the one to punish you. Do you understand?"

"Yes Master."

"Okay, close your eyes and rest. I'll sit here with you until you are able to walk and get dressed."

"Thank you Master."

She closed her eyes and sank deeply against him. He placed another gentle kiss on her forehead and then his eyes turned and looked deeply into Trisha's.

It was obvious he had known she was there but he hadn't taken any of his attention from Simone until now.

Trisha turned and walked away. Her brain was telling her to never return but her body was saying something different. She would decide the following day.

Chapter Seven

He was standing with a flogger in his hand. Everything around them was dark and his arm rose; casting a shadow on the wall. His hand fell. The pain felt incredible and her body responded. He wasn't standing close but somehow she felt him deep inside her pussy. She moaned and awoke from the dream with her fingers buried deep and an orgasm pulsing between her legs.

"Shit."

He invaded her every waking thought and then her dreams too. She had to talk herself out of going back tonight.

Her sexual needs wouldn't subside even after her orgasm so finally she got out of bed, and made her way to the shower. She had to go into work and pick up some things from the office. She was an advertising specialist but did most of her work from home. It would be a busy day but it would keep her mind off the coming evening.

Work was productive but she didn't have time for lunch. She drank a bottle of water on her way home as anxiety slowly took over and apprehension increased as the minutes ticked away. Her fridge had nothing that tempted her nervous stomach.

This was ridiculous. Her relationship with Pat was a two-year disaster because her emotions were involved. She thought she loved him but knew after the first year that she just wanted things simple and easy. So what if he never gave her what she needed sexually? She didn't even know what that was at the time.

Now she did. Could she keep her heart from getting involved and just enjoy the time she had with Kyle? He had looked at her with shock that first night. What was that about? She had never met him before but he reacted as if he knew her and he hadn't appeared happy when their eyes first collided.

She was going back. There was nothing she could do to stop herself and she couldn't resist her body's desire for what Kyle could give her. Hopefully, it would be a while before he demanded high levels of pain and she would be long gone by then. If someone else could give her body what Kyle did then she would find him. She couldn't help but think about the slut she was becoming; give her an orgasm or two and she couldn't get enough.

She dressed with care but her outfit was more conservative than usual. If he wanted her waiting naked then she would enter the club in what she had on and remove her clothes in the private room. She admitted to herself that she was excited and incredibly turned on and forced herself to mentally push back her reservations.

It was a Monday night and like Sunday, there were only about twenty-five people at the club when she arrived. A few of the subs said hello and then Raul stopped her.

"Hey girlfriend, the big gossip here is that you're training with Master Kyle?"

"Yes and I'm running late."

"Not a good idea to make him angry. Is Gloria coming tonight?"

"I'm not sure. She doesn't know I'm here or with Kyle."

"She'll hear soon enough but get going so you're not too late. Try to remember to refer to Kyle as Master or Sir even out here. One of the Doms might overhear you and I promise they'll inform him."

"I will. Thank you for the tip.

The Club employee at the entrance to the hallway smiled and nodded toward the same room she was in the night before. She couldn't help her blush. She didn't have a watch but she knew she was at least a few minutes late. After entering the room, she closed the door quickly and began removing her clothing laying them on the shelf Kyle used the night before. Her contract was gone. She walked to the mirror and went to her knees. There was a cushioned mat on the floor so she could get comfortable. She waited.

Having no idea how much time passed it seemed like forever before the door opened and Kyle walked in. She followed him with her eyes and smiled shyly at his approach. His black dress shirt tucked into tight slacks made her mouth water. The rolled up sleeves were about six inches from his wrists and three buttons were open on his chest. He was fucking sexy, but he continued to stand and stare at her without comment. His facial features looked like they had the night before when he whipped Simone. He was maybe a little more intense and she began to feel apprehensive.

"Kyle, what's wrong?"

He didn't answer for a moment. But finally, he said with no inflection in his voice, "I'm not pleased with you. If there was a problem with being here at eight you needed to inform me last night."

"I'm sorry; I stopped and spoke to Raul."

"I know and thank you for mentioning it. I will go lightly on your punishment for being late this one time. Do you know why?"

"No I don't."

Because you're new, and you don't quite understand what it is I want from you."

She was perplexed. "What do you want from me?"

"Submission. That's what this is all about. It's a power exchange and for complete submission you must give your own power over to me. Obeying my commands unquestionably is part of the deal. You must trust me to take care of your needs. I understand that comes with time but I expect you to follow my direction even if it's something as small as the time we meet. You haven't addressed me as Sir tonight either. Your fantasies need to include my proper name. Sir needs to be part of your muscle memory or I'll be making it a pain memory."

His voice remained unyielding and she was beginning to get angry. This was nothing like her fantasy.

"Stand up."

She had been on her knees for over thirty minutes and when she stood her legs wobbled and she became light headed.

Kyle grabbed her and held on tightly. "When's the last time you've eaten?"

"This morning." She knew she was really stupid. She tried to twist from his hold but his hands were like steel.

"Is there a reason you haven't eaten since this morning?"

Her tone was belligerent, "I was busy at work, and when I got home I was too nervous to eat."

He shook his head slightly and his voice softened, the rough sexiness returning, "What am I going to do with such a wayward sub?"

She didn't say anything just sighed and rested against him. She didn't like his anger it scared her causing a small knot to form in her belly.

He picked her up as if she weighed nothing and carried her to the couch dropping her butt on the cushions. He then walked over and collected most of her clothing.

"Put these on. I'm taking you to dinner."

Startled, she took the clothes and realized her panties were not in the mix. "What about my underwear?"

"That is your punishment for not being here on time. No underwear and I have something extra to add but I want your skirt on first."

She did as commanded thinking no underwear was actually not a punishment at all. When she was finished dressing he told her to stand there and wait. He walked over to a large bag he left by the door, and took out thin black straps from inside and approached her again.

"Lift your skirt."

She did.

"Higher."

She kept her irritation to herself but did as told. If he wanted her bare, he should have done this before she put on her clothes.

A resounding slap hit her backside.

"You are not to argue with my commands."

"I didn't."

Another slap landed and she kept her mouth shut but god how did he always know? His hand on her ass caused instant arousal. What would stop the wetness from flowing down her legs? The lack of panties was turning into a punishment.

He leaned down. "Step into this."

The black straps had two circles to put her legs through and a waste band that he pulled up. The front had a two inch red sparkled butterfly that fit over her pussy. He adjusted it so it rested snuggly against the hood of her clit and then tightened the waist strap before straightening to his full height.

"Is that comfortable?"

"Yes."

"Good." His hand went back to the butterfly and he flipped a small switch.

She almost came instantly. It vibrated directly over her clit.

"You can drop your skirt."

"You're not serious. I can't go anywhere with this on."

His hand went to her hair and he painfully pulled her head up so she was looking directly into his dark brown eyes.

"You were late, you didn't eat, and I have one last question for you. Have you pleasured yourself since I saw you last night?"

Chapter Eight

Trisha pressed her lips together, dropped her eyes, and didn't answer.

His hand grabbed hers and he marched her to the couch like she was a wayward child.

He landed on the leather cushion and pulled her ungracefully across his lap with her butt in the air. He pulled up her skirt bringing his leg from under her and using it to hold down her thighs. The first strike of his palm landed before she could protest.

"I have a reason for everything I do." Thwap. "Your only responsibility is to do what you're told." Thwap. "I want an answer now. Did you pleasure yourself last night?"

The small butterfly vibrator was causing her pussy to gush and his spanking stung but it was the most erotic feeling she'd ever known. Her orgasm was right on the edge of release but before she could say anything, he flipped her and turned off the butterfly. Without missing a beat, he turned her back over and laid an even sharper slap to her ass.

"I can go on all night but I promise you will not come."

"It was an accident. I dreamed you were flogging me and I woke up with my fingers getting me off. I'm sorry."

He placed his hands under her armpits and lifted her off his lap as he rose. He stood her on her feet.

"Lift your skirt and tuck it high and into your waistband and then lock your fingers behind your neck."

She didn't hesitate.

He went to his knees and she inhaled sharply. His hand went to her right ankle and lifted her foot up onto the couch. He then moved the butterfly slightly over and his tongue licked from her slit to her clit. Two fingers entered her slowly sliding in and out. His lips took her clit between them and then sucked the stiff bud of sensation into his mouth.

Her scream resounded through the room as tremors rocked her pussy and then throughout her body. When the last pulse quivered inside her vaginal walls, his tongue passed once more over her slit and then he stood. Taking her hands from behind her head, he held them at her sides and kissed her.

It was there; the flavor of amaretto, him, and her own juices which she had never tasted before. While he kissed her, he pulled her skirt down and adjusted her clothing so she was decent.

When he finished, he pulled back. "You're driving me crazy. You need to eat but I'm still punishing you. You will accept it or I will have food delivered in here and I will feed you in between spanking you on the bench. Do I make myself clear?"

"Yes Sir." Her voice sounded low and husky, and completely sated.

His fingers traveled beneath her skirt, and adjusted the butterfly then turned it back on.

Her pussy was now more sensitized and she wanted to scream. He didn't give her a chance just led her from the room. They took one of the private elevators down to the fourth floor and walked into a very fancy restaurant. It was crowded but the maître d greeted Kyle by name and took them directly to a table.

"We don't need menus. I'll have my usual to drink. My friend will have water. Please let Simon know I'm ready to order."

"Very good Sir." He walked away.

"How are you doing?" His eyes drilled into hers.

Her pussy was going to explode in the middle of the restaurant. "Fine." She put all the Saccharin sweetness she possessed into the word.

He had the gall to laugh full out. He leaned over and kissed her cheek then ran his teeth down and over her jaw, which caused her pussy to clench and she almost went over.

"Are you going to come?"

"No."

"We'll see."

Simon delivered their drinks and then took their order. Kyle never asked what she liked or preferred.

His grin was back, "You lost your chance to choose what you wanted to order when you didn't eat lunch. If I were you, I wouldn't let it happen again. Playing a scene can be very intense and it's quite dangerous if your blood sugar drops too low. You won't like the punishment I have for you if it happens again."

She resisted her snide comeback but knew her feelings showed on her face.

"Okay sweet sub, you have permission to say what's on your mind but only because I know how much the butterfly is turning you on right now."

"Are you enjoying yourself?"

"Of all the things I expected to come out of your smart mouth that wasn't it. And yes, as a matter of fact, I am. More than I have in a long time."

"Does it excite you to make me feel this way?"

"If you mean keeping you right on the edge and being able to smell your arousal, yes it does. Now I want you to put your hand under the butterfly and rub yourself."

"What? Here?"

"Yes, and if you do I'll turn it off while you eat."

"You're bribing me?"

"I'm tempting you."

"I will come and embarrass us both."

"No, you will come but you will remain silent, keep your eyes open, and not let anyone know what's happening."

"I don't think I can."

"But I do. Our food will be here shortly so please get started."

She had no idea why she followed his every command. Her hand went under her skirt and then under the butterfly. He watched and she knew her face was red. He took her other hand, and drew two of her fingers between his lips and sucked them into his mouth. Her eyes shut."

"Keep your eyes open." The words were hoarse but commanding.

The pulsating throb in her pussy became more intense and her hips rose to meet her fingers.

The waiter delivered their food in the middle of her orgasm and she thought she would die. She tried to stay still but it was almost impossible.

Kyle kept a straight face and spoke to the waiter whom he had obviously known for a while. He kept talking and the waiter stayed at the table.

When her orgasm was over the waiter finally walked away. Kyle reached under the table and turned off the vibrator before grabbing the hand she used to masturbate with, and brought her wet fingers to his mouth licking them off one at a time. He then proceeded to cut up her food and feed her small bites. She was still hungry when he told her she was finished.

"I plan on playing tonight and I don't want you to have a full stomach. Drink your water quickly; we're going back to the playroom. She downed it in one swallow.

Chapter Nine

"Remove everything including the butterfly."

He watched her take off her skirt and top. His seductive eyes concentrated fully on her body. When she finished he circled his finger and she turned around.

"Slowly. My handprints look sexy as hell on your ass. I think I'll add some stripes to the mix."

Her eyes obviously looked panicked when she finished turning.

"Don't worry it will be pleasure mixed with pain and nothing you aren't ready for. I promise you'll like it."

"What happens if I use my safe word?"

"I will stop immediately but that doesn't mean I won't be angry if you use it when you can handle more. My job is to make sure you are pushed to your limit but that I stop before you need to stop me."

"I'll try."

"Oh my sweet, you are more likely to safe word over sexual intensity than pain. I plan to keep you on the edge before giving your body release. The pain will focus you away from the sexual sensations and you'll be happy for it. Now let's get your wrist and ankle cuffs on."

He put on the same ones they used the night before followed by a blindfold over her eyes. He tugged on her hand and then led her across the room. He went slowly because of her lack of eyesight explaining that he took away her sight so she would feel the intensity more and she would pay closer attention to his voice.

Going by what she remembered from the day before and the feeling of what he was securing her to, she knew she was placed facing outward on the St. Andrew's Cross.

He finished with her ankles and arms and then placed a strap around her waist.

"Are you comfortable?"

"Yes. I think so."

He came in close and his hot breath passed along her chest. His nose barely skimmed over her neck and face before he whispered in her ear. "I don't want you comfortable. I want your pussy dripping for me."

His words were doing just that. She heard him walk away but he returned within minutes.

"Remember I told you that pain and pleasure go hand in hand? This will feel uncomfortable for a moment."

Her body tensed and then she felt the pressure on her nipple as he clamped it tightly.

"Augh." She couldn't help the sound she made. It hurt.

His voice was husky and soothing. "Shh, ride out the pain it's almost over."

The pain quickly turned into an erotic ache. The pressure was there but the overall sting was slowly leaving. That's when he attached the other clamp.

"Awwwe."

"That's better; you know what it feels like this time. Give it a minute."

She could feel a chain hanging down between the two clamps. It swung between her breasts and hit the top part of her stomach. A longer chain ran down the front of her body, down the center over her pussy, and bounced in a rhythmic brush across her flesh as she breathed.

"You're lovely. I could look at you like this for hours without touching you."

God no. He had to touch her.

"I would love to add a zip line down each side of your body. I didn't talk about that yesterday but it's a series of clamps held on a chain. It pinches, like the nipple clamps, into different parts of your flesh and intensifies when I do this." He tugged gently on one of the nipple clamps, causing a slight sting and instant throbbing to her nipple. "I can bring sensation to so many different places. No zip line today but we aren't done with you yet."

She felt him place his hand beneath the chain hanging between her breasts. The warmth from the back of his knuckles skimmed down her body over her belly and ended between her legs. His fingers spread her labia and his other hand played with her clit. Her breathing accelerated and suddenly she felt a clamp applied to one side of her labia and then the other.

"Awwe, god, aaah."

His tongue replaced his fingers and the hot roughness licked over her folds and around the clamps.

Her body wanted to fight the pinch of pain and the sensations his mouth was causing. One finger entered deep within her pussy.

"Please, I can't. I..."

His tongue stopped and his finger came out. "Yes, my sweet, you can." He kissed the inside of her upper leg and sucked just a small amount of skin into his mouth causing a pinching sting before repeating the process on her other inner thigh. His mouth left her body and she craved for more even if it included pain.

How could he do this to her so easily?

She heard him walking away and tried to get her breathing under control. Did anyone ever die from desiring an orgasm as badly as she did?

"This will be slightly cold but it will warm to your body temperature quickly."

His fingers again went to her pussy lips. She felt the clamps pulled slightly and she tightened her vaginal muscles in anticipation of the pain.

"Relax for me."

"One warm finger entered her again and she allowed her body to untighten."

The cold object slid up inside her as his finger came out. It was a small oblong item of some sort. She couldn't believe she was letting him do this to her. With her hips secured, it was impossible to rock her pelvis into the throb he caused deep within her pussy.

"Now for the fun part."

Thank god he didn't think it was fun up to this point. It was erotic torture.

Soft strips of leather touched the side of her face, and ran down her neck and over her shoulder then traveled across her breasts. Her nipples were beyond sensitive and the added feeling of the leather made her press against the strap across her hips. He continued to run the strands downward, over her stomach and then between her legs pulling slightly on the genital clamps and then continuing down one leg to her foot. He went to her other foot and made his way back up her body.

"This is a deerskin flogger and we'll start with it tonight. I may use less flexible leather another time but tonight we'll see how you do with this.

The flogger stopped its gentle travels over her body and the first strike landed across her breasts. Her back arched. It didn't exactly hurt but her sensitized breasts caught fire and she couldn't help the noise that came from between her lips. He didn't stop and the flogger landed repeatedly with her practically screaming as she fought the sensations progressing throughout her body.

He stopped suddenly and his hand went to her cheek. His lips took her mouth in a soft kiss before pulling away. "You are doing beautifully Trisha. I just need to make a small adjustment and we'll play some more."

"Please, I don't think I can."

"Are you hurting anywhere?"

"No, but I need relief."

"I know you do." The words held a promise.

She felt a very gentle pulsation deep in her pussy and realized the toy he placed inside her vibrated. It started softly but grew in intensity. Finally, her body was hanging over the ledge and almost...the vibration stopped.

"Ahhh, don't please."

"It's set to build and then stop. I'm pushing your body Trisha and you're doing great. A little more now."

The flogger landed on her breasts in a steady rhythm, and traveled down over her stomach then landed on her mound. His strikes were harder and they pulled slightly on her pussy clamps. The vibrator began its slow steady build and her cries were now loud in her own ears. She felt tears dampening the cloth over her eyes and realized she was crying. She was so close but she didn't know if she was close to using her safe word or having the most incredible orgasm of her life.

Everything stopped; the vibes, the flogger, everything.

Her breathing was so harsh she couldn't hear anything else in the room. The clamps on her pussy released and his warm lips sucked gently and took her past the pain. Then the nipple clamps came off and his lips replaced them with sweet torment. She groaned as the ache deepened before fading away to a dull throb.

He released her legs first and then her arms. She fell forward but he caught her in his arms and lifted her. Her need for an orgasm continued to scream through her nerve endings and her body shook uncontrollably. He placed her forward over the spanking bench.

"No I can't."

"I'm going to give you what you want Trisha but this is for me. Only three and you'll get everything your body desires. Hold on tight and I'll make it quick."

She clenched the leather armrests beneath her fingers and continued to cry. The first strike of the cane was so painful she screamed aloud. The next two fell in rapid succession. She felt herself lifted, carried a few feet, and placed on her back. She tried to turn to her side but his arms stopped her legs from twisting and suddenly his mouth was on her pussy and the vibrator started strong without the slow build. He pulled her engorged clit into his mouth and sucked hard.

She had never experience anything like the orgasm that rocked her body. It went clear to her toes and caused her nipples to throb harder. If she were standing she would have fallen. He removed the vibrator and replaced it with his fingers. They rubbed the inside of her pussy and massaged the pulsations inside. The blindfold came off but she didn't open her eyes. She couldn't.

Finally, he stopped and his lips took hers. The kiss was neither gentle nor harsh. It claimed her mouth; sucked, nipped, and explored. His hands came up to her face and his body lay on top of her though most of his weight was on his forearms.

"Oh my sweet. Can you take just a little more?"

"More?" She could barely catch her breath.

"Yes. I want to bury my cock deep inside your pussy but I can wait until tomorrow."

"No, please don't wait."

"Good girl."

He eased away and she heard him removing his pants followed by the tear of a condom package. Then his shirt-covered chest was back against her bare breasts and without giving her time to breathe, his hands took hers and lifted them above her head as his hips thrust and his cock buried deep inside of her. She could feel his knees on either side of her legs and every nerve in her body welcomed him before exploding. While the orgasm continued, he kept pumping in and out. There was nothing slow or sweet about what he was doing. He was fucking her hard and she wanted it. Her ass cheeks stung, her nipples ached, and her mind completely focused on the cock slamming in and out of her body.

His low moan finally sounded above her cries and his weight settled fully on top of her.

He whispered into her ear, "You my sweet sub have hidden depths even I didn't suspect."

He released her arms and carried her to the couch. There was a cabinet beside them and he grabbed a water bottle and tipped it into her mouth.

"Drink and then I need to rub oil into your muscles to help relieve your aches and pains."

"I don't want more pain, please."

"I know love. You have nothing left to give me tonight but I don't want you lying in bed hurting. I want you to have a good night's sleep. Tomorrow when you come here, I won't be as intense. I'll give your body a rest and maybe let you learn a little about mine."

She lifted her head and looked at him for the first time. His shirt remained buttoned but he was naked from the waist down. She looked into his eyes as her fingers went to the buttons. "May I?"

"I think you've earned it, go ahead."

"Earned the right to see your body?"

He laughed, "No earned the right to do what you want within reason."

Oh yes. She was exhausted, her body totally spent but she wanted to look at him. The buttons came undone in spite of her trembling fingers. She pulled the fabric apart and ran her hands over his pectoral muscles, gliding over his nipples. He had no chest hair and she wondered if he waxed. The thought of the pain involved with waxing made her smile.

"And what devilish thoughts are in your head sweet sub."

"Do you wax?"

"Yes, though I have it done."

"I hope it hurts."

His laugh was loud and full out. He pulled her in close and squeezed.

When his arms loosened she asked, "May I take your shirt completely off?"

He leaned forward and let her pull the material over his shoulders. She drew it completely from behind him and snuggled into his chest. His hand came up to her hair and he ran his fingers through the strands.

She had no idea how long they stayed that way. "Do you have another scene tonight?"

"No, I cancelled it after I saw you speaking to Raul. I wanted time to punish you properly."

"Is that what you were doing, punishing me?"

"Only before and during dinner. The rest was because I wanted to test your limits."

"Did I pass?"

"Yes." He pulled her up by her shoulders and looked directly into her eyes. "This world of kink, sex, and need will pull you in and what you thought you couldn't take will become a line you will cross again and again. If, and when, it becomes too much you must safe word. I watched you closely tonight. I knew you were almost to that point. Another Dom may not. People pass out, and are left with physical scars and permanent damage to their bodies. I won't do it tomorrow or even this week but I will force you to safe word so you know you can. It's important you understand your body. I don't want another Dom doing irreparable harm."

His words made her heart ache. She never wanted another Dom doing what he did to her. She refused to let these feelings get in the way of her next question. "Is that why you hurt your subs, because you know they need it and someone else would hurt them worse?"

"Don't confuse what I do with any kind of compassion. I need to feel their pain. I enjoyed your pain tonight. At the same time, I enjoyed your desire also and I haven't felt the need to do what we did in many years. You're like a drug. But even though I pushed you, and you took more pain than I thought you could, what I need is way beyond what your lovely body can give. You don't have the torment buried deep inside that fights to come out through a whip or a spike tipped flogger."

"Is that why people want that kind of pain?"

"Most of the time the need for extreme pain relieves the internal agony but there are the few exceptions. Every once in a while, I run across a person who just simply loves the pain but they are rare. Working with them can be difficult. They don't always have the self-preservation to stop what's being done to them." He moved a lock of hair out of her eyes. "I prefer the tortured souls who need it to feel better."

His lips moved forward and the kiss was gentle but slowly became more. He groaned when his lips finally left hers and he placed a last gentle kiss to the side of her mouth. "We're done for the night but I'm starving. Do you think you could eat again? This time I won't put anything against your pussy and you can actually enjoy the meal."

More time with him—that was not a difficult question to answer.

"Yes please."

He made her stand up while he covered her in soothing oil. "Lydia has the special recipe for this and we all use it now. It'll help with the aches and pains over the next few days."

"I'll feel pain for a few days?"

"Mostly muscle strain from fighting the restraints."

She knew each ache would remind her of him.

They dressed and he placed her panties in her hand. "I would love to keep these but I won't. I'll buy you some incredibly uncomfortable bits of lace and after you wear them all day at work and they're good and juicy I'll keep them for myself."

"You're so kinky."

"You, have no idea."

Chapter Ten

He was worse than any addictive drug and she craved his touch. The pain and ecstasy were part of the same package and she could no longer comprehend the line between the two. Forty-eight hours and her entire sexual world changed. She felt guilty for allowing him to use and torture her body but she couldn't resist going back. She wasn't even sure why she fought it. What more could he do, how much farther could he push?

She had to know.

She dressed casually and arrived thirty minutes early. She was heading to the private room when a voice from across the room stopped her.

"Trisha?"

"Oh shit." She mumbled under her breath. It was Gloria. She turned and prepared herself for the questions.

"Oh girlfriend, you're the talk of the club. Private time with Master Kyle and you didn't even call your best friend and tell her. If I was a Dom, I would punish you."

"Her Dom decides what she's punished for."

Neither of the women heard Kyle walk up. His hand closed around the back of Trisha's neck and massaged lightly. It was an entirely possessive gesture.

"Master Kyle Sir, I'm sorry, I was only teasing." Gloria went instantly into her submissive role.

"I'm aware of that but my sweet sub was late for our appointment last night and I wanted to remind her that it would be my pleasure to punish her again for tardiness. I'll leave you to talk for a few minutes and let you make the choice." His eyes drilled into Trisha's.

"I won't be late Sir."

He walked away but not before giving her a look of mock disappointment.

"Wow, we are having a long talk over coffee tomorrow morning. Now hurry before he gives you a harder whipping."

"He hasn't whipped me yet and I can't believe I'm back here." Her face flushed bright red.

"Hmm, yes a very long talk. You need to get over your puritanical roots and let your body do the talking."

"Believe me; my body has spoken to me all day due to last night's punishment."

"I'm going to have an orgasm right now. Go, I can't take anymore."

Trisha hurried to the room but the staff member monitoring the hallway stopped her. "Master Kyle wants you in room five and he asked me to give you this and said you are to be wearing it when he comes in." He handed her a shiny pink bag with the handles secured by a long pink strip of lace.

The bag jingled when she took it. She hurried to room five and walked in.

She was in another world. It was amazing and erotic all at once. Gauze cloth in pastel colors draped from the ceiling swaying gently from the wind created by ceiling fans. The room was as large as the other playroom but had very little furniture. Pillows lay scattered in one corner of the room. Against the other far wall was a large four-poster bed. The room looked like what you would see in a harem. She opened the bag and found the reason for the jingles.

The bottom piece was an elastic waistband with red silk scarves attached. There was no crotch and she had a feeling she wasn't supposed to wear underwear. She hurriedly changed clothes. There were round delicate gold disks that hung down from her waist and ended directly over the front of her pussy. Her bare thighs and hips showed when she walked. There was no top just an elaborate necklace that hung low over her breasts with the same gold disks.

She wasn't sure where to wait. She pulled a pillow from the pile, and used it under her knees. He walked in shortly after she got into position.

Glancing up, she couldn't take her eyes from him.

His chest was bare but he was wearing black pants tucked into mid-calf black boots. A wide red sash surrounded his waist. In his hand, he carried a long coiled whip. He was sexy as hell but the whip terrified her and once she noticed it, she couldn't stop staring. He came closer.

"Spread your legs wider."

She didn't move. She barely heard the words and continued to gaze at the whip in his hands. The handle of the whip came toward her face sliding under her chin and lifting it so her eyes looked up into his molten gaze.

"Is there something about my instruction that you don't understand?"

"I, I'm, what?"

"Tonight wasn't meant to be a punishment but if you address me incorrectly again I will gladly change the scene."

"No Sir, I'm sorry, I didn't hear what you said."

"Then listen closely sweet sub. You will not be hurt tonight if you follow every direction I give you. I want to play with my whip and I want to use it on your body but not for pain. Are we clear?"

"Yes Sir."

"Then spread your legs farther apart or I will do it for you."

Her legs moved wider.

He placed the whip beside her and leaned forward taking her breasts in his hand. He held nipple clamps with the same gold dangles as her necklace.

"These are not meant for pain but I want them secure because you will be moving in them."

He placed them on after using his tongue on each nipple. They weren't as uncomfortable as the ones from the night before but her sore nipples still protested and she made a slight noise.

"I know they are tender but each night you wear them your breasts will become more accustomed and I can use tighter ones. Now give me your hands."

He took a red scarf from his back pocket and tied one end around her wrist. He left about ten inches of material between her hands and tied the other one.

"Place your hands on your thighs."

She complied.

"You will kneel here while I warm up."

He walked about ten feet away, turned sideways, and unfurled the whip. The area in front of him was a large empty space. His arm lifted and the whip exploded with a loud crack.

She jumped and he looked over with a grin before focusing on an invisible object in front of him. He cracked the whip again. His body was lean but at the same time his muscles were perfectly defined. They flexed and then relaxed though the harder he worked the more they bulged. She watched and became mesmerized by the different movements of the braided leather of the whip. He continued and a fine sheen of sweat broke out on his chest. Wetness spread between her legs and she knew she was probably causing a mess on the pillow.

He stopped and without looking at her walked over to his bag which he placed by the door when he entered. He pulled a red object out and a tube of what looked like ointment. His long legs then walked to the bed.

"Come over here Trisha." He laid the whip across the top of the bed and she stood and came forward on shaking legs.

His hand went to the side of her face, and with his palm holding her in place; his lips came down on hers in a sensuous kiss. His tongue licked at the inside of her mouth and she couldn't help the sigh of pleasure escaping her throat. He pulled away.

"I'm using a rubber glove because we didn't talk about preparation for tonight's play. In the future I want you to use an enema at least two hours before you get to the club. This will be uncomfortable for your first time but like the rest of your body it will adjust. Now I want you to turn and take hold of the bed post."

She couldn't help looking at the items on the bed. The butt plug was red like her outfit. There was a medical latex glove lying with the other items."

Warm hands took hold of her midriff and startled her.

"You aren't listening. Turn."

Her body trembled but she turned away. His hands went to hers, and lifted them to the post putting pressure on her fingers to grab the smooth wood. He moved her back and then placed his hand on the small of her back pushing slightly. She leaned forward.

"Spread your legs."

She moved her feet out about a foot from each other.

His black boot and thigh went to the inside of her right leg and moved it further over.

"Rest your head on your arms looking away from the bed and relax."

A nervous giggle left her mouth but then she heard the plastic glove snap into place and her body stiffened even more. Kisses began caressing her hip, moving to her bottom cheeks.

"Your ass is beautiful. I fantasized about sinking my cock deep inside it two nights ago when I masturbated. This is a small plug and I want you growing accustomed to the stretching and feel of it."

His fingers massaged the cleft of her ass, and traveled over without touching the pucker and moved down further to her labia and swirled around at the entrance to her wet pussy, spreading her natural lubrication over her outer lips.

His gloved hand traveled back up and lightly moved in a circular motion over her anus. His hands left her for a moment and she heard lube squirt onto his fingers. They returned to where they were before but she felt the coolness of the ointment.

She knew it was going to hurt and she tightened her ass cheeks.

"You need to loosen your muscles sweet sub. It won't be that bad unless you stay tight."

"I'm trying."

"Slap." His hand landed hard on her ass, which was still sore from the night before and she suddenly sucked in air with the pain.

"You forgot a key word in your reply."

"Sir, I'm sorry Sir."

"Better."

His ungloved hand went to her pussy and he circled her clit. She felt his lips on her back. He sucked gently then moved to another spot. She already had two hickeys on the inside of her thighs from the night before. He enjoyed marking her body and it was as erotic as hell. She didn't mind as long as no one could see them. She didn't realize her muscles loosened as he continued his assault on her body until his finger slipped past her sphincter muscle and caused discomfort.

His finger worked slowly in and back out but never completely left her body.

"God you're tight. This will feel incredible around my cock in a few weeks." This was said between the suctioning kisses and his other hand rubbing her clit harder.

"Ahhh." She couldn't help it. His hand left her clit and then she felt added pressure against her ass. His finger came out as the plug went in.

"Ahhre. Oh god please take it out."

"Shh." She heard the rubber glove snap off and then his hands were back on her pussy. His sucking kisses moved down over her ass cheeks and continued to the insides of her thighs. She had no idea how many marks he left on her.

"Come for me sweetness, don't fight it."

The butt plug was uncomfortable but her clit was heating up and she felt her orgasm rise to the surface. Suddenly the plug moved out slightly and then reseated. Her pussy clenched and the walls of her vagina throbbed. The butt plug moved again and she screamed.

He continued to move his fingers in and out of her pussy until her muscles stopped pulsating. His hands took hold of her breasts and pulled her upright. His lips went to her neck but he didn't suck. He turned her around and took her mouth. His erection ground forward into her cunt and his hands went to her ass and kneaded her butt cheeks adding pressure to the plug.

"Now it's your turn to please me."

She'd dreamed about giving him a blowjob the night before. Luckily, she woke up before she had an orgasm but her body burned for an hour before she fell back into an exhausted sleep.

He walked away from her and messed with a control on the wall by the bed until music flooded the room. It was Eastern Indian flute, belly dancing music with a low drumbeat in the background. He came back and took her hand drawing her to the other side of the room. She couldn't help but notice he picked up the whip. She also noticed the fullness inside as she walked. It was only slightly uncomfortable now and caused another flood of juice to slide down her legs.

He stopped in the center of the large open area.

"I need you listening very closely." His eyes drilled into hers.

"Yes Sir."

"I will not strike you with the whip but you must do exactly as I say. I used it earlier to get you accustomed to the sound when it cracks. You cannot jump or move suddenly. All your movements will be slow. Do you understand?"

"Ye… No Sir."

He took her hands lifting them over her head. "You sweet Trisha, are going to dance for me. Slowly you will move your hips and legs. I will tell you when to speed up."

"Dance?"

The slap to her ass was sudden and pushed the butt plug in.

"Sir."

"One more time and we will have a punishment session after you please me. Do I make myself clear?"

"Yes Sir."

"Good, now dance sweet sub." His hands went to her hips and he moved them sensually to the music before letting go and walking away. She continued to move but watched as he unfurled the whip. She slowed momentarily."

"Close your eyes Trisha and don't worry about the whip."

"Yes Sir." Her eyes closed instantly.

The snap startled her but she realized it was nowhere near. She relaxed and began to get into the music. She felt sexy and the slight jingles caused by the gold disks added to the sensual feeling.

She didn't jump at the sound of the next snap but she felt the breeze by her thighs. It was close but he said he wouldn't hurt her and she was beginning to believe him. She let the dance take over and the next pops caused the breeze at different points of her body but she didn't flinch.

"Keep dancing but open your eyes."

She did as told.

"Move, just like you're doing."

A few more cracks of the whip struck close but she didn't care.

"Now spin for me."

"She turned."

"Faster, I want the skirt to fan out."

She spun.

The whip sounded and a section of material floated to the floor.

"Keep going."

She felt dizzy but continued to twirl as her skirt continued to disintegrate with every snap of the whip.

"Stop."

She stopped but her head whirled and she took an unsteady step to the side.

"Get your equilibrium back."

"Yes Sir."

He gave her a minute.

"Can you stand very still now?"

"Yes Sir."

"Good my sweet sub, don't move."

His hand rose and the whip spun out over his head. But before she even realized it was heading directly at her the long braid wrapped around her torso and circled her breasts and stomach. The nipple clamps were pushed in and a tightening of the whip pulled her body forward until she stood in front of him. There was no pain, and with a shake of his wrist, the whip slipped to the floor and he took her mouth in an earth-shattering kiss. His body was slick with sweat and so was hers. He pulled his mouth back.

"Come."

He led her to the bed and turned her so she was sitting on the edge. The butt plug pushed in and she squirmed. He laid her back and gently kissed her belly.

"Hands behind your head."

He sat on the side of the bed, and removed his boots and then stood and took off his pants and underwear in one move. He took a condom out of the pocket before he let them drop to the floor. He tore the wrapper and rolled the latex slowly over his cock then stepped between her thighs.

He pulled her body toward him so her ass was almost off the bed.

"This will be hard and fast."

Her eyes opened wider and then he slammed into her pussy going all the way in until his cock hit her cervix and his balls hit the butt plug. He didn't give her time to breathe before he pulled out and rammed in again.

She cried out but he didn't stop. Finally, when she thought she couldn't take any more, his groan accompanied her cries. He slowly sank down next to her body and pulled her in close. His heart was beating rapidly. She hadn't had another orgasm but she knew this fuck was not meant for her. She actually giggled slightly.

"And what could you possibly find funny?"

"I'm sorry Sir."

"No tell me. I seldom have subs laugh after finishing a scene."

"It was something Gloria said."

"I can only guess, go on."

"She said I would improve my oral skills because the male Doms all want blowjobs every night." She took a slow breath "I'm sorry Sir that was inappropriate of me."

He laughed and pulled her in close whispering in her ear.

"I need to remove your toys, and then if you give me a few minutes, I will gladly improve your oral skills."

Chapter Eleven

One week turned into two. He finally took her out to the main floor and began spending time with other Doms and their subs. She sat at his feet, and what seemed so unnatural a few short weeks ago, became second nature. He never took her to a station and only worked with her privately. He pushed her past every limit she thought she had and he knew more about her body than she did. She had two nights off a week and he told her not to come to the club. He wanted her to do something she enjoyed with friends or family. There was no way she could tell him her enjoyment these days came only from pleasing him.

He continued to do scenes several times a week with different subs but he used toys to get them off and never had sex with them or even allowed them to give him blowjobs. She no longer watched the scenes because she hated to see the complete lack of emotion on his face as he hurt the subs that enjoyed his kind of pain. She learned through watching him that when he showed the least emotion was when he felt the most. If she stayed at the club when he was finished, he would leave without speaking to her. It was easier for her to leave early. She hoped he stuck around the club when she wasn't there and talked to someone even if it was another sub.

After the night she mentioned blowjobs, he made sure her BDSM education included oral skills too. He took her out to dinner several times a week and asked her about her day, her job, and her family. She learned not to ask him private questions. She remembered the words he spoke that left her feeling sad and alone.

"Trisha, I told you I would always let you know what to expect from me and be very clear about it. I am not willing to discuss my life outside the club. I work in the company my father started. He's no longer alive. I have no siblings and a mother who drives me nuts though I love her. That's it and it will only make me mad if you continue to ask. You really don't want to make me angry."

That was it. He was in one of his moods that night and she finally used her safe word. He held her while she cried.

"Shhh, you did well. I'm proud of you for what you gave me and proud that you knew your limit." He placed gentle kisses over her face and neck until she calmed down. When it was time to leave they walked passed Simone and Kyle asked her if she was available for a scene. Her eyes lit up. He placed a soft kiss on Trisha's lips, told her to take the next night off, and walked away with his pain sub. That was what Trisha referred to them as now.

She was frantic with worry, but when she went back to the club two nights later, he had set up a pirate ravishment role-play and brought her to orgasm more times in the one night than ever before.

She walked in on a Friday and went to the private room Kyle reserved for them. A note was on a bag sitting on the inside shelf.

"Dress in these and then go out to the carousel and I will collect you later."

She had never been on the carousel before and the thought excited her until she looked at what was in the bag. It was a pair of yellow thong underwear and handcuffs. He had walked her through the club naked and sat with friends but had never had her walk alone in practically no clothing. She worried she had done something wrong and this was her punishment.

She went out and Raul was standing next the spinning toy-land for grownups. "Kyle asked me to assist you on."

"Thank you."

"It's not a problem."

"I'm sorry Raul but do you know if I did something wrong?"

"It wasn't you it was three other subs. They've been given to Kyle to discipline and he's not happy."

"Is he supposed to hurt them?"

"Yes, though not as badly as he usually does. The subs are being brought out one at a time so they don't know what to expect."

"What did they do?"

"All three women are collared and they went to a private party without informing their Masters. One of the regular Doms was there and spilled the beans."

"I see and do you know the particular reason I must wait on the Carousel?"

"I'm not sure but I think he doesn't want you alone in a private room for as long as this could take and he also doesn't want you watching. Those would be my two guesses."

"Why wouldn't he want me watching? I've seen what he does."

"But that's with willing subs. This is different."

"I want to watch."

"He's not handling this very well and I think you should do as he says."

"Too bad."

She walked away and headed to the station he used when he whipped his pain subs. There were about twenty people watching in open fascination. The first woman was brought in. She was shaking and crying. Kyle barely looked at her. Her Dom secured her on the St. Andrews

Cross with her back facing Kyle. After her Dom moved away, Kyle walked up to her and pulled her hair hard to the side so he could say something in her ear. Trisha couldn't hear what it was but she heard the "Yes Sir" response from the sub.

He then proceeded to whip her. His face was completely controlled. As horrible as he wanted Trisha to believe he was, when it came to his need to inflict pain, he did not want to deal it out to anyone that didn't want it. That was perfectly apparent in the control he kept over his emotions.

He gave her ten lashes before her Master unfastened her and carried her off. Kyle would not deal with her after care. Before she was taken away, and while she continued to cry loudly, the next sub was brought in. Again the hair pull and again the "Yes Sir."

This sub took it better than the last but she cried out with each strike. There was no sensual play only pain. On the tenth strike, her cries turned into pleas to stop. Trisha had counted each lash and knew when he reached ten. Kyle looked to her Master and the Dom nodded his head. Kyle gave her one more. Her screams started, not knowing it was finally over. The next woman was carried in kicking and screaming.

"Red, red," Came out of her mouth before they could put her on the cross. Kyle threw the whip to the floor and stormed from the scene. His eyes caught Trisha's and for the first time she was truly afraid. He grabbed her hair and held on as he walked her to the private room.

"Knees."

Her knees hit suddenly but she didn't feel the shock.

"You were told to wait on the carousel but you disobeyed me."

"Yes Sir."

Suddenly, he lifted her from the floor and then picked her up and carried her across the room. He sat on the bed and placed her over his knees. His hand came down hard. She didn't make a sound. Then it came down again.

Silence.

"What the fuck are you doing? Scream."

Tears were running down her face but he couldn't see them.

"No Sir."

"Fuck."

He lifted her up and then wiped her eyes with his fingers. His lips took her mouth in a kiss that sent a punishing zing clear to her toes. He lay back on the bed and brought her with him. Finally, he stood up removing her thong and handcuffs, and then took his clothing off. He took a condom from his pocket and she placed her trembling hand out. He put the condom in her fingers but didn't say a word.

One of the subs had shown her the trick and she had been practicing at home with a cucumber. She placed the condom in her mouth and then placed her mouth on his cock.

"Christ." He said on a long groan.

When the condom was in place, he flipped her over, and pulled her ass up and back. His cock drove inside her pussy in one smooth stroke. He stopped for a moment and his hand went to her reddened ass cheeks and gently smoothed over each. He drove into her again and then continued but with a slow steady rhythm until she was begging him to let her come. His hand went to her clit and he pinched hard. That was it. Her orgasm shook her body from her ears to her toes. He continued to pump into her until he finally cried out with his own release.

After their breathing slowed, he gathered her into his arms. "Why did you disobey me sweet sub?"

"Because I knew punishing those women would hurt you. Why didn't you say no? No one could make you do that."

"Most subs at the club are terrified of me and when I'm called in as punishment their bad behavior is not repeated."

"What about the last sub?"

"She will be banned from the club."

"I'm sorry Sir for disobeying you."

His kiss was ever so gentle and then he made love to her slowly with his hands and mouth. He asked her to put the second condom on with her mouth again and she smiled for the first time that night. She gladly obeyed him.

Chapter Twelve

She arrived early but made her way straight to the private room. Master Damian greeted her when she opened the door and she let out a shrill squeak that made him smile.

"Kyle asked me to deliver a message and give you this."

"What is the message Sir?"

"He has been unexpectedly called away. He doesn't mind if you stay at the club but he wanted you to temporarily wear this." He handed her the box.

She opened it and took out a gold linked collar about three fourths of an inch in width.

"Turn around and hold up your hair, I'll put it on and then you may go out on the floor."

She turned and felt her emotions surge with love for her absent Dom.

"Sir, is everything okay with Sir Kyle?"

"That's something he will need to speak with you about when he returns."

The worried look in her eyes must have affected him, "Kyle is fine, and it's just personal issues."

Feeling a little better, she still worried about Kyle's personal issues. She spent the evening talking to other subs. Raul stuck close by and told her Lydia wanted her watched closely. Lydia's baby was due in a few weeks and she was not at the club that evening but she seemed to know everything that went on. It made Trisha smile and she was glad to have Raul with her.

Gloria ended up sitting and talking with her for a while too. "He collared you."

"No, it's only temporary while he's out of town."

"I have trouble believing that. Kyle keeps you locked away almost every night. You're like the only sub that doesn't do scenes in the stations. Everyone's talking about it."

"I can't believe the amount of gossip that goes on here. Raul has been filling my ear for over an hour, and now you tell me I'm the subject of additional gossip."

"I just thought you might want to know what people are saying. He doesn't do half the scenes he used to and he no longer fucks his subs. That man has it bad for you."

"I'm in training and I'm sorry but I don't think he has anything for me but protective feelings for a sub in training."

"You keep thinking that girlfriend."

Trisha knew she was in love and Gloria's speculation only made her heart hurt worse. It was even harder without Kyle at the club. She needed her Dom drug fix badly just like an addict.

She tossed and turned that night and drove to her office instead of working from home. It helped keep her mind off her missing Dom.

At the club that night, he still hadn't returned. She was miserable. It was five days before she heard from him. While she was taking a shower, she missed his call. She didn't recognize the number on her caller ID but her heart accelerated when she listened to his message.

"Hi sweet sub. I've missed you. I'm exhausted and I'm going to try and sleep for a few hours. I would like to take you to dinner but if you don't mind, meet me in my room. I'm in room 2501 and the code is 7437. Just let yourself in at six if you can make it that early. Wear something nice, I'm taking you to Mark's. I'll see you soon."

His voice sounded husky and tired. Saturday night and he was getting her into Mark's. She needed to go shopping.

The dress was red, seductive, and perfect. Her heels were black. He liked her hair down so she curled it into soft waves. She felt strange entering the code and not knocking but she followed his instructions. The lighting in the large apartment was set low but it didn't hide the elegance. Her apartment would fit in the living room of this one. She saw no sign of her Dom so she decided to look for him.

He was in bed with a sheet partially covering one of his legs as he slept on his stomach. His ass cheek peeked out the twisted covers and she smiled.

Sitting on the side of the bed she ran her fingers over his shoulder and around to the front of his chest. His hard grip closed over her questing fingers.

"You dare to wake up your Dom?" He rolled pulling her fully onto the bed and into his arms.

The kiss was passionate and she felt it lock deep into her heart. He smelled delicious; amaretto, musk, and sleepy male. His mouth nuzzled her chin and neck.

"Mmm, I could eat you. No, I will eat you."

She laughed. "What about our reservations?"

"Do you care?"

"No."

He finally looked at her.

"Stand up. I want to see the dress."

She did as commanded and tried to portray a sexy come-hither smile.

"Turn around slowly."

She spun.

"Exquisite, now take it off."

She laughed and turned her back to him. "I need help with the zipper."

The dress came off and it drifted to the floor as he lifted her to the bed. Her shoes and garter belts were still on but she had worn no panties.

He kissed his way down her legs and then placed them over his shoulders and spent the next ten minutes sucking, nipping, and teasing. He finally used his fingers and looked up past her stomach, over her breasts, and into her sensual gaze.

"Come for me sweet sub."

And she did. When her body stopped trembling, he placed her hands on the gold rails of the headboard.

"Hold on."

His claiming wasn't hard. He used slow steady strokes to drive her wild again. She watched his face when his eyes closed immediately before his orgasm tightened his features; it was the face she loved and belonged to the man she worshiped.

After both their breathing returned to normal, he called room service for champagne and dinner.

"Grab a robe out of my closet. I'm going to take a quick shower."

Her eyes were shy. "Do you want me to join you?"

He smiled softly, "Yes and no. I love the way you smell right now; sex, woman, and spice. I'm not finished with you yet. We can take another shower later."

How could any woman resist a man that wanted her smelling of sex? She put the incredibly soft white robe on and walked around the apartment admiring the artwork and furniture. The kitchen was incredible and she wondered if she would ever have a chance to cook him a meal here.

The bell sounded and she walked to the door figuring the champagne had arrived. She opened it and stood staring at a striking middle-aged woman so obviously not a hotel employee.

The woman looked at her in shock. "Who are you?"

Before she could get any words out Kyle's deep voice spoke from behind her. "Mother this is Trisha. You should have called first."

"I see that." She looked between the two of them and then looked back at her son. "I came to see how your wife is doing."

"Christ." His tone was filled with pain.

Trisha heard the words but for a minute, she stood frozen. Slowly she turned toward Kyle.

"You're married?"

"It's not what you think."

"You're married." All her agony was in those two simple but complex words.

"It's more complicated than that."

Trisha turned, "Excuse me Mrs. Garson, I must be going." She walked past his mother whose eyes had grown incredibly large.

"Trisha you can't walk out in a bathrobe." She stopped and then made her way to the elevator at the opposite end away from the regular hotel elevators. This would take her directly to the club and someone there could get clothes for her.

A solid hand landed on her shoulder when she reached the elevator doors.

"No, you aren't going anywhere. You are staying here and talking to me."

Tears had started falling but with an agonizing breath, she got out the words. "Red, don't touch me."

"Trisha."

"Red."

The elevator door opened and she stepped in. Through watery eyes, she saw him standing there—stunned, barefoot, shirtless, sexy, beautiful, and married.

Chapter Thirteen

She suffered through a week from hell alternating between sadness, depression, and anger. She cried for hours and then screamed into her pillow so her neighbors wouldn't call the police. Going to a bar and picking up a man had never been on her radar because of the chance the man was married. And here she was, in the predicament she swore she would never put herself. She was in love with a married man.

Her heartbreak was interminable. She would never go back to the club and she realized the lifestyle she needed was no longer open to her. The man she loved was no longer part of her life.

She had a project deadline that required her to go into her office. She was actually relieved. She had to get out of her apartment, and just maybe, a few hours would go by without thinking of him. She left work two hours late because she messed up several things by making stupid mistakes. Her disorder carried on in everything she did. Wiping tears from her eyes, glad there was no one around to see them; she took the elevator to the parking garage and removed her keys from her purse. Security cameras monitored the garage, but she liked to be prepared when no one was around.

She looked in the direction of her car and saw a black limo driving slowly forward. Surprisingly, it stopped beside her. The back door opened and Kyle unfolded himself from the interior of the car and stepped out.

Her eyes took in the square line of his jaw, his sleep deprives eyes, and his less than immaculate appearance. He was rumpled which was completely opposite to the strong dominating man he was. She met his eyes and took a step back.

She saw the hurt but he didn't come closer.

"I need you to come with me."

"What? No!"

"Yes, Trisha and I'm not asking."

"That's kidnapping."

"I'm fully aware what it is. You can make this hard and give the security people something to talk about or you can get in the car with me. I will not touch you. This is not about domination and submission. It's about you and me."

"There is no you and me." Her eyes flew back and forth looking for the best way out.

"Have it your way." He stepped forward and lifted her into his arms. He turned and dumped her into the back of the vehicle. She landed on her ass with her legs up in the air. He moved in quickly and she pulled her legs down and shuffled to the far door. It wouldn't budge. He settled across from her.

"Are you seriously going to do this?" Anger pulsated with every word.

"Yes, you've given me no choice."

"Where are you taking me?"

"You'll find out when we get there." He leaned his head back against the seat and closed his eyes.

She could see his exhaustion but refused to feel sorry for him. She knew she probably looked just as bad and felt the tears start to fall. Once they started, she couldn't stop.

Warm gentle hands pulled her sideways and into his lap. "Please don't cry. My purpose is not to scare or upset you though I'm sure that's hard to believe. I just need you to trust me, the same way you did with your body." He moved the hair out of her face and pried her fingers loose. He kissed her gently on the lips.

More than anything she wanted to give into his seduction, wanted to feel his hands on her again. "I'm okay now, please no more."

His hands left hers immediately but he didn't remove her from his lap and when she tried to scoot off, he held her in place. She remained until she noticed the airport traffic.

Her entire body stiffened. "Where are we going?"

"I'm sorry but I won't answer that just yet."

The first chance she got she would scream bloody murder. His wife could bail him out of jail. They drove through winding narrow passages and she finally figured out they were not going to a main terminal.

"You have your own plane?" Her anger and frustration were evident in her voice.

"No, I'm taking advantage of Damian's plane. I use it a few times a month for personal business."

"Is that what I am, personal business? You kidnap women and then hide them away where no one finds them again?"

He actually laughed.

She began to struggle, "Put me down now."

He released her and moved to the other side of the car again. She sat still and seethed.

The limo drove them directly to the plane's airstairs. He tried to take her hand but she got out of the Limo, and went up the steep steps unassisted. Walking as far to the back as she could, she sat down at a dinette table built to accommodate the space.

"I'm afraid for takeoff and landing you will need to be seated in one of the flight seats but you can move back to your spot as soon as the pilot gives the go ahead." His voice held dominant authority.

"Fine." It was the best she could come up with even if it sounded petty and childish. He was kidnapping her for god's sake. She moved to one of the large leather seats and refused to look at him."

"Put your lap belt on." He used his damn Dom voice again.

She began struggling with the buckle. It probably wasn't hard but she was past being able to make her hands work properly. It was taking everything she had to not break down and cry again. If she did, she knew she would never be able to stop.

His hands came down and buckled her in. She wanted to punch him.

A young woman approached, "Good evening Mr. Garson, may I get you and your companion something to drink?"

"Yes Denise, we'll each have a glass of white wine."

Trisha had kept her head down but now looked up. "No thank you Denise, I don't feel white wine goes well with kidnapping. If you have a red I'm sure it's more appropriate."

Denise's eyes almost came out of her head. "Ahh, okay."

"Sorry Denise, she's not crazy, I am kidnapping her, but she will be flying back early tomorrow morning. Damian is aware Miss Carpenter is with me."

"Yes sir, I'll get your wine to you before we take off. The Captain wants you to know we'll be leaving momentarily."

"Thank you." She walked away as quickly as her legs would carry her.

"Was that really necessary?" He seemed exasperated.

If her eyes could strike someone dead, he would be laying in a pile of cinders. She continued her childish behavior and turned sideways without speaking.

Denise delivered the wine and quickly left. Trisha forced herself to drink the red though it wasn't something she cared for.

The flight was two hours long and when they disembarked, another limousine was waiting. She saw a sign and realized they were in South Carolina. The jerk. She figured he was aware he crossed state lines and the FBI would handle the case. Not that the thought made her feel any better.

The drive took about forty-five minutes as they slowly made their way into a less populated country area. It was dark but she could see the large trees. They took a long winding road that seemed to go on forever.

The car finally came to a stop. The grounds of an extremely large mansion were lit up with soft lighting. The house was beautiful.

"Where are we?"

"At my home."

"Seriously? Is your wife in residence?" It was snide and mean but she couldn't help herself.

"Yes she is."

"What? No. Hell no!"

"Trisha, you can make this easy or I can carry you in but you are going in."

"How could you do this to me, to her? I hate you."

He opened the door and got out of the car. His hand came out but she ignored it and managed to get herself standing upright though her knees felt like they wouldn't support her. She walked to the front door.

Chapter Fourteen

Kyle turned the handle and the door opened wide. It was late and there was only a low light glowing from accent lighting displaying artwork. Her heartbeat sped up and dread filled her. He walked to a staircase that went up to the second floor, which overlooked the lower landing. His hand waved for her to precede him but she didn't budge.

"If you don't go up I will carry you."

"Please?" Desperation was in the plea.

"Trisha, up."

Her legs felt like lead but she put one foot in front of the other and climbed each step. She mentally counted them; twenty-six. She stopped at the top and Kyle stepped around her.

"Follow me."

They made their way down the long hallway. There was a room up ahead that had a faint light shining out. All the other rooms they passed were dark.

She heard the odd noise first. It was almost like air swirling in short bursts. Kyle preceded her inside but her legs froze at the entry making it impossible for her to step forward.

"Carol, do you mind giving us a few minutes. I'll come and get you before I leave."

"Yes Kyle, no problem."

The middle-aged woman cast a curious glance at Trisha before closing the book in her lap. Standing, she left the room.

Kyle walked over and extended his hand placing it on the cheek of the woman lying in the bed. There was a soft light shining above her head but the rest of the room remained in shadows. She was small, ethereal. A ventilator breathed for her and numerous tubes ran from her body into assorted machines. Her hands curled into themselves.

"This is my wife Amanda." He leaned forward and placed a kiss on Amanda's pale unresponsive lips. He never looked up just sat on the side of the bed and watched the woman next to him.

Trisha's feet wouldn't move they were completely locked into place.

"I was driving; neither of us wore seatbelts when another car struck us head on. The driver who hit our vehicle had a heart attack. Amanda was ejected and suffered a major brain injury. I remained trapped until the fire department used the Jaws of Life to get me out. I could see her lying there and I knew she was gone. But I was wrong; she was still alive though barely.

Tears trailed down Trisha's cheeks. She could hear the pain in his voice and it tightened her stomach painfully.

"We were married for two years. I was her husband and master and she was my wife and slave. It was a perfect match. We loved each other and were incredibly happy. She was pregnant with my child but lost the baby in the accident." He inhaled deeply and finally his eyes rose to meet hers. "It was my fault. I didn't insist she wear her seatbelt. It was my job to keep her safe. She always obeyed whatever I told her to do. When we started our relationship I promised to always keep her safe." His voice was tortured. "Turn on the light switch beside the door Trisha."

The command was so unexpected that she wasn't sure what he was asking.

"The light switch beside you, turn it on."

Her hand went to the switch and the soft glow stung her eyes for a moment. She allowed them to adjust and then looked around. The walls were a shrine to his wife. Her pictures were everywhere. The person she had once been. Amanda smiled, laughed, and held daisies. She even rode a horse. Her love for life was evident. There were pictures of the two of them together. He was smiling, happy, and incredibly in love.

It took her a few moments but finally she noticed it; the missing piece of the puzzle. His wife, Amanda looked like Trisha. Same hair, similar eyes, and bone structure. They could be sisters.

"The first night I saw you I thought you were her. The way she used to be. You were so embarrassed and shy and I remembered Amanda being just like that. I looked at you and fell in love all over again." His head turned back to his wife. "This is why I give pain. I have so much built up inside and I realized others do to. If they want to feel a whip and take away some of the heartache for just a little while, I can help. It also gives me a chance to escape with them."

Trisha knew her knees were going to crumple, she could no longer see through her tears. Strong arms lifted her body and carried her from the room. He took her into a large room that must have been the master bedroom. He didn't go to the bed but sat in a love seat a few feet away. He pressed her head into his shoulder and inhaled slowly.

"I never wanted to hurt you. I didn't know how to explain."

"You, you need me to replace her." Sobs shook her body.

"No, my love. I knew very quickly that you were nothing like Amanda. Pleasing me was her one and only pleasure. She wasn't feisty and she never disobeyed me. She was the perfect slave. You on the other hand push me at every turn. You gave me back my passion for life and this lifestyle."

Her hands went to his shirt and fisted the material crying even harder against his chest. She felt soft kisses on her hair and then the side of her face. Long fingers lifted her chin and he placed a gentle kiss on her tear-dampened lips.

"I love you for you, but I don't think it's enough. I cannot marry you. I will never divorce Amanda. I couldn't do that to her. Part of my heart will always be hers. She is often unwell and I need to be here. She was hospitalized more than a week ago and that's why I left you."

She looked up. He was so beautiful, so perfect but he suffered unimaginable internal pain. "I need time to think. I'm sorry. I don't want to hurt you more but I can't do it here or even around you."

"I understand. The car is waiting."

Chapter Fifteen

They drove back to the airport in silence. Trisha felt like the biggest bitch on the planet but her brain was on overload. She didn't blame him. She loved him, but could she accept the fact he was married, even when his wife would never be by his side?

The sun was rising when the limo stopped in front of her office. Before she could scoot out of the car, his strong arms brought her close and he kissed her with incredible tenderness. She felt his love, his worry, and she knew he was kissing her goodbye. He released her, leaned back into his seat closing his eyes, and allowing the driver to assist her from the vehicle.

She had slept in short fits on the plane and exhaustion was weighing her down. She drove home immediately. Lying in her bed she was too shattered to rest. Before finding out about his wife, thoughts of Kyle brought dreams of marriage and children; about having more than their relationship at Club El Diablo. When the tears began, they refused to let up. Finally, her mind went numb and she fell asleep.

Her days blended one into another. Gloria tried to get together with her a few times but Trisha always had an excuse. She woke up at night, her body trembling because of her dreams. She loved him and nothing that had happened stopped her feelings.

He would always love his wife but if Amanda was dead it would be easier. Her thoughts made her a horribly selfish person. None of this was his fault and he was just as much the victim as Amanda.

Finally, Gloria called and invited her to Lydia's baby shower the next afternoon at two. The party was sub exclusive. No Dom's but Lydia herself. "I'm picking you up. No arguments."

She wore a dark blue skirt that ended an inch above her knee with a pale peach blouse. Nothing like she would wear to the club. Lydia's stomach had grown in the two weeks since Trisha saw her and her cheeks were fuller. It only made her more beautiful.

Trisha received curious glances but no one mentioned Kyle. They ate, talked, and laughed with one horrible labor story topping another. Though Gloria and Trisha were childless, it was hard not to commiserate with mothers everywhere. Finally, the women began to clear out but Trisha insisted on staying and helping with the cleanup.

When they finished, the words Trisha had not wanted to hear came from Lydia, "I'm heading up to collect Damian from the club would you both like to come?"

"Sure." Gloria answered at the same time Trisha said no.

"He's not there. You can go to the club without seeing him." Compassion showed in Lydia's eyes.

Trisha took a deep breath. "The problem is I want to see him so bad it hurts."

"Damian told me about his wife, I didn't know."

"It's okay."

"Come to the club and work with another Dom. You'll feel better. It's not only about sex. Anna is there and she would do wonders for your mood."

"I just can't. Maybe next week. Do you know when Kyle is coming back?"

"His wife has been in intensive care and I'm not sure but I know he won't return until she's out of danger."

Trisha felt like a dull knife stabbed straight into her heart. "What happened?"

"Apparently she came down with a temperature and fluid formed in her lungs. The last I heard she was in stable condition."

"I need to get to South Carolina."

"What do you mean?" This question came from Gloria.

"I've been really stupid and I need to be with Kyle. He shouldn't be alone."

"It's about time. The plane is here in Houston and I'll call Damian to have it placed on standby. My pre-pregnancy clothes will fit you and I'll have housekeeping bring up a toothbrush and other necessities. You don't even need to go by your apartment first."

"Were you planning this?"

"No, but Kyle needs you and you need him."

"Yes, I do. Gloria, will you drive me to the airport?"

"Not a problem girlfriend. It's about time some life came back into your voice. I was getting sick of your moping."

"I don't know his address."

"We'll have a driver meet you at the airport in South Carolina and he'll have all the information."

The flight took forever and though she needed sleep, she couldn't. Her biggest fear was that Kyle had given up on her. With all his pain, she had only added to it.

It was eight-thirty at night when the limo turned down the long drive. The house looked the same; dark and silent. Damian called before Trisha's plane landed and informed the limo driver that Amanda was moved home earlier in the day and was no longer in the hospital.

Her hand grasped the cold door handle and it turned. She walked up the stairs and at the top, she saw the light coming from Amanda's room. She could also hear the voice that haunted her dreams. As she drew closer, she realized he was reading aloud. How could she not love this man?

She didn't make a sound just stood at the door and absorbed the sight of him while he melted her heart. He wore flannel pajama bottoms with no shirt. The book was propped on the bed by Amanda's head. He read slowly in his deep Dom voice that sent shivers down her spine.

Trisha looked around the room but it was hard to see the pictures. His voice stopped and her eyes jerked to him. He was looking at her with such intensity she felt her knees grow weak.

"Don't hate me Kyle. I'm sorry."

He closed the book and placed it on the nightstand. His hand ran lovingly over Amanda's hair and he kissed her on her cheek. He whispered something into her ear and then stood and came toward the door.

His arms pulled her in and wrapped her within his warmth. His nose went to her hair and he inhaled. His body rocked while he held her tightly.

A few minutes passed and then she felt herself lifted. He carried her down the hallway to his room. Laying her on the bed, he picked up the phone and pushed one button. "Carol could you please stay with Amanda, I have a guest."

Trisha didn't hear the reply just watched as he disconnected. His hand ran down the side of her face, his intense eyes following the same path. One finger wiped her tears and he brought them to his lips.

She reached up and took his hand. "I love you."

She was in his arms again and his mouth consumed her. Finally, he let her come up for air and pulled away slightly. "Share my life. I'm not perfect but I love you. I can't promise to protect you always. I want you to think for yourself and tell me I'm stupid when I am. I want to tie you up and do unmentionable things to your body. I want pain mixed with pleasure but never so bad you stop me."

This time she brought her lips to his. She drew back after only a moment and looked into his eyes. "Yes." Her smile grew and she kissed him again.

Finally, he pulled away. "Thank you."

"Will you take me to meet your wife? I need to speak with her alone."

"She would like that."

A few minutes later, Trisha sat next to the bed and heard the door shut softly behind Kyle and Carol. She took Amanda's hand and felt stupid for expecting it to be cold. It was warm. There was still life in the small hand.

"I will take care of him for you Amanda. I will love him and help soothe the pain he's suffered since losing you. I will be his friend but I will be your friend too. My heart is big and I can love you both and accept that he loves both of us." Tears streamed down Trisha's face. "You will never be alone and you have two of us now."

She sat for several more minutes before she went in search of Kyle.

"Is the driver still out front?"

"I wasn't sure if you would want to stay here in the house."

Her smile was gentle. "Why wouldn't I? This is your home and Amanda is a part of our life. I can love you both."

A single tear rolled down his cheek.

She walked to him and trailed her finger against the wetness before bringing it to her lips.

When his mouth came down over hers, it was no longer gentle. It was possessive and passionate. "I need to send Carol back with Amanda and dismiss the driver.

Please come with me, I don't want you out of my site for at least the next fifty years."

She laughed, "Fifty years sounds good."

Chapter Sixteen

Club El Diablo was crowded. Her back was against the St. Andrews Cross where she was restrained spread-eagle. The clamps he used were tight and the pinch wasn't going away. His grin was merciless. He used his tongue but knew it wouldn't relieve the pain. Each nipple received his attention until he finally grasped her hair and positioned her mouth for his taking.

One hand traveled down and stopped between her thighs. He pulled away slightly so he could look in her eyes. "I have a special toy for you tonight."

Her breath was coming in short gasps because he never stopped playing with her clit, running his fingers around and over the super sensitive flesh.

"Don't you want to know what it is?"

"Ahhh, I just want you to fuck me Sir. Fuck me hard."

He laughed and she knew it wouldn't be that easy. She was purposely late joining him at the club so he would punish her. She knew it and he knew it but she would make sure the punishment affected him as well as her.

"Fuck me hard Kyle."

He walked away returning with a red butt plug covered in lube. It was larger than what he normally used and his evil grin told her he knew it would make her nervous.

"After tonight it will be my cock buried deep in your ass. But I thought you needed a bit more stretching my naughty sub."

His slippery fingers found her flowered pucker, and gently massaged and then pushed passed the muscle. He used them to stretch and apply outward pressure.

"That's two of my fingers and you're doing so well."

"I won't scream." She was panting harder.

"Oh, you'll scream but not until I want to hear it."

Her jaw clenched and her teeth ground together. She could play his game.

His fingers slipped out and the plug pushed in.

It hurt, "Ahhre, no Kyle."

"Oh my sweet sub, how soon you've forgotten you manners." He applied more pressure. "Bear down and it will help."

Though she wanted to call him names, she did as her Dom commanded and the plug slid in. He immediately walked away and she wished he would get a part of his body close enough so she could bite it. She heard him washing his hands and the burning in her ass eased slightly though the fullness remained.

"How are you doing Trisha?"

"I'm thinking of ways to make you suffer later tonight Sir."

"Interesting but I don't think you'll be in any shape to do anything more than fall asleep from exhaustion."

He picked up a leather flogger with knots tied at the end. "We haven't used this one yet. But before I start I forgot one special function of my new toy." His hand slipped inside his pants pocket and the plug began vibrating.

He lifted the flogger and snapped it across her stomach.

She was biting down hard refusing to make a sound. He went to work and let the strands travel up and then back down her body. It stung but it was also erotic and caused juice to flow between her legs. He stopped and stepped forward bringing his fingers to her clit. He pinched and at the same time turned up the power on the plug.

"Ahhh, god, ahhre." She finally screamed. The pulse of the vibrator thrummed with the pulse in her pussy. Every nerve ending ignited and flowed steadily to her clit, which finally his fingers released, causing even more sensation to explode in her center.

Her breathing eventually slowed and he removed his new toy, the nipple clamps, and her restraints. He carried her to the couch and sat holding her. His fingers traveled through her hair. "You are entirely too stubborn my dear."

"You love it."

"Yes I do."

The low lights in the club suddenly blinked out, the carrousel stopped, and all sound but the nervous laughter of the patrons ceased. It was only dark for a moment before the backup generator took over and the lights came back on.

Employees walked around and checked on everyone. There was a storm forecasted for their area and apparently, much worse than expected.

Trisha giggled, "We may be stuck here for a while."

He placed a soft blanket over her. "I can't think of a better place to be." He kissed her cheek.

"Are you both alright?" Damian asked a short time later.

"Yes, we're fine. I'm assuming the elevators are out until the power is back on?"

"Yes, but I think the club can entertain our guests for a few hours if needed."

"I'm sure you can."

"Damian." It was Raul and he looked slightly ill.

"Yes Raul."

"Umm, well, umm."

"What exactly seems to be the problem?" His Dom voice showed his impatience.

"Lydia just asked me to tell you her water broke."

"Well fuck!"

Trisha couldn't help herself. "With all the Dom's in here tonight I'm sure one will know what they're doing."

"We'll fireman-carry her down the stairs if we need to. I am not delivering a baby." Damian's usual strong voice actually croaked.

"Yes daddy." Trisha couldn't help herself.

Both Dom's looked at her with utter terror.

She stifled her laugh. "We need to check on Lydia and then you big bad men can figure out what needs to be done next."

She tightened the blanket around herself and got to her feet. Damian headed to the stairwell. He had to climb four flights to get to his wife. Hard hands pulled her back and Kyle's strong arms brought her in close. "I Love you but when my baby arrives we won't be anywhere near here. I promise." His kiss was gentle and loving.

"I love you too."

"I'm scared shitless with this whole baby thing. Don't leave me."

"I would never leave my dom."

The beginning…

Book IV

Domination in Pink

Chapter One

Club El Diablo was crowded and one problem after another took Damian away from his wife. Lydia was expecting their first baby and he would rather be doing something kinky, watching television, or even playing a game of chess rather than settling disputes over which sub belonged to whom.

When he wasn't around, Lydia had a way of getting into trouble or at least doing things he expressly forbidden. He laughed at the thought. "Forbid," was considered the "F" word as far as she was concerned. He learned that the hard way and now, with her advanced pregnancy, he tried a little harder using gentle persuasion.

It was getting late but he needed to pick up a few things from his office before making his way to the penthouse and the seriously chubby hot body of his wife.

He opened the office door and then stopped dead. How she managed to tie herself up to be displayed for him was almost impossible to figure out but then he realized she would only let one other man touch her and that man was her ex-sub Raul.

"Mommy's been bad, Master." Her wicked smile told him how bad she wanted to be.

"Oh, she has, has she?" He gave her a leering grin.

With her largely rounded tummy, there was no way she could lean over the desk for a nice spanking but she was tied to his office chair with her legs secured wide apart using a spreader bar. Tape held her hands to the chair arms and a pink ribbon surrounded her stomach with a large pink bow slightly to the side of her bellybutton.

The bulge of her stomach kept his eyes from her smooth pussy but she would be able to slide forward and give him better access if he commanded. He knew her pussy was smooth because since her fifth month he was the one that shaved it.

Lydia herself was a Domme but after strict negotiation, bets with the odds stacked in his favor, and lust; lots of lust, they reached a compromise. She stood beside him equally as a Domme in the club but he dominated in their bedroom.

It didn't matter that she loved him and wanted him to Master her in bed; she continued to try and top him every chance she got. It was in her blood and god was she sexy when she did it. She was sexy now; with her chubby cheeks and swollen fingers and ankles. Her additional weight only gave him more to nuzzle.

After this child he planned to talk her into another baby quickly. She would want to lose her baby weight but he wanted her plush and smushy.

"Is Daddy afraid Mommy will make him cry when he comes?"

Her voice brought him out of his extra-curricular thoughts. "Make me cry huh?" He lifted his eyebrows.

"Your mind was a million miles away while your fat wife is displayed in all her glory. I think I'd like to make you cry." Her voice was now petulant.

He laughed and walked closer, leaning over the chair, and putting his lips by her ear. "You know the word 'fat' gets you punished more."

"I've been very bad Master."

"Yes you have. You promised me you would rest and not come down to the club." He licked the side of her neck and let his tongue travel up to her ear. His teeth gently bit her earlobe as he listened to her sexy sigh which she knew aroused him. He gave a chuckle, "You think I'm that easy. I have a hard punishment planned for my naughty little wife."

He didn't give her a chance to respond. Turning the chair, he wheeled her to the corner of his office and pushed her as far into the corner as she could comfortably fit.

Her voice held disgruntlement. "What are you doing?"

"Well my disobedient sub, first I'm giving you the rules…you will not speak or I will place a ball gag in your mouth, you will not have an orgasm until I give you permission, and you will scream loudly throughout your punishment."

"I think Master has lost his fucking marbles."

He didn't reply. Her dirty mouth caused him endless trouble and it would be silent for a while. When it was time for her to scream he would take the gag out. She wasn't making a sound and he knew she realized she was screwed. She hated being gagged but for some reason she just couldn't control her lush, delectable, potty mouth and he usually had to control it for her.

He was proud of her though because she knew begging did nothing. He took the gag out of his desk drawer. He had several in their private suite but he kept one handy in the office. It was just for her and no matter how many times she hid them he just continued to buy more.

His hot breath landed on the side of her neck. "If you kiss me first I'll take the gag out sooner."

"You're getting soft Master but put those lips to mine and I'll fuck your mouth."

She was in a mood tonight and his cock went rock hard. Spinning the chair, his lips claimed hers and their tongues played and sucked while their teeth nipped at each other. There was no one in the world that could kiss like her.

Finally he pulled away and his hand went to her tummy, rubbing gently. "Is there anything you and Abigail aren't ready for?"

"Leave her out of this, Mommy needs to come."

He lifted the small red ball to her mouth and then secured the tie behind her head. "I think you look damn sexy like this; unable to speak, bitch, or tell me what you want."

Her eyes went from sensual to snappy just like he knew they would.

"You've been resisting what I have planned as punishment but it's been my fantasy for a while. Tonight, you will please me greatly. Now, with your mouth controlled I'm going to let you use your fingers. One finger lifted means it's getting to be too much and two means stop." His fingers trailed over her delightfully chubby knuckles, and lifted one off the arm rest and then lifted two. "Do you understand?"

Her middle finger came up and he turned away fighting his laughter.

Chapter Two

He walked to the cabinet on the far side of the room and took out the items he needed; three candles in three different colors, a lighter, and a medium sized knife in its sheath. When he approached his desk her blue eyes darkened and her breathing accelerated.

"Mommy's been bad and Daddy knows the perfect punishment. I've missed clamping your nipples because they've been so sensitive but I think this will give us both what we want."

A small bit of saliva ran down from the corner of her mouth and he wiped it with his finger and then licked his tongue over the wetness. "You always taste so good no matter where the moisture comes from."

Her eyes closed and when they opened the dark blue irises expanded.

He lit the candles one at a time and then turned to his captive. "I want your ass a little more forward in the chair but I don't want our baby uncomfortable. Do you understand?" His Dom voice came through loud and clear.

She nodded her head up and down.

"Good girl." He knelt between her legs and grasped her hips in his hands. "Lift just a bit." He pulled her bottom out so she was propped slightly back in the chair.

He stood and unbuttoned the sleeves of his black shirt and then removed it while she watched. He opened his desk drawer and removed a rubber band. Walking behind the chair, he gathered her thick red hair. It was hard for him to believe but her hair was actually fuller during her pregnancy. He placed the band around the heavy strands and let it hang down her back in a single ponytail. He then pulled the chair closer to his desk so the candles were in easy reach. Moving to the side, he took hold of the bottom lever on the chair, lowering the back to a one-hundred and twenty degree angle. Her eyes followed every move he made.

"With pain there is always pleasure." His voice dropped lower as he went back to his knees in front of her.

His hand came out and he used his fingers to part her labia. Just the one digit traveled from her clit to her tight sheath and entered the waiting moistness. He was unable to help himself and brought the silky juice to his mouth.

"Emm, you are both sweet and spicy at the same time. There is no taste on earth quite like you."

His finger went back to work on her pussy and he spread the wetness up to her clit rubbing and teasing until her hips came off the chair. He bent forward and kissed her stomach then untied the bow to unwrap his gift. Bringing his hands up, he cupped the underside of her breasts. His tongue went to one nipple and licked softly before moving to the other. His thumbs circled the moisture he left behind.

"When our baby arrives, she will be sharing her morning feeding with Daddy. I could come right now thinking about how your milk will taste."

Her breathing became more erratic and he released her breasts and let one of his hands travel down past her stomach and in between her thighs again. He used one finger to slowly ease into her pussy watching the sweet torment on her face as her eyes closed. His other hand reached for a candle. Leaning forward he wet the tip of her breast with his mouth and then spilled the first drip of red wax directly on her nipple.

"Ahhh." It came out behind the gag.

He watched her hands closely but they only clenched the chair arms tighter. His finger continued its work on her pussy but his thumb now rubbed over her clit. He blew gently on the wax as it cooled and then he repeated the process on her other nipple.

The wax ran down the nipple and past the areola. He blew softly until it was dry. Lydia's eyes were looking down and watching the same erotic play he was. Next he used blue while he kept up the steady glide of his heavily lubricated finger. He refused to pick up his pace even when her hips came off the chair to meet his hand.

"After the baby is born and you are healed, I will strap your hips down and not let them move for a few hours while I play."

He looked into her eyes then looked at her breast. The blue wax started at her nipple but then took a different path than the red. Where the two met the color went purple. He used a little more and allowed the wax to slide over the soft pillow of her breast leaving a sensual trail. She was a work of art. He never stopped the movement of his finger and thumb on her pussy.

Suddenly, he removed his hand from between her legs and walked behind her. She let out a groan until she could feel his hands untying the gag. He used his palm to wipe her face and then he kissed her lips before resuming his position between her legs.

"Do you have anything to say my dear?"

"God, hurry please."

"Tsk, tsk. You are always so impatient."

"I need to come. I've craved it all day but you stayed away and left me on my own. I want your cock buried deep in my ass, sliding in and out slowly while your hands squeeze my breasts."

He inhaled sharply and even knowing she was teasing him so he would move faster he couldn't help the image her words conjured in his mind. He stood and removed his pants. They were suddenly too tight and he no longer wanted his cock confined. He held himself in his hand and slowly let his fingers travel from the head down to his balls.

"I want to taste Sir."

Now she was throwing out the big guns. "Soon but I haven't properly punished a bad Mommy yet."

"Argh. I hate you."

"No my love, you love everything about me. Now, I want to use the yellow and see what colors we come up with."

The yellow turned orange and green when it hit the other wax. She was beautiful this way and this playtime would be repeated when he could cover her back from the top of her thighs up to her neck. Wax pooling across her ass was another fantasy he was determined to fulfill.

Chapter Three

He began stroking her again and increased the slide of his finger adding a little more pressure with his thumb. "Are you close my dear?"

"Oh god yes. Please."

All movement stopped and his hand glided gently from her pussy up and over her stomach.

"What are you doing?"

"I need to remove the wax." His other hand went to the knife sitting on his desk. He used both hands to unsheathe it.

"Oh hell no! You are not putting that knife near my breasts."

"Trust me." His eyes held intensity and pure sexual longing. He knew how to use his voice and eyes against her. She knew she could use her safe word and he would stop.

Her eyes closed tight.

The knife was dull but half the fun was her not knowing. He lifted her breast in his left hand and pulled the skin with his thumb before sliding the edge of the knife between the wax and her flesh. She didn't move but her eyes opened and she stared at the knife as it ran along her skin. He didn't use the knife on her nipples. When she was no longer pregnant he might try but for now he just wanted to play, a little.

He performed scenes out on the club floor with subs but he and his wife rarely watched each other. Once she became pregnant the oddest thing would set her off and she would be in tears. She told him she didn't know why she suddenly became so jealous. They agreed to stay away from the other's scenes. The further her pregnancy advanced the hornier she became. She was every sub's wet dream and her play became more intense which only upset him because he felt she was overdoing it.

No watching for now. It worked for them both.

He finished with one breast and moved to the other. She rested her head back and let him have his fantasy. When he finished he walked over to the cabinet and took out a bottle of massage oil and a soft cloth. He worked the oil into her skin and then gently removed the wax from her nipples.

"We're finishing this upstairs." He said softly in her ear.

"Hurry." She groaned.

He used scissors to cut the tape on her arms. The spreader bar was next. He grabbed a blanket out of his kink cabinet and covered her and then lifted.

"I keep telling you you're going to break your back."

"Only if you squirm, now hush and be still."

He walked into his private elevator and pressed the button for the penthouse.

She wasn't that heavy and even pregnant she fit perfectly in his arms. His quick strides ate up the carpeted floor as he carried her to their bed.

They had a long talk with her Obstetrician about their lifestyle. There were safety concerns for mother and child. A lot of their play was toned down but some parts had become more intense. Her hormones added a wilder streak than she possessed when she wasn't pregnant and he loved every nuance though it made him nervous worrying about the baby.

He laid her gently on the bed but there was no gentleness in his tone. "Remove your hair from the band

and then get on your knees; I want your ass in the air." He went to his dresser and pulled out what he needed.

When he walked back over he couldn't help but admire the well rounded globes displayed for his pleasure. They were missing one key erotic turn on and his hand landed with a resounding slap.

"What was that for?" Her groan was sexy and low.

"For being naughty and because my handprint looks so good on your skin." Another blow landed and her groan was louder this time. He got onto the bed behind her and placed his hands on her hips using his thumbs to gently glide over the red prints caused by the slaps. He then bent forward to kiss and lick the marks.

Her bottom squirmed and he gently nipped with his teeth. "Hold still."

"You're killing me. I want you fucking my ass."

"That's not going to happen until after the baby's born but I have a toy that will give you what you want while I take what I want. If you argue I'll just delay longer."

"Please." Need, longing, and frustration sounded in her voice. For a woman who listed anal sex as a hard limit in the beginning of their relationship she now loved it as much as he did. The doctor gave good solid advice on the subject and like all things told them to use care. Her pregnancy was now so far advanced that Damian had his own reservations and they were playing his way.

He sat back on his knees and picked up the lube applying it to his hand and the plug. He then ran his fingers over the cleft of her ass cheeks, and inserted his greased finger past her sphincter and massaged in and out feeling along the tight muscles that grasped him. Her breathing was growing erratic and he knew she was trying to quiet her little sounds of ecstasy.

"Hold on baby." He removed his finger and slid the plug in place. He grabbed her hips, squeezing the extra bit of love handles she hated and he worshiped. His cock had no trouble locating home and in one forward thrust he buried himself inside her warm pussy.

"Awwe."

"Scream for me, I want to hear you." His strained voice demanded.

"Faster, please!"

He pulled out and slid his hand against her clit using his other to move the plug. "Your cunt is so hot around my cock but you need to slow down and give me those sweet sounds I love to hear."

His finger remained on her clit as he slid back into her warmth.

Her head went to her forearm and she finally stopped fighting the delay of her orgasm and let her vocal cords express her yearning. This is what he wanted and the sounds she made turned him on even more. His hips picked up their pace and his finger circled the hard nub that was now swollen with need.

He was having his own trouble holding back but finally he gave his command, "Come for me sweet sub." And she did, burying her mouth against her arm to stifle her yelling.

He grabbed her hair and pulled her head back. "I want to hear you. Don't make me stop and punish your sweet ass."

"Ahhwe," and her scream echoed from the walls.

He was able to thrust twice more before his shouts matched hers.

He shifted them to their side and lay spooned behind her. His fingers trailed over her abdomen and lovingly kissed her shoulder, nuzzling her hair out of the way so his nose was resting against her skin. He loved the smell and taste of her skin after they made love and though she needed sleep, he couldn't stop touching her.

Finally her soft snores rumbled from her chest. He hadn't told her about the sounds that came with her weight gain, it would only bother her, but it just made him love her more. He removed his arms and tried to leave the bed.

Her voice cracked with sleepiness, "Don't leave me."

Placing a soft kiss on her brow he whispered in her ear, "I'm taking a quick shower and then I'll tuck you in with Alexander and join you."

"K, don forget ATG." She was barely coherent.

Alexander the Great was her five foot pillow that became the most comfortable way for her to sleep once lying on her back became impossible. She had named the pillow and Damian didn't quite get the connection but he smiled thinking about her peculiarities since the pregnancy started. He showered, dried himself off, and then went to the closet and grabbed a bright pink ATG. Carrying the monstrosity to the bed, he gently squished the softness between her thighs and up against her breasts. He joined her beneath the covers and pulled her tightly against his chest, spooning his body around hers. His tender smile gave way to nothingness.

Chapter Four

A long hot tongue brought him awake and he realized Samson must have stayed the night with Raul. Sam was Lydia's one-hundred and fifty pound Rottweiler and had to be contained when Damian wanted to play with his wife.

Lydia continued to sleep and Damian quietly untangled himself from the covers and left the room. Sam gave a short whine as he looked to his mistress buried beneath the covers but followed Damian. Raul was sitting at the kitchen table drinking coffee and reading Damian's newspaper.

"Make yourself at home but hand over the business section." He managed to grunt out.

"I haven't been kicked out so the little seduction scene last night must have worked."

"The further advanced her pregnancy gets the hornier she becomes. She hasn't done a scene at the club in two weeks. I may be chafed raw in a few more days."

"You could be the only man on earth who would complain about the situation."

"Oh believe me, that's not a complaint." A little pain, even for a Dom was okay with Damian. "Did you by any chance let Sam out to do his business?"

"He's been walked and fed. I lost a bet with your wife and he's mine at night until the baby's born."

Damian's laughter startled Samson who was lying on the floor a few feet away causing him to jump before he settled back down. "You haven't learned betting is futile against Lydia?"

"You bet against her all the time."

"Yes, but I cheat. All the time."

"She'd kill me if I was caught."

"You're probably right. Will you be able to handle things at the club for a few weeks after the baby's born?"

"Yours could be the only BDSM club in the country run by a sub."

"I'm only four flights away and if I need to come down I'll be sure to pound a few heads."

"Bran will be back soon from his honeymoon and he emailed me and said he would be glad to help." There was relief in Raul's voice.

"See, you worry about nothing."

"Worry about what?" Lydia walked in wrapped in a bathrobe with tousled sleep hair. She looked at the two men and picked up Raul's coffee cup taking a drink of the hot liquid. "Needs sweetener."

"You need your own cup."

"Yes, but mine won't have caffeine and it's not nice to remind me." Her hand went out to Samson as he came over for mistress love. The dog nuzzled against her stomach as Lydia scratched behind his ears.

"What are your plans today my love?" Damian was getting a hard on and wanted to be rubbing against her belly.

"I think I'm just going to lie around and get fatter." She sulked.

"The 'F' word so early in the morning? I'm keeping track and I won't go as easy as last night's punishment."

"I was hoping you would say that."

His smile was seductive and promising. "Let me put a few hours in at my desk and then we can picnic at the park and take Sam with us. We'll give his dog sitter a break until this evening."

"I love you."

"I'll love you more tonight and you have my promise on that."

Raul finally broke into the lovey dovey talk, "Thank god I have a significant other, and your seriously sugary sweet words don't make me puke."

Two pairs of dominant eyes drilled into the daring sub and he made a hasty retreat.

Chapter Five

A week later they ate dinner and it was delicious even though it came from the hotel kitchen. Lydia wanted to cook but she looked tired and slightly depressed so Damian insisted on ordering in. He invited Raul and his boyfriend Paul to join them. Keeping his wife content was his top priority until the baby came.

They talked and laughed but Damian noticed Lydia picking at her food. He would make this a short evening and get her tucked into bed early.

They all joined in to clear the table, planning a round of cards to pass the time over the next hour.

Suddenly, the power flicked off and everything in the suite went dark.

"Lydia, do not move." He didn't want her falling. "The backup generators will kick on the emergency lighting in a moment."

His last word came out and the low lighting came on throughout the suite.

"It's a nasty storm." This came from Paul.

"Yes, there have been weather warnings all day. I need to go check on the club."

"I'll come with you." Lydia put a touch of demand in her voice.

"You're tired and there is no way you are going down to the club and then walking the stairs back up if the power doesn't come back on soon. Argue and I'll handcuff you to the bed and give Raul the key while I'm gone."

"Once this baby is born Mister, we're having a talk."

"As long as you begin the conversation with Mister, you may be able to avoid a red ass."

"Argh, keep dreaming."

"Oh I do baby, I do." He turned to Raul. "If you don't mind I want you and Paul here with my irritating wife while I check things out."

"No problem we'll keep her busy and out of your hair."

"Raul!"

Sheepish eyes turned to Lydia. "Only while you're pregnant."

"I'll be teaching Paul a few things when I'm not pregnant and you won't be sitting comfortably for a week."

"Promises, promises." Raul smiled and batted his eyelashes.

Damian walked to Lydia, kissed her, and at the same time ran his hand over her extended belly. "Relax sweetheart, I'll be back as quickly as I can."

Thirty minutes later Damian stopped to talk with Kyle and his sub Trisha while they cuddled on a couch next to the scene area. He was almost finished with his rounds.

"Are you both alright?" Damian asked.

"Yes, were fine. I'm assuming the elevators are out until the power is back on?"

"Yes, but I think the club can entertain our guests for a few hours if needed."

"I'm sure it can."

"Damian?" It was Raul and he looked slightly ill.

"Yes Raul." Why the hell did he leave Lydia?

"Umm, well, umm."

"What exactly seems to be the problem?" His Dom voice showed his impatience.

"Lydia just asked me to tell you her water broke."

"Well fuck!"

Trisha couldn't help herself. "With all the Doms in here tonight I'm sure one will know what they're doing."

"We'll fireman-carry her down the stairs if we need to. I am not delivering a baby." Damian's usual strong voice actually croaked.

"Yes daddy." Trisha couldn't help herself.

Both Dom's looked at her with utter terror and Raul's face went green.

He looked at Kyle, "If you don't mind, will you see if anyone here knows anything about childbirth? Raul, call the fire department and let them know what's going on." He didn't wait for an answer just walked away without saying another word.

Chapter Six

Damian ran up the four flights of stairs. They would need to carry her twenty-nine flights down if the power didn't come back on. Whatever it took he would keep his wife and baby safe.

Lydia was walking across the carpet when he entered the front room. She looked up with large worried eyes. He wanted to yell at her for being on her feet but couldn't. He walked over and scooped her into his arms bringing her into his body and pressing his lips to her neck and cheek.

"I love you and our baby will be fine. You have my word."

He felt her body relax and she squeezed his neck. Suddenly her arms stiffened and her breathing increased.

He waited for the contraction to stop. "How long have the pains been going on?"

"I'm so sorry, a few hours."

"You should be sorry. Why didn't you tell me?" He was angry but kept his voice gentle.

"I wasn't sure it was the real thing and I didn't want you worrying until I was positive."

He had so many punishments saved up for after the birth but this one would be the end all. He kept his voice gentle. "Silly momma, daddy needs to know these things. Where do you want me to sit you down; the bed or couch?"

"The couch please."

Damian noticed Paul. "Have you ever delivered a baby Paul?"

"No Damian but I'm here for whatever you need."

"Raul should be back in a few minutes. He's calling the ambulance and Kyle is checking around the club for anyone with delivery knowledge."

Damian felt the stiffening of Lydia's body again and decided against taking her to the couch. He headed back to their bedroom and waited for the pain to subside before placing her on the comforter. He grabbed ATG from the closet and propped it behind her back. Voices could now be heard coming from the other room and Trisha stuck her head inside the bedroom door.

"You can come in Trish." Lydia smiled but the strain in her voice was clear.

Trisha entered with a small trail of people behind her.

They were friends and most felt like family. Kyle kissed her on the cheek. "You okay princess?"

"You're only calling me that because I can't take a whip to you right…" Her voice caught as another pain hit her.

Damian took over and grabbed her hand.

When the pain diminished a single tear ran down her cheek. "Please Damian I need to talk to you alone."

Everyone heard the plea and made their way quickly from the room with no prompting from Damian.

Raul whispered in his ear when he walked by, "At least an hour for the ambulance."

Damian inhaled deeply and took Lydia's hand bringing it to his lips. When everyone was gone and the door closed he looked into her pain filled eyes and knew even more why he loved this woman.

"I'm afraid. I didn't want anyone else to know. I'm so afraid."

He leaned over and kissed her gently on the forehead. Her hand constricted on his and her breathing picked up. "Slow my love, ride it out." He breathed along with her.

When the contraction ended, he wiped the moisture from her brow. "I love you. I will not let anything happen to you or our baby. In a few hours you will be holding Abigail at your breast. I promise."

Her smile was small but it was there. "A few hours? I may kill you by then. I want her out now."

"I know you do, but, my tough little Domme, you can handle this."

"Please Damian, let Raul hold my hand, I want you delivering our daughter."

"Whatever you want. I may as well begin being a daddy sooner than later. But, if you want her to come quickly you have work to do."

"I know and it hurts again."

Her grip tightened and he held her through another pain. Maybe the electricity would come back on but he realized changing her location to a hospital might be impossible at this point. As much as he liked pushing her limits this wasn't in the same ballpark and he just wanted her and the baby safe.

Tears slowly trailed down her face and he wiped them away when the majority of the pain passed. He could see by her facial features that even without the contraction she continued to suffer.

"Who do you want in here with us?"

"If none of them have ever delivered a baby then just Raul and I guess Trisha."

"Okay I'll get them."

"We need towels and." Her voice came out on a groan as another contraction hit. This one was closer to the other and they were noticeably getting stronger.

When it was over, Damian didn't wait to talk but left the room to give orders. Paul already had a collection of what they needed and carried it into the room. When

Damian walked back in with Trisha and Raul, Paul was holding Lydia's hand while she breathed through her pain. Damian went to the far side of the bed, and pulled the comforter down and then walked to the other side picking Lydia up.

"Get the sheet exposed and place the blue blanket down and then a few towels."

Everyone went to work organizing the bed.

Paul left the room without being asked but Damian lay Lydia on the bed and stopped him in the hallway, "Go grab my Ipad out of the office and Google childbirth, it has its own Internet and should still be working. I want step by step directions and you also need to gather everything else we need."

Damian walked back into the room. "Raul, you get the honors of holding Lydia's hand. Trisha, follow me and we'll wash up."

Damian washed his hands with soap and water and then watched as Trisha did the same. She was a tough woman and didn't seem to be thrown off by midwife duty. If Kyle chose her as sub she had to be strong.

He walked back into the bedroom to the sound of Lydia panting. He waited and when most of the tension left her face he kissed her forehead. "I'm going to remove your clothes and put you in a nightshirt."

"One of your t-shirts, please."

"Yes my love, not a problem."

He made short work of her clothes and acting quickly, placed a soft white t-shirt over her head. His lips met hers for a quick hard kiss then he placed her hand in Raul's and walked to the end of the bed.

"As soon as the next pain is over, we're going to move you closer to the end of the bed." They waited and when the pain passed everyone helped to guide her bottom to the foot of the bed leaving room for her feet to rest on the edge of the mattress with her knees bent.

Paul entered the room again bringing a large bowl with items resting inside. He placed the bowl on the dresser and then stood out of Lydia's sight.

Damian walked over, "Words of wisdom?"

"The baby should pretty much deliver itself. Don't pull on the head, it will turn to the side naturally, and then the body will come out. Place the baby face down on Lydia's bare tummy and cover it with a blanket or towel. Don't worry about the cord right away. If the paramedics aren't here shortly after the baby's born, we'll go to the next step."

"Thanks, I need to have a look and see what's going on. Any advice there?"

"If you can see the baby's head it's time. Have her push between pains but not during the worst of the contraction."

Lydia started groaning loudly and Damian walked back over, "When this pain is finished, I'm going to have a look."

"Shut the fuck up and just let me deal with this pain."

"Yes my dear."

"Oh fuck you."

"I knew your potty mouth would activate sooner or later."

Her panting kept her from replying but he knew if she was cussing she was doing okay. He waited her out and as soon as her body relaxed on the bed he moved her knees further apart. No head showed but he didn't know if he was relieved. His hand went to her thigh.

"Don't touch my legs." She said sharply.

It was like touching a hot surface and his hand jerked away.

"Yes ma'am." He couldn't help the laughter in his voice.

"I swear if you're laughing at me we're getting a divorce." Another pain took over.

They seemed to be coming faster and lasting longer. Damian changed places with Trisha for a moment and took his wife's other hand. She released Raul's and rolled slightly toward her husband. He sat on the bed and let her dig her fingernails into his flesh as she rode out the pain.

Her breathing slowed. "I don't think I can do this."

"Oh baby, I have no doubt you can do this."

"But I had it all arranged and they were giving me an epidural as soon as I got to the hospital. My doctor promised."

He kissed her cheek and used his fingers to remove her hair from the side of her eyes. "I love you and you will be a wonderful mother. You're almost there."

Her breathing picked up along with the pressure on his hand. They stayed like this as time passed and the pains were almost on top of each other.

He needed to check her again but would wait until the end of this pain. She was moaning in a low keen. He felt helpless.

"Red, red, oh god." Her voice came out on a cry.

It broke his heart, "Your Domme is the baby right now and she's stubborn like mommy and not listening."

"Mommy always listens to red. I can't take this please help me."

Damian looked at Raul. He walked around to Damian's side of the bed and Damian went to check if she had made any progress.

A small tuft of hair could be seen and he breathed a sigh of relief. "The baby's coming."

"No shit Sherlock she's killing me and I need to push."

His eyes went to Raul who was fighting laughter. Trisha looked at them both with chiding angst and managed to hold back her own smile.

Another pain began and Damian could see more of his daughter's hair. It was short, wet, and red. *Oh Abby he thought, you will give your father a merry chase.*

"She's almost here Lydia, push between pains and then stop when I tell you to."

"I will do no su...ahhh, it hurts."

"Raul, get on the bed behind her and help her sit a little."

Raul moved fast.

"Trisha, come down here and prepare a blanket. Hand it to me when I ask." He was using his authoritative voice because he knew it would calm his wife. He wouldn't let her see his shaking hands.

The pain slowed and his coaching began. "You need to push Lydia, push hard."

"I can't please, I can't."

"I'm going to slap your ass for that one. Push damn it!"

Her face tightened and she pushed. He could see more of the baby's head and it was slowly coming out when the next pain began.

"Hold on Lydia, no pushing right now wait for the pain to stop."

"I'm going to kill you. It's your fault the power went out and you got me into this mess with your wiggly squiggles. I'm better off swallowing."

Damian glanced down. He was incapable of looking at anyone else in the room or his laughter would break through. When the next pain started his daughter began to emerge. She knew how to follow unspoken directions because her head turned to the side and the remainder of her body began to slide out. He didn't force it but had his hands under her small slippery frame.

Lydia screamed as the rest of Abigail's body came out. Lydia opened her eyes just as Damian looked up at her.

Tears fell from his face as he held his daughter. Her eyes were open and her tiny face scrunched as a short cry sounded and then grew louder.

"I love you." Damian said meeting his wife's gaze and then he placed a kiss on his daughter's bloody head and moved the t-shirt up to expose Lydia's belly and lay the baby down stomach to stomach with her mother. His hand reached out and Trisha put the blanket into it. He covered his daughter and wife, and then walked to the head of the bed.

Paul walked over, "She's good. You have about ten minutes until you need to do anything else. We'll go check on the ambulance and give you some time."

Damian never took his eyes off his wife as Raul slid from behind her and Damian took his place. The door closed quietly. He kissed Lydia's hair and gathered it in his hand. "You are my world. Thank you for my daughter."

"She's beautiful." Her hand smoothed over the soft crown of red hair.

"You're breathtaking Lydia; I want another one next year."

She laughed, "Not going to happen." She glanced over her shoulder with tears of her own.

His arms tightened but his pulse slowed for the first time in two hours.

Chapter Seven

A short time later the electricity came back on and within five minutes the paramedics took over the room. Damian grabbed his wife's pre-packed travel bag and followed them out, staying by her side as her and the baby were cared for.

More work was required after they arrived at the hospital. Doctor Pastavich showed up and Lydia noticeably relaxed. All their preplanning was out the window but he let Damian cut the cord. A nurse took Abigail away to be checked out completely. Lydia delivered the afterbirth and required stitches due to tearing. Damian held her hand but she didn't make a sound and only appeared lost without the baby.

A short time later, tightly bundled in a pink blanket, the nurse placed Abigail back into Lydia's arms. She was sucking dramatically on her fist.

"She's doing wonderfully considering how she made her appearance. A pediatrician looked her over. He'll be in to see you soon. Right now this little one needs to eat." The nurse helped Lydia with her hospital gown.

Lydia brought the baby to her breast and pinched her nipple rubbing it against the small pert mouth. Abigail latched on.

In all his life it was the most amazingly sexy thing Damian had ever seen. He laughed to himself acknowledging he was one kinky bastard.

The room cleared and he was left alone with his family. Damian's finger went to his daughter's tiny hand and she gripped it tightly without letting go of her food.

Damian bent over and kissed Lydia's lips gently. "I love you so much and I'm so proud of you. She's beautiful and looks just like her mommy. I hoped for red hair and got all my wishes in one six pound bundle."

"I thought she would weigh at least fifteen pounds with all the weight I gained."

He leaned over his wife and brought his nose to hers. "If you use the "F" word I'll gag you here at the hospital. You are beautiful and every pound gave me more to love. I will miss each one you lose and rejoice in every pound I can convince you to keep."

"Yes sir."

"Your breasts look good enough to eat and I'm quite jealous of our daughter."

"It will be a few days before my milk comes in but as soon as it does, you can have a taste."

"It's going to be impossible to keep my hands off of you over the next six-weeks."

"Well good. I have no intention of keeping my hands off you and I'll enjoy driving you crazy for a change."

"I have a feeling you'll be securing my hands to make that happen." His sexy smile held promise and silent laughter. The last time Lydia tied his hands he broke the headboard and she was quite unhappy with him.

She ignored his reference with only a slight smile, "We still need a nanny."

His soft groan made her smile deepen. "I know. Our lifestyle doesn't make it as easy as one would think. I wish my mother lived closer, I dislike the thought of taking turns at the club but we may have no choice. We'll start looking again next week. I thought money bought everything."

Now she laughed out loud. "We'll find someone and I'm sure your money will buy a great nanny." A yawn followed this statement and her eyelids closed.

He rested his hand on the baby and watched over the two of them while they rested.

It was the afternoon of the third day before they returned home from the hospital. Both parents looked forward to uninterrupted family time. The hospital staff was wonderful but they had to check vital signs, test Abigail for everything under the sun, and inquire how the new family was doing on a regular basis. Home was perfect.

Raul and Paul arranged everything and a bassinet and baby monitor were set up in the master bedroom. There were easily prepared meals in the kitchen and a hotel staff at their beck and call.

Samson met the baby and whined non-stop whenever she was out of his sight. There was really no need for the monitor because as soon as Abigail stirred, Samson barked and made sure she was awake and that everyone else knew it. He watched everyone that got near his human child with a promise of violence if the baby was mistreated.

A week after the birth they held a small gathering in the penthouse and Samson stayed in Raul's suite so there would be no mishaps.

When the night was over, Damian tucked his wife and baby into their perspective beds and went down to the club for an hour. Raul and Paul were doing a great job.

He walked over to a station and saw Bran working with his wife Willow, Damian's sister. Definitely not something he was comfortable watching even with their recent marriage. He took his private elevator back to the penthouse, checked on Abigail next to the bed, and then crawled in beside his wife; pulling her close and kissing the back of her head. She never stirred. He exhaled in contentment and fell asleep.

Chapter Eight

Week four "post Abigail" arrived and their lives surrounded the recently weighed seven pound bundle of fluff. Her feeding schedule gave them about two and a half contented hours and then she let the world know she needed mommy.

Her eyes were blue like her mothers and her hair was getting curly, thicker, and a more defined red. She followed her admirers with her eyes and graced them with quick smiles and contented gurgles when they least expected it. She was quite stingy with her grins.

Damian was spending the next hour alone with her highness while Lydia went to the gym to work out for the first time since Abby's birth.

"Do not overdo it and that is an order." His voice held an absolute promise of punishment if she disobeyed him.

"Yes Master."

He growled in response because she knew the use of the word master turned him on. Abigail was on his shoulder and he was burping her after her feeding. Samson walked beside him as Damian crossed the room and then turned back around to repeat his carpet march.

Everything went fine and he received an unladylike burp for his patience. He sat on the couch and placed his large hands beneath Abigail's arms jumping his knee up and down slightly. Samson stayed two feet away keeping a close eye on his baby's movements like a mother lion.

Suddenly, with no warning, at least a gallon of curdled milk spewed from Abigail's dainty mouth.

"Oh damn." Was Damian's startled announcement as he jumped slightly while realizing he had nothing at hand in which to wipe them off with..

His sudden exclamation caused Abigail to let out a loud cry and Samson began whining loudly.

Damian looked at the dog, "Really, you think you're helping?"

Samson came forward and before Damian could stop him he slurped up a large section of chunky breast milk.

Damian began gagging as he jumped up and headed to the bathroom with a screaming Abigail in his arms. Samson let out a howl and proceeded to pretend he was a wolf during a full moon.

Cleaning the baby up with a wet washcloth only made her angrier and Damian did the only thing he could think of. He dialed Raul's suite number.

Damian didn't get a word out and barely heard Raul over the background noise.

"I'll be right up."

Lydia was gone fifteen minutes and the man that made woman scream in ecstasy was reduced to calling in the big gay guns.

Raul arrived, and took the screaming between hiccups child from her daddy's arms and carried her to the nursery. He ignored her wails and changed her clothes and diaper. Lifting her to his shoulder he soothed her back. He gave a stern look at Samson and the dog went quiet. One instant Abigail was crying and the next she went completely silent.

"I can't believe you did that. I spend more time with her than you do." Damian wasn't angry just relieved.

"It's a gay uncle thing."

"And Samson?"

"I've known that dog since he was Abby's age. He just needed to know his baby was safe."

"And her daddy doesn't keep her safe?"

"Not in dog language."

"Christ! He licked up her spit and I almost lost my lunch."

Raul could no longer contain his laughter.

"What's it going to cost to keep this quiet and not let Lydia know?" Damian knew the score.

"I'll think of something and collect another time. Do you want me to put her in the basinet, I think she's sleeping now?"

"Yes, put her down and I'll let Sam outside. Maybe he'll regurgitate baby puke on the grass and I'll have another picture that needs to be exorcised from my head."

"You need to change your shirt. You smell a little spoiled."

Chapter Nine

Two more weeks went by and all interviews for a nanny were unsuccessful. Damian was back at the club most evenings and Lydia was getting grouchier each day.

It was the busy season if you could call it that and Damian performed two scenes with experienced subs. He enjoyed sexually stimulating them but he was ready to have his wife back. The blowjobs Lydia gave him were wonderful but he craved full out kinky sex. Besides holding his subs during aftercare they were not allowed to touch him. He gave a few quick kisses and found pleasure in dominating the women but controlled himself and saved his own orgasms for his wife.

He finished with Celia, making her drink water and eat a few orange slices before letting her go to the bar and visit with her friends. He noticed a crowd gathering at one of the stations and decided to check it out before calling it a night.

"Damn." He said under his breath when he was able to see what had everyone's attention.

It was Lydia; a fuller, sexier, and more luscious Lydia. Her thick red hair was hanging lose down her almost bare back. She was dressed in a black leather bra that barely contained her large nursing breasts. The black leather short skirt only covered the top of her ass and he wasn't sure if she was wearing a thong or nothing underneath. Her boots were the same material and ended just below her knees. A softly rounded post-baby belly poked out slightly and added to the hot wet dream she created.

She had a male sub face first on the St. Andrews Cross. Gripping his hair; she pulled his head back and kissed him with aggressive passion and then took his bottom lip between her teeth and pulled slightly. Damian almost came in his pants when she released the subs lip and ran her tongue up the side of his jaw.

Damian knew she was playing this game for him and he also knew he was putty in her hands and would be fucking his wife tonight. Standing back, he enjoyed the scene. Lydia took a metal anal ball cock ring from a tray, and placed her hand to the front of her lucky sub and put the ring around his balls. She then inserted the ball into his ass while he squirmed; the lucky bastard. A sharp slap landed on his ass cheeks and he stopped moving.

She grabbed her torture device of choice and unfurled the leather whip. Her shoulders rotated and she let the whip release with a resounding snap though it landed nowhere near her anxious sub.

Then she started in earnest. Red stripes appeared across his back, ass, and upper thighs. She never broke the skin but his body twisted and his loud moans filled the club.

Her precision was impeccable and Damian realized she was probably practicing daily during her forays to the gym. The club was quiet at that time of day and he would bet she was using one of the private rooms. His wife had mad skills with a whip and his cock was ready to blow.

Lydia took her time and gave full concentration to her sub. The show finally stopped as suddenly as it began and Lydia removed the anal plug and then unfastened her sub from his bindings. The sub was not blessed with an orgasm and Damian's cock swelled further.

It occurred to Damian that Raul, who usually helped with her scenes, was babysitting and unavailable. He owed Raul another favor.

Taking her sub's hand, she led him to the side couch, passing Damian while giving him a wink. She would pay for that. Damian stood to the side of the large planter, and watched every second his wife soothed and spoke to her sub. She ran oil over his body and talked to him about his daily life. They loved her; men and women both. She always made them feel special even when her husband stood a few feet away.

Damian waited patiently though his erection refused to subside.

Finally she wiped her hands on a towel and helped the sub to his feet. She kissed him on his cheek. "If you like, you may schedule with me next week Caleb. Just see the front office again and they will set you up."

"Yes Mistress Lydia, I will."

"Enjoy yourself the rest of the evening."

"Thank you Mistress." He walked away with a look of absolute worship on his face.

Lydia organized and cleaned her area without looking at Damian. He waited.

When she finally turned he was a foot away. His arms went to her back and pulled her hard against his chest. "Put those four inch heels around my back. We are going to our own private playroom but I'm carrying you out of here."

"Yes Master." Desire oozed from her voice and her pupils became noticeably larger.

Her legs locked around him and his strides ate up the floor heading to his office. None of his employees were dumb enough to stop him and he went straight to his private elevator.

"Who has Abigail?"

"Our new nanny."

"Really, do I have any say over this?" He kept his voice even, trying not to show his irritation.

"Her name is Raul and she finally turned in her application today. She has every qualification we want. She's giving notice at her current job tomorrow."

"Why didn't he apply months ago?"

"He didn't think we would want a gay man helping to raise our daughter."

"That's the dumbest thing I've ever heard. He's perfect and quite frankly more natural at it than her own father."

"Don't worry, mommy has better uses for daddy, and he'll be really good at what she has planned."

"Mommy's had enough planning for a while. Her Dom is making his demands for the next year or so and she'll need to wait."

"Emmm, that sounds like kinky fun."

He didn't reply just carried her inside the penthouse and made his way to their private dungeon.

"I can feel my milk coming in and it might be a better idea if I pumped first."

"Thank you for the information but I'll take care of everything and fair warning I'm in the mood to gag you tonight if your requests get out of hand. Seeing you run your hands over that sub's body is more than I can stand after leaving you alone for six weeks."

"I told you two weeks ago that I could play."

He leaned back and glared at her. She pressed her lips together and didn't say another word. Smart little sub.

Chapter Ten

He sat her on a high bench and then went to his knees, unzipped her boots, removed them, and then massaged the instep of each foot. The small sounds she made were nothing compared to the ones she would be singing later. He pulled her hands forward and stood her in front of him. His fingers went to her hips and he slowly drew the skirt down her legs and let it fall to the floor displaying her bare ass. Standing, he turned her and unclipped the bra, sliding the straps over her arms and down. The black material also pooled on the floor. Taking her hand he led her to the cross and secured her facing him. He then placed a black cloth over her eyes shutting out his movements.

He next turned on soft sultry music, and then walked out of the room. He knew it would drive her crazy and he needed several items from their bedroom. Abigail wasn't in her basinet so he peeked into the nursery on his way back to the dungeon. There was a private bedroom off the nursery and he could see Paul's legs on top of the covers. Samson sat by the rocking chair where Raul was gently moving back and forth with Abby in his arms.

"She had a bottle of breast milk and I'll put her down in a minute." Raul whispered.

"Thank you. You know, you and I will need to talk about your delay in taking up the nanny or should I say manny job. I'm glad you finally tapped into that brain in your head." Damian's voice was just as soft.

"Yes Sir." Raul smiled.

"Right now there's a very dirty job I must attend to in the dungeon and this could take a while."

"You have all night."

"Then get some sleep because you might have baby duty in the morning." Damian's grin was wicked.

Entering the dungeon he made noise so Lydia knew he was back in the room but he didn't say a word. He knew she was fighting to keep her mouth shut and keep a ball gag out of it. The thought made him smile.

Approaching his wife, he admired her engorged breasts. He knew they were becoming painful and he used one finger to slowly trace the blue vein just under the skin of one hard globe.

"Ahhh, they hurt."

"I know and I plan to make them hurt more."

His lips went to her nipple and he sucked gently, drinking the sweet milk she produced. When it flowed freely he placed the breast pump on her nipple and suctioned the white liquid into the bottle. His eyes went to her other breast which was dripping milk.

Only a few years ago he would not have understood his fascination with her breast milk and the eroticism of nursing his wife. Now, he hoped she continued to breastfeed for many more months.

He finished with the first breast and put his lips to her other one.

Her body squirmed and her sighs were sweet desire to his ears. He finished filling the bottle and bringing the pump with him, he left the dungeon and went to the kitchen. He twisted a top to the bottle along with a dated label and placed it in the freezer. He then took his time rinsing the pump and setting it on the bottle drying mat.

He knew Lydia probably wanted to kill him by now but this was one of her punishments for making him watch her with a sub after weeks of celibacy. Just thinking about it had his cock raging again and he returned to his naughty wife.

"I'm surprised you've managed to stay quiet." He said when he entered the dungeon.

"Will it do me any good to scream?" Her voice was sulky.

"No, but I enjoy having your mouth covered by a gag or filled with my cock. Both bring me intense joy."

"I'm being good Master."

"Yes you are, if I can forget the play scene you performed earlier tonight."

"I wanted you worked up and your cock hard."

"You got your wish and now I get more of mine."

He walked away and pretended he didn't hear her sigh of displeasure when he didn't touch her.

Approaching her quietly he whispered in her ear, "These are tweezer clamps and shouldn't be too uncomfortable or cause problems with your milk production." His instructional reading told him he had to go lightly on her breasts or he might cause her milk production to slow.

"Master has done his homework." Her words ended on a low moan when he attached the clamps.

Without touching her anywhere else, he walked away and then came back with one of his favorite toys. It was a vibrating butt plug and occasionally he could make her pussy milk when he used it. He lubed the plug and his fingers. Her pussy was displayed nicely and he put his hand between the cross and her ass cheeks to tip her further out so he could place his finger at the entrance of her anus and slide it slowly in. Her hips jerked.

"It's probably uncomfortable because you've had no action back here for a while."

"It's hurts because my Master isn't playing anywhere else."

"Umm, I'll take that under advisement."

He slipped another finger inside and watched her wiggle as her body became accustomed to the stretching. When he knew she was ready he replaced his fingers with the plug which was bigger than she liked.

"Ahh, you bastard."

"Shh, you're one word away from the gag."

Her teeth clamped shut like he knew they would. He walked away and washed his hands before picking up his next toy and approaching her.

"These clamps have a little more bite but I want your pussy open for the flogger."

He clamped her labia lips and then used two soft strips of cloth with Velcro on her upper thighs. They attached to the clamps and spread her red swollen pussy fully for his admiration.

He planned to make her beg for release. He picked up one of the soft floggers. It could produce a bit of sting but only if she misbehaved.

The sounds she made when she was excited turned him on and he was fighting his need to fuck her into next week. His plan was to take things slowly so he turned up the music.

The first strike hit her on her belly and she squealed.

"Does my sweet little sub like that?"

"Yes." Her breath left her when he struck the side of her hip.

The displayed folds of her pussy were waiting for him but they would continue to wait. He switched between her stomach, hips, and thighs though occasionally he would softly strike her breasts knowing the nipple clamps added to the sensation.

It took her fifteen minutes to start begging.

"Please, oh god, please I need to come."

It was exactly what he was waiting for and he hit the switch that caused the butt plug to vibrate.

Her hips pumped forward, "Arghhh, please, ahh."

He placed two well-aimed lashes to her dripping pussy and then switched off the vibrator.

"Fuck you, I'm punished already please just fuck me. I'll suck you off if you want but please FUCK me!"

He didn't say a word just turned the anal plug back on.

This time he stood back and observed. When she got close he turned it off and let her settle. Going to his knees he ran his tongue between the pussy clips from back to front. He received the desired scream and did it again. Moving away he hit the power on the plug again.

Her hips were grinding back and forth but he stopped the vibrations and released her legs and then her arms from the cross.

"I'm carrying you to the spanking bench and I don't want you wiggling." Her heavy breathing was his only answer.

He arranged her on the bench with her legs spread and the clamps pulling on her drenched pussy.

"I'm doing the counting because I have every transgression you've committed over the past few months stored in my brain. I'll know when I'm done."

"Are you going to fuck me when you're finished with my punishment?" Her voice was trembling.

"I'm thinking about it."

"You had better think hard."

His palm landed with a sharp thwap. He mentally counted everything he could think of and felt his built up aggression slowly recede. She was begging and screaming loudly when he was down to his last five. She had not used her safe word even though he knew her red bottom was burning.

"We're almost done sweetness but I just remembered something." He turned on the butt plug and his hand landed the final five times.

"I don't know about you but I feel better." His words were a lie because his cock was in severe pain.

"Fuck you." She gasped.

"Oh I think you will."

He quickly removed his clothes and then the butt plug. In one hard lunge he buried his cock in her ass until his balls settled against her spread pussy lips.

"You feel so fucking good." He breathed out against her back.

"Please just give me a minute. Please."

"You're punishment's over, I can afford to be nice." Moist kisses trailed along the center of her back as he gained control of his breathing.

His hand went to the Velcro at her thighs. He then squeezed the end of the clamps and let them fall to the floor. Blood rushed into the lips of her pussy and she arched against him.

"Ohh, that wasn't nice."

"But this is."

She was so tight around his cock and her muscles pulsed even before she came. He slid nearly out and then slowly back in. His hands went beneath her body to her nipples and released those clamps too, slowly soothing the stiff peaks and then rubbing the rounded globes. Milk released and he used the silky wetness to massage her nipples.

"Please Master, may I come?" She was shuddering and gasping for air.

"Yes, come for me sweet sub." When her muscles finally began their heavy contractions he picked up his intensity but she was past caring.

He could no longer hold back his seed and he filled her ass with everything he had to give and then collapsed over her.

Eventually, he was able to carry her to the shower where he gently washed her sticky breasts and then her entire body.

"Do you need to pump again?"

"I would prefer your kinky lips to do the work."

He pulled her around and took her mouth bringing his chest firmly against her swollen breasts.

In between nipping kisses he spoke in a low seductive voice, "My kinky mouth will always be at your disposal. I love you and I'm so glad you're ready for me because daddy's hungry."

Her sighs of pleasure filled the shower.

The End for now…

A note from the author:

Thank you for reading the Club El Diablo Box set. The next two books, Two Doms for Angel & Caught By Two Doms, are also available as a combined set to save you money. I love hearing from readers and all my contact info is available at www.wickedstorytelling.com along with other goodies and info about my pen name D'Elen McClain where I write about vamps, werewolves, and dragons.

Bibliography

Writing as Holly S. Roberts

Completion Series – New Adult Romance
Play
Strike
Kick

Crimson Series – Vampire Erotic Romance
Crimson Warrior (novella: Kept An Erotic Anthology)
Crimson Brothers (coming soon)

Club El Diablo Series – Kinky Romance
One Dom at a Time*
Piercing a Doms Heart
Touched by a Dom
Domination in Pink (short and kinky sequel to One Dom at a Time)*
Two Doms for Angel
Bad Boy Dom (Bad Boys of Rock)
Loving Two Doms (Bad Boys of Rock)
Caught by Two Doms (sequel Two Doms for Angel)
Temporary Dom (Bad Boys of Rock)

Writing as D'Elen McClain

Fang Chronicles – Paranormal Romance
Amy's Story*
Emily's Story
Zenya's Story
Mandy's Story

Dmitri
Ivan

Fire Chronicles – Paranormal Romance
Dragons Don't Cry
Dragons Don't Love (coming soon)

Writing as Suzie Ivy

Bad Luck Detective Series – Non-fiction Humor/Inspirational

Bad Luck Cadet

Bad Luck Officer

Bad Luck in Small Town (coming soon)

CPSIA information can be obtained at www.ICGtesting.com
Printed in the USA
LVOW04s2100151214

418944LV00040B/2856/P